KING
OF
Chatham

Book 2 of the Kings of the Castle Series

London St. Charles

LS Charles Publishing Group
Chicago, Illinois

King of Chatham by London St. Charles Copyright ©2019
Trade Paperback ISBN: 978-0-9993288-5-9

LS Charles Publishing Group
P.O. Box 198778
Chicago, IL 60619-8778

Cover Designed by: J.L Woodson: www.woodsoncreativestudio.com
Interior Designed by: Lissa Woodson: www.naleighnakai.com
Editor: Lissa Woodson: www.naleighnakai.com

KING
OF
Chatham

Book 2 of the Kings of the Castle Series

London St. Charles

♦ ACKNOWLEDGEMENTS ♦

All praises to the Man above for giving me the gift to create, the opportunity to live my dream, and the perseverance to push through when the going gets tough.

Writing *King of Chatham* reminds me of a snake shedding its skin. As the snake grows, the skin becomes stretched, and the only way to allow further growth is to shed the old skin. Writing this story, my literary palate was stretched further than I could fathom. It expanded with each word typed, minutes that turned into hours of research, and tapping into a genre that I don't usually pen. This process has allowed me to grow as a writer and discover a deeper level of my craft.

That being said, I couldn't do all of this alone.

To my husband and daughters, who accept me in all my introverted splendor when I'm in the writing cave. Who've excused the messy house, lack of cooking, and choppy conversation. Thanks for not holding my misgivings over my head while I crushed my goals.

To my mom, who I love more than anything. Thanks for understanding my hustle. I feel guilty when I can't get by there over the weekend, or our conversations are cut short because I have a deadline.

To MarZé and Gwen, thanks for getting me over the hump during the trying times. Encouragement and plotting sessions, coupled with gut-busting laughter, are recipes for success. I couldn't have done this without you ladies.

To the Queen Writers of The Kings of the Castle Series, you ladies are some of the best storytellers I know. The love and support that we show each other is unmatched. I was beyond thrilled to meet most of you at the Cavalcade of Authors.

To my literary team, thanks for putting that flair on my story via edits, beta reads, and cover design. Naleighna, I smiled as I typed your name. Thanks for everything you do. I can't say it enough. Deb, your feedback propelled me to the moon. J.L, I'm loving this cover. You got Reno looking sexier than a …

To my readers, I love you. Thanks for every book you've read, every review posted, every Facebook shout out, every recommendation, and so forth.

One Love,

London St. Charles

ABOUT THE KINGS OF THE CASTLE SERIES

Books 2-9 are standalones, no cliffhangers, and can be read in any order.

Book 1 – Kings of the Castle, the introduction to the series and story of King of Wilmette (Vikkas Germaine)

USA TODAY, *New York Times*, and National Bestselling Authors work together to provide you with a world you'll never want to leave. The Castle. Powerful men unexpectedly brought together by their pasts and current circumstances will become a force to be reckoned with. Their combined efforts to find the people responsible for the attempt on their mentor's life, is the beginning of dangerous challenges that will alter the path of their lives forever. Not to mention, they will also draw the ire and deadly intent of current Castle members who wield major influence across the globe.

Fate made them brothers, but protecting the Castle and the women they love, will make them Kings.
www.thekingsofthecastle.com

King of Chatham - Book 2 - Reno
King of Evanston - Book 3 - Shaz
King of Devon - Book 4 - Jai
King of Morgan Park - Book 5 - Daron
King of South Shore - Book 6 - Kaleb
King of Lincoln Park - Book 7 - Grant
King of Hyde Park - Book 8 - Dro
King of Lawndale - Book 9 - Dwayne

CHAPTER 1

The touch of Baba Godfrey's arms encircling Zuri's body caused a bone-wrenching chill to course through her veins despite the sweltering African heat. She froze, becoming almost as stiff as Mama Suby, who lay beneath the graveyard's red soil.

"Your Mama loved you so much," Baba said, his sweaty round face pressed firmly against her cheek. The thick accented English tinged with a hint of confidence that made Zuri's insides cringe. "I know she feels your presence and is happy that you are home to take your rightful place as Djimon's wife."

Zuri didn't respond, digging the heels of her shoes into the manicured grass of the family's elaborate home garden, filled with multi-colored sunbirds perched on the morning glory bushes with white and purple flowers and cloves that left a pungent aromatic spice in the air. All sights, scents, and sounds she left behind. The last words Mama said to Zuri before helping her flee Tanzania five years ago were, *"I may never see you again, but at least I know you will be alive and safe. You will be free of what will bind you here."*

She had broken her promise never to return, but despite the dangers of being on Tanzanian soil again, there was no way that Zuri would miss her Mama's funeral.

Mama Suby's eternal soul could rest in peace; knowing the sacrifices she made for her only daughter were not in vain.

Zuri tried to ease out of Baba's fleshy arms, but he tightened his grip. The black Kaba and slit-style African dress that cradled her hour-glass curves, melted against her skin under the pressure of his intense hold.

She didn't need or want his comfort. Zuri knew every bit of it came with strings attached, and she was no one's puppet. Had it not been for Baba, she wouldn't have been separated from her Mama and the rest of the family for the past five years. Trying to force her to marry Djimon Aku, a man she hardly knew, was something her mother would have never done.

"You have skirted your responsibility long enough," Baba whispered in a stern voice. "It is time to let go of that school foolishness."

"Never," Zuri shouted, louder than intended, breaking free of his embrace. "I graduate in two weeks."

The sea of older women and men cloaked in black and red dress garments and head ties, turned to face them, most with perplexed expressions. Zuri's cheeks burned hotter than the sun that penetrated the overhead tent. The last thing she wanted to do was dishonor her Mama's celebration of life. But the thought of not being there on her journey to the spirit world was unimaginable.

Zuri's second-level teacher and clandestine guardian angel, Mama Winnie, swooped in and grabbed her by the hand. "Godfrey. Let me talk to her," she suggested, guiding Zuri away from her father before he could protest.

The robust woman with a snatched waistline, smooth charcoal skin that belied her age, and teeth whiter than pure snow wrapped an arm around Zuri's shoulder. "My love. I know it hurts. Try not to draw attention to yourself. It will make your departure less noticeable."

Zuri nodded and forced the unshed tears to remain at bay.

"Thank you for always knowing what I need, even after all this time." Zuri smiled, sliding her hand in Mama Winnie's. "No wonder you and my Mama worked so well together."

"We still are," she said, winking at Zuri as they strolled hand in hand

to the opposite side of the garden where fewer mourners had gathered. They sat on wooden white folding chairs along the concrete ledge that separated the garden from the man-made pond filled with lily pads and koi fish.

Mama Winnie swept a gaze across the people who were seemingly engaged in conversation, but a good majority of them kept throwing suspicious glances in Zuri's direction. Several men, who she only remembered from childhood to some extent, had somehow managed to encircle the garden where they now had become a human net or spider web. They had no reason to be this close, and Zuri could only suspect that her father had something to do with this not-quite-so-subtle watch guard.

We still are.

"What does that mean, Mama Winnie?"

"You will see soon enough, my love."

"Zuri," Djimon's heavily accented voice interrupted, and her heart lurched at the abrupt sound. He smoothed out the imaginary wrinkles in the crisp black shirt, then stroked a hand over the red tie that adorned his medium frame. "Can I talk to you?"

Before Zuri could respond, Mama Winnie said, "Give us a moment. She will be right there."

Zuri wanted to scream, *"No, I will not,"* but remembered the advice Mama Winnie had given only minutes ago.

Djimon grimaced, frustration evident in his chiseled face as he turned on his heels and joined a group of twenty-somethings congregating near the gazebo several feet away.

Zuri observed in silence, wondering *why her?* Some of the women, most from the tribe, yearned to be in her position. She'd gladly allow them. Becoming a man's token wife was not on Zuri's radar, and it had never been, hence her current situation. She coveted education and the freedom to choose her path more than anything.

Mama Suby came from a wealthy family, and they had set Godfrey up quite well, establishing long-lasting prosperity. Zuri's parent's thirty-year marriage started with a $500,000 dowry, a herd of cattle, and a five-bedroom house where Godfrey still resided. The embellishments to the home over the years have increased the value of the property that resembled a resort more than a single-family dwelling. Godfrey invested half of the dowry in the construction industry, which included, real estate and transport infrastructure. He worked closely with the government in the development of the road network, reconstructing bridges, and building a reliable railway in East Africa. Godfrey's investment had gained him ten times the fortune he started with, over the three decades, making him an extremely wealthy man in his own right.

"What is wrong?" Mama Winnie asked, placing a hand on Zuri's lap.

She gave Mamma Winnie a half-smile as her heart swelled with emotion. "I miss you already. You are the only real connection I have to Mama—— her life, her thoughts," Zuri mused, laying her head against Mama Winnie's forearm. "It feels like I am leaving for the first time all over again; sneaking off to escape the danger from my own Baba, who is supposed to love and protect me." Zuri lifted her head, gazing into Mama Winnie's chestnut eyes filled with wisdom. "I have heard of fathers being their daughter's hero or their daughter's first love, as they say in America. Why am I not allowed the same love?"

"You are, sweetheart." Mama Winnie cupped a hand to Zuri's cheek. "I do not think Godfrey is capable of showing you. He only knows the way of our ancestors. That is his way of expressing his love for you."

"But Mama did not agree."

Mama Winnie angled her body toward Zuri. "Suby wanted better for you. She risked her life to make sure you did not have to endure certain cultural practices."

"Like being forced to marry and remain uneducated," Zuri commented, shifting on the folding chair causing it to squeak from her efforts. She felt the heat of the elder's orbs bearing down upon her and wondered why they were so fixated on her presence. Did they not expect Zuri to attend her mother's funeral?

"Those are only part of it."

Zuri leaned forward, catching Djimon gazing, almost glowering at her, shifting as though preparing to move in again. She lifted an index finger to ward him off. He frowned, and it caused his handsome features to take on an ugly state. She would get to him when she was ready and not a minute sooner. Placing her focus back on Mama Winnie as whispers of conversations echoed across the garden, Zuri asked, "What do you mean by only part of it?" A chill whipped through her so strong, she shivered.

"Suby sent you away so you would not have to undergo circumcision."

"You mean mutilation," Zuri countered in such a tone it caused the mourners to zoom in on her outburst, for yet a second time. Lowering her voice, she said, "That practice has been banned for over two decades."

"As with *forced marriages, but they still exist*." Mama Winnie shot a wary glance at Zuri. "We have to protect ourselves because the men will not. They welcome this practice because it almost always guarantees them a young virgin and a faithful wife. They prize those above all else."

Female genital mutilation was common practice amongst their tribe in Tanzania. Most girls were cut days after birth to puberty to control their sexuality. The belief was rooted in ideas about remaining pure, modest, and beautiful for their future husbands. They were cut, removing some or all external female genitalia, then sewn what flesh was left back together, leaving a small hole for urination and menstrual passage. Then later, the girl was forced open by their husband's penis or sliced open by a midwife for intercourse. The act was so painful and inhumane that the girls would rather swallow coal before having sex with their husbands, let alone, another man. The elder women of the tribe performed the ritual cutting. They viewed circumcision as a source of honor and a way to protect their daughters from social exclusion.

Zuri wrung her hands, frowning. "I remember some of the girls at school talking in a hushed manner about a secret initiation into womanhood where they learned about the duties of a wife. One of them said her older sister had it done and told her that sex hurts."

Mama Winnie nodded. "That is how it starts. At least it did for me." She winced, rubbing her hands in a circular motion on each of her thighs. "Suby overheard Godfrey talking with the Aku family about getting you *prepared* for Djimon. You were only eleven then. That is when Suby reached out to me, even though it put her life in danger, going against Godfrey's beliefs."

Zuri inverted her lips. The bitter, chalky taste of lipstick whirled on the tip of her tongue. "Mama could have been killed for helping me?"

An uncomfortable silence permeated around them.

Mama Winnie wrapped arms around her midriff, lowering her eyes to the ground. The implications of what Zuri's mother had accomplished settled into her soul. "Suby suffered for a long time, but she died at peace, knowing you were safe. That gave her joy. She would not be pleased you undid her life sacrifice by setting foot on Tanzanian soil. Even for her."

"What are you saying?" Zuri whispered, failing at the attempt to control her breathing. "Did … did Baba kill my Mama?"

Mama Winnie grabbed Zuri's hands. She squeezed so tight that Zuri's fingers throbbed all the way to her nailbeds.

"You are scaring me," Zuri said between her teeth, her entire body trembling because she was well aware her father valued money and status more than the rights or happiness of his daughter.

"Hello, Zuri," a lady with crow's feet approached them, using a wooden staff for support. "I am so happy you are home. We missed you. Come walk with me, child?"

Zuri hesitated for a moment, trying to place the older woman who seemed vaguely familiar. She didn't see any harm in complying with her request. Maybe she could tell Zuri stories about her Mama. She attempted to pull her hands away from Mama Winnie, but the grip she had on her fingers became even tighter. Zuri glanced down as the veins in Mama Winnie's knuckles protruded. Her eyes shifted upward to search the face of the woman who had protected Zuri her entire life. However, the exchange would manifest, Zuri would follow Mama Winnie's lead.

"Hello, Amidah," Mama Winnie said in a pleasant tone that contradicted her body language. "She is good here. With me."

Amidah chewed on her inner jaw. "Come see me later. Do not forget," she warned.

"Yes, ma'am." Zuri's gaze darted around the garden as Amidah moved at a snail's pace in the opposite direction. "Why does it feel like everyone is staring at me?"

Mama Winnie rose from the seat, gravitating forward, placing her forehead against Zuri's. "Regain your composure and stay solemn for the remaining of the celebration. Do not wander off with anyone. *Especially* Godfrey," she whispered. "We are coming to get you before sunrise, so be ready."

We?

"I have a flight back to Chicago first thing in the morning. Baba will not have a chance to …"

"My love, first you have to make it to the airport," Mama Winnie countered, kissing her on the forehead. "But, *we* have that covered."

Zuri remained seated, dazed, trying hard to instruct her brain to do what Mama Winnie asked. Unfortunately, fear and not knowing who to trust, she struggled to rein in her thoughts, then the gut punch struck her without warning.

"The answer to your question is yes."

Zuri's head snapped to attention, her eyes closing in on Mama Winnie's forlorn expression. "How do you know that for sure?"

"Because Suby refused to summon you here as he demanded. She took her last breath in my arms after a beating from your father." Her expression turned dark. "Now, you have played right into his hands."

CHAPTER 2

Zuri's eyes flew open, and her head jerked from left to right. As the haze clouding her sight dissipated, the outline of her Baba's face came into clear view. She attempted to rise, but the weight pressing against her shoulders kept Zuri grounded to the soft surface beneath her body.

"What happened to my daughter?" Godfrey asked, looming over Zuri.

"Noooooo," she cried writhing, kicking her legs.

"Look at me. Zuri," Mama Winnie said in a soothing tone, applying more pressure to her shoulders. "Follow the calming sound of my voice and turn your head to the right."

Zuri's chest expanded and caved at a rapid rate. Once she stopped thrashing, her eyes were lasered on the beige stucco ceiling and crystal sphere raindrop chandelier that she had admired as an adolescent. She was in the guest bedroom on the bottom level of the family home; one of the rooms that were always off-limits. Things must have gone awry if she were placed in that bed.

A breeze whisked through the coveted space, sweeping whispers of hair across Zuri's cheek.

She lifted trembling fingertips to her head and felt the moisture surrounding her hairline. Finally, turning her head to the right, she asked Mama Winnie, "What happened to my head tie?"

"It fell off when you blacked out in the garden," she responded, stroking Zuri's face with a damp cloth. "Do you remember?"

Zuri shook her head in protest, but she instantly recalled the last thing Mama Winnie told her, making her insides rumble. She winced in disgust.

"What is wrong with her?" Godfrey asked again. "Why is her face moving like that?"

His voice didn't seem as loud to Zuri as when he spoke the first time. She was tuning him out for the sake of her sanity.

"Sometimes grief strikes people in different ways," Mama Winnie explained, sitting on the bed at Zuri's side. "I also think the heat may have made Zuri weak. I should stay with her tonight to make sure she is okay," she suggested, angling her face in Godfrey's direction.

In addition to being an educator, Mama Winnie was a traditional healer which is how she knew first-hand that Godfrey had abused Suby. After every incident, she'd end up in Mama Winnie's care to be put back together, just so he could do it again and again.

"Do what you think is best," Godfrey said, observing his daughter.

"I can take her back to my place since you have a house full——"

"No. She stays here," he shouted, and the bass in his voice bounced off the far corners of the room.

"That is fine," Mama Winnie countered, getting to her feet. "I need to grab some items from home, and I will be back."

Panic rose so fast it flowed into the veins pulsating in Zuri's neck. She didn't want to be alone with Baba. Not after what she'd just learned.

"Hurry then, so you can get back," Godfrey ordered.

Standing in front of the window, his large frame eclipsed the natural light filtering into the room—— almost as a sign of how his will and might had overshadowed her mother's life. He turned to Zuri and said, "Djimon will stay with you until she returns. I will go get him."

Soon as Godfrey crossed the threshold into the hallway, Mama Winnie kissed Zuri on the temple and whispered, "This works out even better. Do not say anything while I am gone. The staff will look after you."

Lying in the room alone for the few minutes between Mamma Winnie's departure and Djimon's arrival, Zuri's emotions boiled from sadness and anger. She felt orphaned. Her Mama by death and her Baba might as well be dead after what he'd done. She would never forgive him.

Stewing in her thoughts of ways to make Baba pay for his crime, rapid footsteps getting closer by the second, jolted her heart rhythm. She quickly rolled onto her side, closed her eyes, and pretended to be asleep.

"Zuri," Djimon called out, tapping on the door as he entered. His spicy scent greeted her nostrils, and it wasn't a pleasant thing.

Her body tensed at the soft click of the door being closed. Zuri was familiar with the sound of *that* door easing closed, as she had snuck in the guest bedroom many times as a child before being caught. The spanking she received left a welt on her backside, a constant reminder of the damage Baba's bare hands could cause. She never entered that room again, until now.

"Zuri." Djimon's fragrance became even stronger as he sat alongside the bed, placing a hand on her hip.

She almost came undone by Djimon's touch. The fact that it was tender repulsed her even more. It took every ounce of willpower not to flinch. He had no right to put his hands on her body.

"I will be a good husband to you. Stop fighting what is destined to be from our ancestors." He sighed. "You already belong to me."

Djimon's hands traveled from the hip, then down her thigh to the hem of her dress. Zuri clamped down on her tongue to keep her breathing steady, but if he inched one finger underneath her clothing, she would strike him. She had never been touched sexually by a man, and her first experience would not be like this.

"You are so beautiful," Djimon whispered, caressing her thigh. A guttural moan rattled in his throat.

Zuri couldn't take much more of this unwanted attention. She shifted but never opened her eyes. He drew his hands away.

Thank you, Allah.

"Hey. Are you awake?" he asked. Zuri felt the warmth from his body as Djimon inched even closer. His rear end propped against her stomach.

Djimon must have leaned over because now, his minty breath swept across her lips and chin.

A couple knocks, followed by the door creaking open, Mama Winnie asked, "How is she?"

He shot up. His footsteps became a little distant. Zuri parted her lips slightly and released a long pent-up breath without making a sound.

"Hopefully, better. She has been sleeping the whole time," Djimon replied, and Zuri swore she heard sincerity in his tone. "I hope the rest helps. I will be with the family if you need anything."

"Thank you," Mama Winnie responded, closing the door behind him.

The click of the knob locking sprung Zuri from her make-believe slumber, gasping. "I am glad you came back when you did," she whispered, sitting upright. "He was about to kiss me."

"Did he touch you anywhere?" Mama Winnie inquired, her dark brown eyes narrowing to slits. She claimed the spot next to Zuri that Djimon vacated.

Inhaling through her nostrils and exhaling through pursed lips, Zuri said, "I am just glad you returned when you did and not a minute later." She reached over and embraced Mama Winnie with all her might.

Time stood still. In her arms was the safest Zuri had felt since she'd been back home.

Rubbing Zuri's back and putting a little space between them, Mama Winnie asked, "What did you bring with you? Where is your luggage?"

"The clothes on my back and a small carry-on duffel bag are all I have. Just enough room to carry a change of panties, toiletries, passport, boarding pass, money, and keys."

"You traveled light."

"I do not plan on staying longer than intended," Zuri shot back. "And now that I know what happened to Mama, I wish I could leave right now."

"Soon enough," Mama Winnie replied, pulling a phone from her purse and tapping the screen in rapid-fire with her thumbs.

After five minutes, Mama Winnie responded to a light tap on the door. Zuri observed the woman move across the floor. Unlocking the door, Mama Winnie grabbed a midnight blue duffel bag from the longtime housemaid, Mama Olivia then closed the door behind her.

"How did she know to bring my bag?" Zuri inquired, pushing her palms into the plush mattress.

"Because she is helping us," Mama Winnie said, handing Zuri her duffel bag. "You have allies all around you. We made a promise to Suby to continue her life mission of protecting you."

Zuri's heart was filled with gratitude and appreciation for the village of women who banded together.

Mama Winnie dumped the contents of the bag onto the bed, then pulled out a switchblade and cut the lining along the seams.

"What are you doing?" Zuri stared in disbelief.

Mama Winnie didn't respond right away. Once she finished slicing the seams on both sides with a skilled hand, she stood, hiked up her dress, and pulled a beautiful gold pistol from a holster strapped around her thigh.

Zuri jumped to her feet. A sudden pain shot through her right temple, and her mouth gaped as Mama Winnie placed the firearm in Zuri's hands.

"Close your mouth, chile. You will catch a fly," she teased, pinching Zuri's chin. Mama Winnie held one hand under Zuri's and slid the other one over the weapon. "Listen to me. This is made of fourteen-karat gold. It is one-hundred percent undetectable by airport security. I am padding and sewing the gun into the seam of your bag, distributing equal weight on both sides. You may get randomly pulled out of line by customs, and if they search your bag, I want them to come up empty." She paused for a moment. "Are you following me?"

"Yesss," Zuri said so slow that it seemed as if merely speaking caused her excruciating pain.

"Because this is not made of steel, the gun is only good for *one shot*," Mama Winnie gazed into her eyes and lifted a brow. "One shot. So, make it count if you ever have to use it."

* * *

A tap on Zuri's shoulder interrupted an already unrestful slumber.

"It is time," Mama Winnie whispered, dressed in all black, appearing like a thief in the night. She handed Zuri a pair of pants and a long black caftan with a hood. "Put these on and hurry."

Zuri hopped into the clothes, keeping a watchful eye on Mama Winnie standing guard at the door. Zuri searched the floor for her heels. They were the only shoes she had brought.

"I am ready," Zuri whispered, scanning the room. "But I cannot find my shoes."

Mama Winnie whisked over, grabbing Zuri by the wrist, and guiding her toward the moonlight peering through the glass. "They are in your bag. Tuck the caftan in your pants," she instructed, slowly lifting the window.

"Where is the bag?" she asked, stuffing the flowy material in the waistband.

Mama Winnie placed a hard glare on Zuri, and she knew to be quiet. "Kassanna, Bupe, Lillian, Agness, and Eunice are waiting for you on the ground. You climb out first, then I will follow."

Once both women made it to the ground, Mama Winnie untucked Zuri's caftan. She retrieved Zuri's duffel bag from Agness and placed it on Zuri's shoulder. She had created a make-shift strap with Velcro, wrapped it underneath Zuri's breastbone, and fastened the straps on the opposite side.

"This way, if we have to make a run for it, your passport and boarding pass will be with you," Mama Winnie explained as the women gathered around. "We have to walk a mile and a half to clear the property grounds and another half a mile to reach transport. Anything closer than that, Godfrey and his security will notice."

Mama Winnie put her focus on Zuri. "High heels leave distinct markings in the dirt, so we are all traveling in flip-flops. You can switch your footwear when we reach our destination."

Zuri nodded, understanding the meticulous planning of the situation. She flipped the hood over her head.

"Ladies, you know what we have to do if we encounter any trouble along the way," Mama Winnie said in a low tone.

Eunice, a middle-aged, athletically built sprinter, pulled a machete from the invisible sheath under her caftan. "Armed and ready."

Kassanna, a silver-haired woman with the energy of a twenty-year-old was another healer of the tribe. She opened a kangaroo-styled pouch on the front of her caftan. "I have twelve syringes filled with a fast-acting agent that will cause delirium, then knock a person out for up to three hours."

Each woman flashed her weaponry. These women of the tribe were risking their lives to protect Suby's daughter. They, because of her mother, believed in women's rights and were willing to sacrifice for the next generation.

Tsetse flies, buzzing cicadas, chirping crickets, and an occasional cool breeze accompanied them on their tense-filled journey. They walked in a single-file line, holding onto the caftan of the person in front of them. Fading lights from the houses helped gauge the distance traveled.

Within twenty-two minutes, they crossed the property grounds without any snags. Pausing for a quick water break, Lillian said in a trembling voice, "Lights are coming toward us."

"Everybody down," Mama Winnie ordered, yanking Zuri by the arm.

Zuri laid in the brush, the shrubs and small trees scratched her face. She was thankful more than ever for the long caftan that protected her body.

The jeep moved at a slow pace, stopping only feet away from them. Zuri's heart was pounding so hard that she thought the men nearby could hear it, too.

"I am sure I saw movement out here," a man said, his voice dark and husky; the only outstanding trait because his features were hidden in the darkness. His feet crunched as he stepped on the undergrowth.

"In the middle of nowhere," another man replied with a questioning tone. "Probably one of the cattle got away from the herd."

"Let's go check it out," the first man said, the sound of his voice getting closer by the second."

Mama Winnie squeezed Zuri's arm as the curious man stood in front of them. If he took one more step, he would kick Bupe in the head.

"Come on, Rashid. There is nothing out there," he called out. "Let the next shift do a search and find mission. I am tired and I do not feel like wrestling cattle in the middle of the night."

A strange silence filtered the air above them.

"Rashid. What are you waiting for?"

Zuri closed her eyes and prayed.

"Something peculiar is going on. I just do not know what it is," Rashid mumbled, turning on his heels and maneuvering back to the jeep. The crunch of the brush under his feet was a welcomed sound.

The vehicle sped off, kicking up sand in its wake. The women muffled coughs, by drawing hands to their mouths as they got to their feet.

Zuri took in a sudden inhalation of air, panting.

"It is okay," Mama Winnie reassured, grabbing Zuri's hand and helping her stand. "We anticipate the guards patrolling the grounds. That is why we left at three-thirty, so I could time their runs," she explained, squeezing Zuri's arm. "We have to keep moving. By the time they circle around again, we will be long gone."

"I thought I would have to gut that man like a kudu," Bupe said, sliding a scalpel underneath a black wristband, then pulling her sleeve over as a camouflage. "One slice to the peroneal artery at the back of his ankle, and he was a dead man."

Bupe was in medical school to become a cardiovascular surgeon, a once male-dominated profession in Tanzania.

"I am glad it did not come to that," Mama Winnie commented as they trekked the final stretch of the terrain with the stealth of a lion stalking its prey.

For twelve minutes, only the sound of their feet and nature filtered their ears until Mama Winnie halted. The women came to a complete stop.

"Shhhhhh," Mama Winnie whispered.

Zuri scanned the darkness and wondered why they had ceased movement. She couldn't see anything—— not even a hand in front of her face.

A low-hum percolated nearby, and the smell of exhaust wafted through the cool breeze.

"Do you hear *that?*" Lillian asked, tugging Eunice's caftan.

"Sounds like a car," Zuri said, not giving anyone a chance to answer.

"Quiet," Mama Winnie ordered, moving forward. "This way, ladies."

"Winnie. Are you sure?" Kassanna inquired. "I thought the jeep was supposed to be on the other side of the valley."

"No. That is a decoy to throw off the guards," Mama Winnie countered.

"Then who is that?" Lillian asked, scooting closer to Zuri.

Mama Winnie parted her lips to answer when a series of whistles rang out. "Right on time," she mumbled under her breath, then faced the women. "Listen closely. That is our ride. Be prepared to fight just in case our driver was hijacked by the guards. We will not know that until we get close enough to board the back of the Humvee," Mama Winnie said as the women grasped their weapons. "The mission is to get Zuri to the airport by any means necessary. If we have to fight off the men, make sure one of you take over the Humvee and drive Zuri directly there. We will deal with the fall out later."

"Yes, Mama Winnie," the women replied in a low tone.

"One more thing," Mama Winnie said, grabbing Zuri's hand. "Put this away. Do not open the note until you get on your flight back to America," she instructed, shoving a small piece of paper into the palm of Zuri's hand, then bending her fingers closed.

CHAPTER 3

The hour drive to the airport in the back of the dark Humvee seemed never-ending. Zuri was quite surprised to learn that the two men helping them were Baba's groundskeepers. She questioned their loyalty from the moment she learned their identity, but if Mama Winnie enlisted them, then they must be legit.

They made it to the airport with only a few close calls of being caught. Sadness enveloped Zuri, gazing at the women who had risked their lives to ensure her safety.

"Until we meet again." Mama Winnie pulled Zuri into her bosom. "I love you."

"I love you back and thank you for everything," she replied, fighting back the tears before breaking the embrace and facing the other women. "Thank all of you. Much love and appreciation for all you have done for me."

The women said their goodbyes, then Mama Winnie and Zuri climbed out of the Humvee and entered Kilimanjaro International Airport in northern Tanzania that served the cities of Arusha and Moshi. Zuri went straight to the security checkpoint since she already had her boarding pass.

After several minutes of looking over her shoulder, Zuri finally made it to the front of the line. She turned and waved one last time, then scanned the immediate area, handing the security agent her boarding pass and passport. Mama Winnie waved emphatically.

Zuri maneuvered into the next set of security checkpoints to scan her body and luggage. While waiting in line to put her items on the conveyor belt, she turned around a second time to catch a final glimpse of the woman who loved Zuri as her own daughter, and her legs almost gave way.

Godfrey had grabbed Mama Winnie and was shaking her by the shoulders.

"Miss, you're holding up the line," said the man in a brown suit holding a briefcase standing behind Zuri, gesturing for her to step forward.

Frozen solid, Zuri stared past him, her eyes locked on Baba handling Mama Winnie like she wasn't a woman. "Excuse me." She nudged the man out of her way and pushed through the crowd toward Mama Winnie, her heartbreaking with every step she took.

Approaching the third passenger in line, she came up short as she stared into the gentle eyes of Mama Olivia. "I cannot let you do that."

"What are you doing here? You did not come with us," Zuri asked the housemaid who cared for her as a child, glancing over the short woman's silky braided white hair. "We need to help Mama Winnie."

"Turn around and walk. You are next," Mama Olivia said, prompting Zuri to move forward. "Winnie *knows* what she is doing."

"But." Zuri pointed a trembling finger.

"Next," the pudgy TSA worker said in a loud voice.

As Zuri moved forward to put her items on the conveyor belt, she prayed the surprise Mama Winnie embedded in her duffel bag remained hidden or else she'd end up behind bars, and Baba would be the least of her worries.

Zuri stepped into the body scanner as her belongings glided in a gray bin through the thermal scan demodulator. A loud beep made Zuri jump, and the impatient man who came through before Zuri glanced in her direction and winked just as police officers swarmed around him.

"What are you doing with a knife in your carry-on, sir?" an officer asked the man, grabbing him by the arm with such force it might break.

"You are good, Miss," another TSA worker with shoulder-length locs said, waving Zuri through. "Do not forget your belongings."

"Um. Okay." She hesitated, frightened by the commotion, but relieved that the sensor hadn't told the world her secret.

Mama Olivia came through security right behind Zuri.

Zuri leaned in and whispered, "Did you see that man wink at me?"

"He is with us, too." Mama Olivia smiled. "A decoy to take the focus off of your luggage, just in case it was flagged."

Zuri was still amazed at the meticulous planning Mama Winnie had orchestrated with the help of the tribe and others.

"I will stay with you until you board," Mama Olivia said as they headed toward the gate. "I know you are worried about Winnie. She is fine. We anticipated Godfrey either following us or showing up at the airport. He may suspect Winnie helped you, but he does not have any proof."

"But what about you, Mama Olivia Zuri asked, as a sadness coursed through her heart. She didn't want Baba to take out his frustrations on any of the women. "What will happen if he finds out you helped me?"

"Chile, you do not have to worry about this old woman. I am on a two-week vacation to visit my great-granddaughter," she explained. "I only came to the house for Suby's home-going celebration." Pausing for a moment to catch her breath, Mama Olivia said, "I promised your mother I would always look after you, so I was more than happy to help and grateful to see your beautiful face, if even only for a minute."

Finally, making it to the gate, Zuri sat with her back to the window so she could see the travelers who walked past and hoped none of them were her Baba. Unzipping the pouch inside her duffel bag, Zuri pulled out the note and unfolded a worn paper on one side, then she heard Mama Winnie's voice in her head telling her to wait, so she put it back.

Flight 834 to Chicago is boarding now.

"This is it," Zuri said, releasing a breath she wasn't aware she'd been holding. She wrapped her arms around Mama Olivia and kissed her soft-wrinkled cheek. "I love you."

"You make your Mama proud. Be everything she knew you were

destined to be," she nodded; her cloudy dark-brown eyes were glistening.

"Yes, ma'am."

The pool of tears in Zuri's eyes, cascaded down her cheeks as she walked over and stood in line. This was the last time she'd see her homeland, but intuition told her this wouldn't be the last time she'd see her Baba.

Zuri handed her boarding pass to a female TSA worker with a smile that could light up the darkest of days. The woman scanned and gave it back to Zuri. One final glance over her shoulder at Mama Olivia who blew a kiss and waved, then she faded from view as Zuri traipsed down the ramp to board.

Sitting in a window seat, she placed the duffel bag in her lap, then retrieved the note from Mama Winnie. Zuri glanced at the woman who claimed the middle seat next to her, unfolded the paper, and angled it toward the window so the passenger couldn't read the contents.

Zuri instantly recognized her mother's handwriting.

If you ever need an emergency place of refuge, go to the Second Chance at Life Women's Shelter on Seventy-Ninth and Cottage Grove in Chicago. Ask for Mariano DeLuca and no one else.

How did she know I would need this?

Zuri folded the piece of paper, placed it back in her bag, and committed the name and address to memory.

Who is Mariano DeLuca?

CHAPTER 4

Zuri deplaned the twenty-hour flight from Tanzania, spent the night at O'Hare International Airport because of the eight-hour time zone difference, then took an Uber to the Second Chance at Life Women's Shelter the following morning.

Her mind raced during the fifty-minute drive as she took in the sights along the Edens Expressway on the north side of the city to the Dan Ryan Expressway on the south side. She never knew how different the two sides of town were since she'd never been on the south side in the five years that she'd lived in Chicago.

Zuri's life had consisted of going to class on UIC campus in the West-Loop, working in the university bookstore, and patronizing the local eateries. Occasionally, she and a few classmates would venture over to Millennium Park or Buckingham Fountain in the downtown area or catch a Cubs Game at Wrigley Field on the far north side during the summer months.

The driver traveled up the exit ramp on Seventy-Ninth Street, and Zuri didn't know what to think. Droves of young men hung out in the corner parking lot of a fast-food restaurant. Their pants hanging off of their backsides, loud music blared, and the smell of marijuana engulfed the car.

She had second thoughts and almost asked the driver to take her back to her dorm on campus, but two things stopped her. One, she trusted her Mama. If this was a place she recommended, Zuri knew she did it for a reason. Secondly, Baba might have taken a flight out of Tanzania and followed her. The first place he would check would be the University of Illinois at Chicago.

"Thank you," Zuri said to the driver as they pulled in front of a massive white building on the corner of Seventy-Ninth and Cottage Grove. The place had large picture windows and a glass door with Second Chance at Life Women's Shelter above the entrance. She clutched her duffel bag under her arm and left the vehicle.

The driver pulled away from the curb, leaving Zuri entranced by the questionable surroundings. Backing toward the building, a red muscle car pulled into the intersection and came to a screeching halt. Two men jumped out of the backseat and yelled vulgar obscenities and ran in her direction with guns in their hands. Zuri yanked the door open and dashed inside, bumping into a man, knocking him to the floor.

"I am so sorry, sir," Zuri said, pushing the door closed and turning the lock.

"Boss, are you okay? asked a copper-toned woman in a white blouse, polka dot circle skirt, and red heels. She rushed from behind a desk to the man's aid.

"Yes, Skyler," he responded, getting to his feet and wiping off his slacks. Moving forward, he asked, "May we help you?"

Zuri gave the man a once-over. His green eyes seemed kind, especially for someone who had just been knocked down by a stranger. No form of anger was present in his handsome sun-kissed face with a five o'clock shadow that gave him an edge or in his body language.

"I am looking for Mariano DeLuca," she said, squealing from the police sirens zooming down Cottage Grove.

"No need to worry about that. You're safe in here," he reassured, gesturing for Zuri to come further inside. "I'm Mariano. How may I help you?"

Zuri scanned the lobby. She'd been in a shelter before in Tanzania while volunteering with her school, and it didn't look anything like this. Where were the cots? Where were the workers? Soft elevator music played in the background, reminding her of a hotel lobby.

"I am not sure," Zuri countered, slowly stepping backward. "This does not look like any shelter I have ever seen."

"Our first floor is designated for client intake. We want to make the women feel as comfortable as possible in an uneasy situation, hence the mellow music and homestyle seating and lighting," the woman said as she came over. "I'm Skyler Pierson, Mariano's assistant."

"Zuri Okusanya," she said, moving forward and claiming a seat on the round sofa chair.

"Okusanya," Reno repeated, narrowing his eyes as he lowered his bottom in the seat across from Zuri. He placed a hand under his chin and gazed into her dark brown orbs, putting Zuri on edge.

She felt transparent as if he were looking right into her soul.

Skyler observed for a moment before she continued, "The living quarters are upstairs so the women can have maximum security and privacy. Safety is our top priority."

Reno's hand slid into his lap. "You're Suby's daughter."

Zuri flinched, causing every hair on her body to stand at attention. "How did you——?" She paused, taking a deep breath and shifting in the seat. "You knew my Mama."

"Knew," Reno echoed, leaning forward with a bewildered expression.

"She passed away a few days ago," Zuri whispered, lowering her gaze to her lap.

"Sorry for your loss," Skyler said, touching a comforting hand to Zuri's shoulder before walking away.

"Me too," Reno added, reaching his hand toward her, but pulling back before contact was made.

Zuri saw the gesture. It was sweet of him to try to comfort her, but all she wanted to know was how Mariano knew her Mama. How and when did someone like him and her cross paths? What made her trust a man? The men from where she came from only wanted the women for sex slaves, childbearing, and to work from sun-up to sundown, all while pleasuring them and raising their kids. The women's happiness never factors into the equation.

"I appreciate that, but how did——?"

"I met Suby at a women's conference at McCormick Place a little over five years ago."

"Sorry for interrupting, but how did you meet her at a women's conference?" Zuri asked, gazing at Reno. "I thought you had to be a woman to participate."

"True, but the founder of the conference was aware of the service I provided for women and allowed me to speak," he explained, putting his weight on the arm of the chair. "After the conference, Suby introduced herself. I could never forget that moment."

Intrigued, Zuri asked, "How so?"

"The tenderness in Suby's voice through her thick African accent was different than any other I'd ever heard before," Reno said, smiling. "And she smelled like berries. Not perfume, but fresh berries picked from the garden. Kind of the way you smell right now."

Heat rushed beneath Zuri's cheeks, and she was grateful that she had a dark complexion, or else Reno would have seen her blush.

"Suby asked me about the shelter and the programs I ran to help women get back on their feet. She told me she had a daughter and that one day, you may need my help. She asked for a business card and said, *"I am trusting you to do right by my girl if she ever graces your door."* And then she left. She never told me your first name," Reno stated, shaking his head. "But when you said your last name was Okusanya, and the fact that you have Suby's soulful eyes and the same exotic dialect, I just knew."

Zuri placed a hand over her heart. "I am still learning about the depths at which Mama has gone to protect me."

They sat in silence for a moment as Zuri absorbed Mama's foresight. She loved her more every day and wished things could have been different.

Skyler resurfaced with a serving tray and a sympathetic expression.

"Zuri. Would you like some coffee, tea, or water?"

She reached for the bottle of water, nearly knocking it over at the loud voices of men swearing as they hovered around the entrance.

"You don't have anything to worry about," Reno reassured. "That's normal."

"Baba may have sent them …" Zuri said with a trembling voice, brushing past Skyler and hiding behind the front desk.

Reno and Skyler rushed over.

"Zuri," Skyler said in a tender tone. "You're safe. We keep the door locked. No one's coming in here. You have my word."

"But I came in without any issues," Zuri shot back.

"That's because you caught me on the way out," Reno explained, moving closer to the desk. "I unlocked the door, then realized I left my phone in the office. I had gone back to retrieve it and was leaving out when we collided. That was my mistake. One that won't happen again," Reno added, extending a hand, hoping Zuri would trust him enough to grab hold. "I won't let anyone hurt you. I promise."

"You can trust Mr. DeLuca," Skyler soothed, her manicured hand stroking the woman's trembling one. "He helps women every day who need a safe place to stay."

Zuri knew she could trust Mariano because her Mama had. That was all the confirmation she needed. The element lurking outside the door was another thing.

Reno turned on his heels and maneuvered briskly toward the entrance. He swung the door open and shouted, "Take that mess down the street before I call the police."

Zuri peered over the desk while Skyler kept hold of her hand.

"Ain't nobody scared of you, white boy. Go help them strung-out chicks in your hood. You don't belong here," the man spat in Reno's face.

"Dude. You got one minute or else I'm putting in that call, and they'll be here quicker than you can move your ass off the curb."

"Man, please," another guy chimed in, waving Reno off. "The Po-Po don't move that fast around here. You got your zip codes mixed up."

He slapped hands with his buddy and laughed.

"But they will if *I* call them. Do you wanna find out?" Reno glanced down at his watch. "Thirty seconds."

"Whatever, with your privileged ass," the first dude said, pursing his lips. "I'll see you around."

Once Reno closed and locked the door, Zuri stood and glanced in his direction. "Thank you."

"We'll take good care of you," he vowed, returning her gaze. "Can we start your intake paperwork, and you can tell me in further detail why you think your father's after you?" Reno's phone chimed. He shoved a hand in his pocket, and the ringing subsided.

"Sure."

"Come with me," he instructed as they moved into a small corner with a desk, Mac, and two swivel chairs, and a partition for privacy.

Reno's phone rang a second time, then a third. He ignored those calls, too.

"I can wait if you need to answer that," Zuri said, taking a seat and pulling the duffel bag into her lap. "I do not mind."

Reno parted his lips. "Let's get——"

"Excuse me," Skyler said, stepping halfway inside the cubicle. "Here's your water."

"Thank you." Zuri twisted the cap off, then took a few sips.

"If you need me, I'll be at my desk."

Reno nodded, settling into the office chair. Skyler smiled and sauntered away. The clicking sound of her heels faded into the background.

Things had started off a bit rough when Zuri first arrived at the shelter, but she was starting to feel more comfortable, especially after witnessing Reno handle those men. She believed him when he said he'd protect her. This was the first time she trusted a man *ever*.

"Why would your father send men after you?" Reno asked, resting his hands on the desktop.

Before she could reply, they both zoned in on the fast approaching clicking sound against the floor.

Skyler knocked on the partition and rushed in. "You have an important call."

"Take a message. I'll call them back."

"The man said to tell you it's Kaleb Valentine. I'll finish," Skyler insisted. "Go on. We'll be okay."

"Thanks," he said, then turned to Zuri. "I'll be right back." Zuri nodded and gave him a wan smile.

He maneuvered from behind the desk and jogged out of the cubicle.

"What is your job here?" Zuri asked, glancing at Skyler.

"I help Mariano with whatever he needs. Intake, place orders, phone calls, but mostly, I'm here to serve the women and make sure they're doing okay."

"It is so quiet," Zuri commented, scanning the immediate area. "Kind of hard to believe this is a shelter."

"I can see how you've come to that conclusion, but we're definitely in the business of helping women. During the day, most of the clients are at work, job placement programs, trade school, individual and-or family therapy," Skyler explained, leaning her backside against the desk and crossing her ankles. "The kids are in school, but now, during the summer months, they're at day camp or have tutoring sessions to keep them on task for the following school year."

"That is a lot for one person to take on," Zuri said, sipping more of the water.

"I'm happy to do it," Skyler countered, moving to the empty seat next to Zuri and lowering her bottom into it. "I was once a client of the shelter after my husband kicked us out to play house with his mistress. Pregnant with one child and another one in tow. It took me two years to get back on my feet. Mariano helped me in ways I could never repay him for, like giving me this job. So, I'm more than happy to give back to him and be whomever he needs me to be for the women that are here."

"I understand."

Skyler's empathy for the women oozed into Zuri, and she knew exactly why this was the right place for her. At least, until she graduated and could find an apartment in an area that was nowhere near campus, which would throw Baba off of her trail.

"What forms do I need to fill out?"

Skyler rose, moving around the desk when Reno rushed in, almost knocking her down.

"I have to go," he said, pulling keys from his pants pocket.

"What about me?" Zuri shot back, confused by the man who just entered the cubicle. He wasn't the person who left five minutes prior. His demeanor and facial expression were panic-stricken.

"Please don't leave," he begged, taking her hands in his. "Someone close to me has been shot. I have to get to him." He waited a few moments for that to absorb. "I can help you. Promise you'll stay here with Skyler until I get back."

Zuri gazed into his pleading green eyes and got lost in the trance. Hypnotism was real. If she wasn't a believer before, she was now. After holding his stare for what felt like an eternity but was closer to a few seconds, Zuri glanced downward.

"Reno, you need to go," Skyler reminded him, clearing her throat.

"Not until I get an answer," Reno insisted, squatting beside Zuri and lifting her hand into his.

Zuri quivered at the unfamiliar surge that ran through her body from his touch. She'd never felt that before. She liked it. Channeling her focus back on Reno's face, Zuri pulled her hands away and responded, "I'll stay."

"Great." He smiled and shot out of the cubicle faster than an Olympic sprinter.

CHAPTER 5

Thirty minutes into Reno's drive to The Castle, an urgent alert came through his phone. The silent alarm at The Second Chance at Life Women's Shelter had been activated. He pulled onto the shoulder, threw the gear in park, and dialed the shelter to reach his assistant. When Skyler didn't answer, he opened the security app to check the surveillance cameras, but that function was interrupted by an incoming call from an unknown number.

"Hello."

"Mr. DeLuca, this is Sergeant Michaels with the Chicago Police Department. I'm calling because your alarm was tripped, and I want to make sure everything's okay."

"I don't know. I'm not there," Reno responded, putting the gear in drive, then exiting the off-ramp. He made two quick left turns and entered the expressway in the opposite direction. "I can't reach my assistant."

"Don't worry, Mr. DeLuca, there are several cars in the area. I'll send one right over."

"Thank you," Reno replied, flooring the gas pedal. "I'm on the way."

"There's an active shooter in the area, so be careful. The perimeter is a mile long in each direction," Sgt. Michael said, releasing a sigh. "I shouldn't have told you that, seeing as though you're a civilian, but

Lieutenant Knox said to keep you in the loop."

Knox and Reno had a private arrangement. Reno protected his daughter from her drug-addicted mother and made sure she and the entire family received counseling under the radar while keeping the façade of the Lieutenant's happy home intact with the department. In return, the police and their resources were at his disposal.

"Continue," Reno urged, whizzing through traffic like a professional Nascar driver.

"I've already sent your information over to the officers guarding the perimeter. Just show them your driver's license. They'll have a protective vest and a two-way radio waiting for you."

Reno shaved fifteen minutes off the return trip to the shelter. He made it through the security checkpoint. After stepping into forensic shoe covers so the crime scene wouldn't be tainted, he slid on the protective vest. Detective Xavier Carter gave him a personal escort to the doors of the shelter. Immediately, Reno noticed the spider cracks in the bulletproof glass door and window.

"Smart move, installing bulletproof glass to your building. Especially since your business sits in the middle of a crime-riddled neighborhood," the burly dark-skinned Detective Carter said, signaling the other cop to join them. "This is my partner, Detective Jason Sharpe. We're going to do a sweep of the building before granting entry." Detective Carter took a two-way radio from the clip on his belt and switched it on. "Wait here. If you see something, call out."

"Is there anyone in the building?" Detective Sharpe with the cobalt blue eyes and short-spiked hair inquired, retrieving his service weapon from its holster.

"Yes," Reno said quickly. "My assistant, Skyler Pierson, whom I haven't been able to reach, thirty women who reside upstairs, cleaning, and kitchen staff … and Zuri."

"Zuri," Detective Sharpe echoed.

Reno realized that he had singled her out. He shouldn't have done that. According to Zuri, her father's connections had a wide range. Even though these Detectives were part of the lieutenant's handpicked team, he didn't know them well enough to trust them with Zuri's life.

"Anyone inside who isn't a female is an intruder."

"Got it," Detective Sharpe countered, following Detective Carter into the building.

They returned within eight minutes with Skyler in tow. "It's safe to enter."

"I'm so glad to see you," Skyler said, flinging her copper-tone-skin arms around Reno. Her curly hair was covering his face. "I'm okay. Everyone's okay."

Reno raised an eyebrow.

"Yes. Everyone," Skyler replied, putting emphasis on the last word.

Reno was glad that Skyler, who had been with him for six years, knew how to read between the lines. He didn't want to repeat Zuri's name again and put the detective on notice.

"Do you know what happened?" Detective Carter asked.

"I was working at my desk, then rapid shots rang out of nowhere, followed by an alert that there was activity at the rear service door," Skyler explained, twirling the cross-shaped charm dangling from her necklace. "I thought someone was trying to break-in. Next thing I know, I heard two explosions, which turned out to be the bullets hitting the door and the window. I reached to hit the panic button, but it had already been activated—— probably from the force of the impact. We locked ourselves upstairs in the panic room."

"Quick thinking," Detective Carter said, facing Skyler. "We're going to check your service entrance to make sure there isn't any damage."

While the detectives triple-checked the premises, Reno was already on the phone, making arrangements to relocate the women to his family's estate in Rockford. He had several acres of land sectioned off for emergency housing if the need ever arose.

"Adali Automotives, Cadence Goldsmith speaking."

"Cadence. This is Mariano."

"Hey, Reno. What's up?"

"I need you to send a bulletproof charter bus to The Second Chance at Life Women's Shelter, ASAP. Do you have one available?"

"Let me check."

Reno waited as he listened to the recognizable sound of keys being punched on a keyboard.

He met Cadence when his firm drew up the plans for the European auto conglomerate's cutting-edge office building. He was impressed to meet the youngest Chief Design Officer, female automotive engineer *ever.* They became friends over the three years it took to build the fifty-two-story skyscraper.

"You know there are two bus companies in your immediate area," Cadence informed him.

"I know, but they don't provide what you offer."

After several minutes, she responded, "I have a bus that's on its way back to the barn. I'll send the driver your way."

"Please do. Bill my account and take an extra grand for the inconvenience."

"That's not necessary."

"Take it anyway. I'll have the bus back to you by the end of business today. Thanks."

"Mariano, I have a suggestion," Skyler said, inching forward after he put the phone away. "I'm going to remain at the shelter——"

"Absolutely not."

"Someone needs to be here for intake."

"I understand that, but not at the risk of your safety." Reno frowned, pointing toward the front entrance. "Our security has been compromised."

"No, it hasn't," she rebutted, walking to the door and sliding her manicured fingers across the glass, then repeating the action along the window. "If anything, today's activity has proven that the extra precautions you took actually work. The bullets didn't penetrate the glass at all. The cracks are on the outside layer only." She paused, facing Reno. "Which is what it's designed to do."

Reno pondered what Skyler said as he strode over and swiped a hand along the clear pane where the ammunition hit. The surface was smooth with no abrasions. "I'm still not comfortable with the glass in this state."

He pulled out his phone and placed a call to the glass company, leaving a message on their voicemail.

"I'll make you a promise. Once the potential clients are safeguarded, I'll bring them to the Rockford estate with the rest of the women." Skyler extended her hand. "Deal?"

"The service door is secure and hasn't been damaged," Detective Carter announced as he entered the main lobby with Detective Sharpe at his side.

"Then it's settled," she remarked, glancing at Reno for approval.

He shook his head, giving Skyler a half-grin, then turned his attention toward the detectives. "Thank you very much."

"Anytime." Detective Carter said, shaking Reno's hand. "Here's my card. My personal number's on the back. Call if you ever need anything."

"Will do."

Once they left the building, Reno contemplated Skyler's suggestion. He still was against her staying behind, but Skyler's passion for helping women in need was deep-rooted, especially since she was a former recipient of the shelter's services.

"Okay, Skyler."

"Thanks, Mariano. I promise I'll be careful."

"I know you will," he said nodding. "But don't think for one second I'm leaving you here alone." He plucked his phone from his pocket and scrolled through his contacts. "You'll have a personal security detail here within the hour. In the meantime, let the women out of the panic room, so they can gather their things. The bus will be here soon."

"What about Zuri? She hasn't finished filling out the paperwork."

"No worries. She's riding with me."

CHAPTER 6

Khalil's fighting for his life and they want to question Kaleb's loyalties.

Reno played back the phone conversation he had with Kaleb four hours earlier as he trailed Vikkas to the private waiting room at Northwestern Hospital. Vikkas was on the same darn page as the other guys, questioning Reno's connection to Kaleb. Reno would give Vikkas a pass, considering the circumstances. He'd play it cool, at least until he got a status update on Khalil, but after that, he couldn't be held responsible for what came out of his mouth.

Vikkas grabbed the door handle and stopped abruptly, causing Reno to step on the back of his heel.

"My bad," Reno said, taking a few footsteps backward.

"Just be cool," Vikkas warned, placing a hand on Reno's shoulder. "We're all here for the same reason."

"So, you're a mind reader now," Reno shot back, lifting his chin upward, casting a side-eyed glance at Vikkas.

"It's been a long time since we've been in each other's presence, but I think I, of all people, still know your tendencies."

"Hmph," Reno grunted, slamming his hands into his pockets. He wouldn't deny or confirm the judgment, even though Vikkas was on point. His insight had always been superb, except for when it came to Kaleb.

Vikkas opened the door, then stepped inside and said, "Not quite Cali."

"And not quite Vegas," Shaz chimed in, sweeping his locs over his shoulder.

"It's Reno, all the way, baby," all of the men chanted, then laughed and welcomed Vikkas and Reno into the circle of their embrace.

The familiar brotherhood mantra reminded Reno of their younger days when the only concerns they had were maintaining their GPAs, Khalil's life lessons, martial arts, weapons training, and girls.

"How's Papa K?" Reno asked, straightening his collar.

"He's in recovery," Dro answered, rubbing his hands together. "They were able to remove the bullets and most of the fragments. Now we have to see if any permanent damage was sustained. We asked to see him, but the nurse said she'd let us know when we could."

Daron checked his watch. "That was several hours ago."

"Where've you been?" Grant asked, closing the gap between them. "Khalil wanted to speak with all of us individually before the surgery. He damn near jeopardized his survival rate waiting for you to arrive," Grant huffed, his breath danced on Reno's face. "They couldn't delay any longer. The anesthesiologist was forced to put him under."

Reno did not appreciate Grant's tone, but he answered anyway, "I had to evacuate the women from the shelter and take them to my family's estate in Rockford."

"I told them this already," a voice that Reno knew better than his own, said from the far corner of the room.

"Kveeeeee," Reno crooned, turning his back on Grant and walking over to give Kaleb a brotherly hug.

"Always, Mr. GQ," Kaleb cracked, breaking the embrace, wiping the pretend dust off of Reno's shoulder, then tugging on the lapel of his suit jacket. "I see some things don't change."

"Whatever, man." Reno grinned, popping Kaleb in the back of his head full of brush-waves that would make the ocean sea-sick. "How's your mom?"

They claimed two seats in the area where Kaleb had been sitting.

Kaleb parted his lips to speak, but Reno held up an index finger, silencing any further speech. The looks of disdain on his brother's faces gave him pause and brought Reno back to the reason he'd felt some kind of way about the snide comments that were made toward Kaleb before he arrived.

"Let me holla at y'all for a second," Reno said, raising out of the chair.

"This is not the time," Vikkas shot back, approaching Reno and grabbing his arm.

"It's the perfect time," Reno countered, shaking him off. "Who knows when we'll all be together again."

The men gathered around, some with their arms crossed, while others leaned against the wall.

"I'm not sure why some of you are having a problem with Kaleb, but if he has Khalil's stamp of approval, the rest of you need to back up and get on board."

"He's never been one of us," Shaz commented, giving Reno an intense glare.

"Does he have to be?" Reno fired back.

"I'm not my past," Kaleb defended, standing in front of them, and stroking his full-beard. "You can't judge me off of the fourteen-year-old kid you barely knew at Macro. We all have things in our background that we aren't proud of; the only difference was that my foolishness was on display."

The creak of the door opening snapped everyone's attention toward the sound. "Mr. Germaine is awake, and he's lucid," the dark-haired nurse announced with a smile. "He can have visitors, but only one at a time as he still needs his rest."

"Thank you so much," Vikkas said, as Jai pulled him into a hug.

The two men looked so much alike that they could have been brothers.

"Understood." Daron nodded.

"Great. Thank you." Reno and Kaleb exchanged a look and winked.

"Thanks a lot," Grant, Shaz, and Dro, said, shaking her hand.

"We appreciate your kindness." Dwayne beamed at the woman whose cheeks flushed a shade of pink.

"You're all welcome," the nurse replied, sliding toward the hallway. "Is there someone here named Mariano?"

"Yes," Reno, said, moving forward.

"Mr. Germaine's asking for you."

Reno didn't miss the flash of concern in Vikkas' eyes. Anger? Jealousy?

CHAPTER 7

Reno entered Khalil's spacious recovery suite. The place was almost as big as the master bedroom in his penthouse condominium on South Shore Drive overlooking Lake Michigan. He eased the door closed, then stood with his back against the wall. He'd been in a hospital twice in his life, not counting his entry into the world. The only thing familiar between the two was the smell of hand sanitizer and death.

He glanced over at Khalil, laying in the bed and had a vision of his high school friend, Ebony. At the time, her face had been several tints of black, blue, and purple. Secretly, she was beaten by her father but passed it off as her boyfriend's doing because she was afraid of what he'd do if she reported him. Ebony had nowhere to go for help. She refused to stay with friends for fear of their parents calling the police. Reno's breathing hitched, remembering Ebony's last words before succumbing to her injuries. *Don't cry for me. The afterlife has to be better than this.*

At that moment, Reno knew he'd have to do something to honor her memory. Had a place like, The Second Chance at Life Women's Shelter existed, Ebony might still be amongst the living.

"Are you gonna hold-up the wall?" Khalil teased, his voice shaky and weak. "Or are you gonna come over here and talk to me?"

The corners of Reno's lips turned upward as he peeled off the plaster, walked over, grabbed a chair, and pulled it to Khalil's bedside. "Hey, Papa K."

Khalil didn't move his arm, but he opened an unsteady hand as it rested on his chest, extending his fingers. Reno lifted Khalil's hand with caution.

"You know it takes a lot to keep me down," Khalil said, tightening the grip on Reno's hand. "I've got plenty of gas left in the tank and several miles to go."

Silence permeated the air as the men shared a head nod and a confident stare. That was all the reassurance Reno needed. Khalil was going to be all right.

Lowering into the seat he brought over, Reno asked, "What's this I hear about you wanting the complete Macro crew to run The Castle?"

"In my absence, while on that spiritual tour, the board went rogue. Everything The Castle represented in the past has been tainted with all kinds of illegal activity. The latest rumor being that some members are using it for sex trafficking. I hired private investigators to look into it since local law enforcement can't be trusted."

Reno frowned, shifting in the seat.

"All of these new developments can't be happening without the help of customs at border patrol," Khalil said, amid a mild coughing spell.

Reno heard the gurgling sound at the back of Khalil's throat and handed him some Kleenex, but Khalil shook his head. "It just itches from the intubation," Khalil explained, rubbing the front of his neck. "The doctor told me that's expected."

He nodded, reaching over and adjusting Khalil's bed to a more upright position, then grabbed a bottle of water from the counter and offered it to Khalil. He took several sips of the clear contents.

"Is that better?" Reno asked, taking the bottle from his hands and placing it on the side table.

"Yes, thank you."

"I'm going to leave now," Reno said, pushing the chair back. "I'm sure Vikkas is eager to see you. I don't want to drain all of your energy."

"Not yet," Khalil shot back, his voice much stronger.

The commanding tone forced Reno to park his behind back in the seat.

"I need a confirmation that you'll at least think about what I'm asking. I want you on the Board of Directors, a managing partner. Find out what the current members are doing so we can force them out." Khalil's brows knitted. "By any means necessary. I've been following all of your lives, and every one of you possess a certain something that can be useful in this undertaking. Jointly, we can turn The Castle around."

"I will give it consideration," Reno replied, standing. "I'm going to head out, but I'll be back to check on you tomorrow."

"Send Vikkas in, please."

With that, Reno left the room.

Re-emerging in the waiting area, Vikkas came to his feet. "How's he doing?"

"Khalil's good. And he's asking for you."

"Yeah, but what are you prepared to do?" Vikkas fired back, glaring at Reno.

"What?"

"About The Castle."

"It's a lot to think about in such a short time. I need to mull it over."

Vikkas gave a weary sigh. "If any of you had opened the letter he sent; my father may not be lying in that hospital bed. The men who orchestrated this attack——"

"Excuse me a sec," Reno interrupted, lifting a finger, cutting Vikkas off mid-sentence as he answered his ringing phone, walking toward the exit.

All of his Macro classmate's heads snapped upward.

"¿De verdad?" Dro blurted, squaring his broad athletic shoulders.

"Yes, really," Reno answered in English. "My assistant wouldn't call unless it was important."

He vacated the room before anyone else could object. They were all businessmen and should understand that work sometimes trumped current situations.

"Hi, Skyler." He jump-stepped to the side and flattened his body against the wall as two nurses pushed an electric bed on wheels with a patient down the corridor. "Is everything okay?"

"Zuri's here."

"How is that possible?" he shouted, ignoring the *Hospital Personnel Only* sign on the door, then dipped into the room filled with shelves of bandages, syringes, and other hospital paraphernalia. "How did she get from Rockford to the shelter within such a short amount of time? That's at least a two-hour drive."

"I don't know," Skyler replied. "Zuri won't talk to me, but she seems more frightened than she did when she first arrived hours earlier. How fast can you get back here?"

"Soon. Don't let Zuri out of your sight."

He ended the call, then made a beeline into the private room. "Fellas, I'm heading out. Keep me posted of any changes with Khalil."

"What?" Vikkas eyes expanded to the size of flapjacks. "You're not staying."

"I have to get to the shelter."

"You need to be here." Shaz's chest inflated. "What's so important that you can't stay in support of your brothers, especially Vikkas?"

"I have an emergency that can't wait," he stated, turning on his heels and aiming toward the door.

"That's very selfish of you," Dro shouted over Reno's shoulder. "We all have businesses to run, but we're here."

Reno turned around and swore he saw steam shooting from Dro's ears. "This isn't about me," he hissed. "You of all people should understand given your line of work ..." Reno paused to let the meaning carry, then glanced over at Vikkas. "I'll be back as soon as I can."

"Make sure you do," he shot back. "My dad's counting on you."

"Hold up." Kaleb bounded from his seat and rushed to Reno's side. "I'll go with you. Two emergencies, in the same place, only hours apart—— you may need an assist."

"That's not necessary." Reno waved him off.

"We won't know that until we get there. Now, will we?"

"Cool," Reno responded, glancing around at the disapproving faces of the other guys.

They gave each other a fist bump and dashed out the door.

CHAPTER 8

"What do you think about Khalil's offer?" Reno asked Kaleb during their twenty-five-minute drive to The Second Chance at Life Women's Shelter.

"I'm intrigued, but it would require moving back to Chicago, and that's something I never considered. Memories are timeless, especially bad ones. The last thing I need is for someone to recognize me."

Reno merged onto Lake Shore Drive. "It would be nice to have you around."

"Khalil suggested that I move into The Castle." Kaleb shrugged an action that mirrored a perplexed facial expression. "I wouldn't be in the city, and I'd be able to get insight into the shady dealings he's speaking of firsthand."

"Let me know what you decide. As for me, I don't know. I'm already stretched thinner than a used condom."

The men shared a glance and burst into laughter.

"You've always had a way with words," Kaleb teased, shifting his focus out of the passenger's side window. "The neighborhood looks so different—— and not in a good way," he said as they rode down a street filled with boarded-up storefronts.

"I know. It was heartbreaking when I first came back from Cornell. None of my friends lived in the area anymore. They either moved to the north side, suburbs or to another state." Reno marinated on his thoughts for a moment as he parked his Porsche several blocks away due to police re-routing traffic. "By the way, thanks for coming with me, but let me forewarn you, we have a delicate situation, and your discretion is a must."

"Understood." Kaleb slid his fingers around the door handle. "If I hadn't said it before, let me say it now. I'm proud of the work you're doing; changing women's lives."

"Thanks."

"No, really. You took your architecture degree and built a state-of-the-art women's shelter in the hood. Not many would do that. I know you walked away from multi-million-dollar projects to pursue this."

"Don't get it twisted. I closed several of those deals before handing the firm my pink slip." Reno smirked, exiting the car. "And you better believe, the growth stock I purchased is doing quite well. But I needed to do something more meaningful—— something that would make a difference."

"Ebony inspired …" Kaleb whispered as they briskly strode along the pavement toward the shelter.

He gets it. Reno couldn't help his friend, Ebony, back then, but he could help several women in her situation and worst, now. This is what gave his life purpose.

"Whoa, man. What happened here?" Kaleb asked, pointing to the extensive damage of the door and window. "Who would shoot at a women's shelter?"

"We were a casualty of the neighborhood gun violence. I guess they wanted to switch it up," Reno said, pulling on the handle, but the door didn't budge. "The foolery usually happens at night."

"I see why you got the women out of here this morning."

Reno fished the shelter's keys from his pocket and unlocked the door.

"Sorry it took so long. Police were still redirecting traffic, and I had to walk——"

He froze, scanning the lobby area that resembled an upscale hotel lounge. All the furnishings, modern paintings, and lighting were still in place, but no sign of Skyler or Zuri.

"Skyler," Reno called out, lifting a hand to halt Kaleb's movement. "Something's wrong. She would never leave the front desk unattended. *Never*—— unless there was a reason."

In the six years, Skyler Pierson had worked for him, this was the first time she'd ever done that.

"And where in the hell is the security detail I hired?" Reno scowled, scanning the area.

Reno scanned the open area, then took swift steps behind the front desk. He opened the bottom drawer, then pressed in a code to the safe, retrieved a Smith & Wesson, and inserted the loaded clip. Standing with the pistol at his side, Reno pressed the crisis mode button on the keyboard that locked all the windows, exit, and service doors.

The only time they've had to activate that button was during practice drills. In the event of a real emergency, there were several locations strategically placed throughout the shelter where anyone could press the silent alarm that would alert the security company and the police.

If an unauthorized person was in there, the only way they were leaving was in a body bag. He'd be more than willing to shoot first and ask questions later if anyone had harmed Skyler or Zuri.

"You strapped?"

"Nah, man, but I'm quick with my hands. They don't want none—— I'm good. Let's go."

"Follow me," Reno said with a tilt of the head.

He eased along the wall with his pistol drawn, making his way to his office in the rear of the building. Closed-circuit television monitors with video and audio surveillance were housed in many of the rooms. A slight smirk twitched his lips. He'd be able to get the upper hand on the intruder if that were the case. Then a frown replaced the expression just as quick. The living quarters were upstairs, the only place in the building *without* video cameras. He wanted to give the women as much privacy and dignity as possible.

Gripping the pistol, he inched the office door open.

Shrieks and squeals pierced Reno's eardrums.

"Don't shoot. It's me," Skyler shouted, raising her right hand, while her left one was wrapped around the petite woman cringing in her bosom. "Don't shoot."

Reno crept into the room, never lowering the pistol. "Is anyone else in here?"

"No. Just me and Zuri," she said, looking at Reno, then eyes widening at the sight of Kaleb.

Reno lowered the pistol and slipped it in his back waistband.

"Where's Boris and Donovan?"

"I sent them away," Skyler admitted, still keeping a tight grip on Zuri.

Reno folded his arms across his chest, then covered his mouth and gazed at her with every ounce of incredulity he felt. "They were here for your protection. What if something happened to you or Zuri?"

"They made her uncomfortable. What choice did I have?"

Reno didn't have a comeback. Skyler did what she was trained to do; honor the client's needs above anything else, unless there was a direct threat to the staff's personal safety. She outright ignored the latter part.

"Don't be mad, man," Kaleb chimed in, gazing at Skyler in a manner that was pure admiration. "Your assistant did what she thought was best for the client."

"But at her expense."

"I'd do it again if it brought Zuri peace," Skyler countered with a hint of defiance in her tone.

"I bet you would," Kaleb said, nodding but lowering his gaze, extending his hand.

Reno didn't miss the not-so-subtle once-over he slid in Skyler's direction.

"By the way, I'm Kaleb Valentine."

CHAPTER 9

Reno inhaled deeply and held his breath for ten seconds. When he exhaled, he blew away the circumstances that he didn't have the power to change. Reno would channel his focus and energy on Zuri and what she needed.

Stepping forward, Reno asked, "Would you like to sit down?"

"Why is he here?" Zuri slowly lifted her head and faced him. "I thought this was a female-only shelter?"

"It is," Reno assured. "Kaleb is a long-time friend of mine and he accompanied me to make sure you, and Skyler were okay. You don't have to worry about him."

"Talk to Mariano," Skyler encouraged, grabbing Zuri's hand and guiding her from behind the desk. "You'll never meet a kinder man who cares more about protecting women the way he does. You can trust him. If he brought Kaleb into the shelter, that means he's an honorable man as well."

Skyler's gaze latched onto Kaleb.

Zuri clutched her bag.

"Would you two give us a minute?" Reno asked, glancing at Kaleb and Skyler.

"Sure thing," Skyler replied. "I'll give Kaleb a tour of the place."

Kaleb's eyes flashed brighter than the sun at high noon. Reno made a mental note to talk to him later. He'd seen that look directed at a woman before, and things did not go well. Her name was Liana Steed.

"I activated the crisis mode button. Could you reverse it, please?"

"Sure thing," Skyler said, with a reassuring squeeze of Zuri's upper arm, then walking toward the door with Kaleb on her heels.

Once their footsteps faded into the background, Reno spoke candidly, "Thanks for trusting me, reaching out for help is a big first step. I will do my best to accommodate and understand your needs. And of most importance, protecting you at all cost," he said, searching her reddish-brown eyes. "But I can't do that effectively if you disappear on me. How did you get back to the shelter?"

She swallowed hard, still clutching that duffel bag as if her life depended on its contents. "After you did a headcount and assigned us rooms, I snuck out and hid on the back of the bus while the driver unloaded the women's luggage from the compartment underneath. I laid in the back until he stopped for gas. He had gone inside to pay, and that is when I hopped out and ran across the highway to the Shell station and waited for the bus to leave. I called an Uber."

"You took a big risk, Zuri. You could've been killed."

"I know, but the bigger risk would be staying out there. Everyone saw us get on that bus. It would've been easy for my father's people to follow us. So, you see—— I am safer here."

Her deductive reasoning made sense, but only if he understood why her father would send people after her.

"Why would——"

"Godfrey——" She halted, cutting her eyes. "My father and Djimon are after me."

"Djimon?"

"My fiancé," Zuri hissed.

Reno was certain the confusion in his brain must have shown on his face. He'd heard many peculiar circumstances, just not that particular scenario.

"I am from Tanzania, and I am being forced to marry."

She is an African Goddess.

"I am here on a visa, studying at U of I at Chicago to get a degree in International Relations," Zuri shared, twirling the gold bracelets on her arm.

"That's my alma mater. I graduated summa cum laude with my Masters of Architecture Degree," he boasted, then clamped down, reprimanding himself. This wasn't about him. He knew better than to interrupt a potential client while she's disclosing information, especially since she was getting a feel for him and the facility. What was it about Zuri that made him lose his head? "My apologies, please continue."

After a slight pause, she peered at him and said, "Mama passed away three weeks ago, and I went home to celebrate her home-going."

"I'm so sorry for your loss." He leaned forward, resisting the urge to reach for her hand to provide comfort. Reno had to keep reminding himself that she was a client. Why was he drawn to her in *that* way?

"Thank you," Zuri continued, shifting on the couch, her heart-shaped face a mask of beauty and sadness. "My father refused to let me return to the States, saying that I had to take my rightful place as Djimon's wife," she said, holding two fingers up, making air quotes. "I do not know him. I do not love him. My father accused me of letting modern women and the Western world brainwash me. I never wanted this. My mother never wanted it either. She is the reason I am in America."

Reno was surprised to hear that in today's time with so many advances, arranged marriages were still part of some cultures.

"I know my father," she mumbled, lowering her eyes to the floor. "I have two weeks left before I graduate, and I cannot even take my finals or return to the dorm because I know the first place he will check is the university." Lifting her head and squaring her shoulders, Zuri placed an unwavering stare into Reno's eyes.

Instantly, he noticed the change in her demeanor. Tough. Assertive.

"I will die first before I marry that man. I do not care how much of a dowry he paid for me."

This time, Reno did reach out and touch Zuri's hand. A strong flutter of desire tingled in his fingertips, traveled up his arm, and into his chest. The current was so intense that she had to feel it, too.

"I'm not going to let it come to that."

Zuri locked a gaze on him; that same mesmerizing one she had when first entering the shelter. "Now, what do I do?"

Trapped in her vortex of beauty, he was speechless. The connection was paralyzing, and if it were anyone other than a client, Reno would welcome the feelings. This wasn't safe, and he made a mental note to keep an ocean's distance between them once Zuri got settled.

"Mariano," she called his name, squeezing his hand, sending another wave of electricity through his body. "What should I do?"

"You can stay at the transitional housing apartments."

"Where?" she asked, narrowing her eyes.

"It's four safe haven apartment complexes with six units in each. They are mostly used for the women who come to the shelter that require anonymity."

"I do not understand," she proclaimed.

"In some cases, they need protection from abusive husbands and boyfriends. Sometimes, they're fighting nasty custody and divorce battles. Some are rape victims trying to find their way back to normalcy and need a place not associated with their current life," he explained. "The apartments are part of the Chatham Village Cooperative Community. They look just like the other buildings, so they don't stand out, which is a good thing. The only difference is that I own them and have a separate management company running the day to day operations. No one knows the buildings are connected with Second Chance at Life."

Skyler tapped on the opened door before entering. Reno drew his hands back into his lap, but not before he caught the examining glare from Skyler's piercing orbs.

"Yes."

"It can wait," she spat, swiveling on her heels and stalking off.

"Excuse me," Reno said, rising from his seat and following after his assistant. "Skyler. Slow down."

She spun around. "What the hell are you doing?"

"Skyler, you know me. I would never jeopardize the work we do here by getting involved with a client."

Sighing, she pursed her lips. "I know I don't have a right to question you, but it looks like I interrupted an intimate moment."

"No," Reno countered, shifting his weight from one foot to the other. "I was telling Zuri about the transitional apartments. It's the best alternative for her since she isn't comfortable with staying in Rockford. What do you think?"

Skyler's expression softened, and so did her tone. "That's an excellent suggestion. One of the units opened up three days ago. Carly's husband was convicted and sentenced to two consecutive life terms without the possibility of parole. She and the kids moved back into their home."

"I'm so happy for them." Reno clasped his hands together. "Justice has finally been served."

"Sorry for questioning your morals," Skyler said, interlocking her fingers and placing them under her chin. "We've got such a good thing going here. You've helped so many women——" She paused, clearing her throat. "Speaking from experience, I know firsthand how this place saves lives, and I wouldn't want you to compromise the shelter's integrity."

"There's no need for that. We make a good team. You've always had the leeway to ask questions and say what's on your mind. No need to stop now."

They moved toward Reno's office, stopping just outside the door.

"What were you coming to talk to me about?"

"I was checking to see if you all wanted something to eat. The kitchen staff's in Rockford, and it's almost seven o'clock. Kaleb and I were ordering shrimp from Haire's Gulf. Did you want any?"

Reno's mouth watered at the thought. "Most definitely. I'll check with Zuri, but let's get her settled into the apartment first, then we'll place an order. My treat." Reno winked, crossing the threshold to his office.

"Perfect. I'll let Kaleb know," Skyler said as she traipsed down the hall. Somehow there was a different pep in her step.

"Is everything okay?" Zuri asked, scooting to the edge of her seat.

"Everything's fine."

Reno wished that were true. On the surface, everything was great, but those unexpected feelings bubbling on the inside needed to check themselves before he found himself and his life's mission spiral so far down a hole that they couldn't find their way out.

CHAPTER 10

After scoping out the immediate area to make sure they weren't followed and to put Zuri's fear of her father lurking close by to rest, Reno, Kaleb, and Skyler drove Zuri to the transitional apartments.

Exiting the car, Reno walked with Zuri through the quad of the Chatham Village Cooperative. The landscaping was moderate with cement benches, fresh-cut grass, and beautiful rose bushes lining the walkways. Kaleb and Skyler brought up the rear, engrossed in their own conversation.

Tenants of the other apartments assumed Reno was the landlord showing potential renters the property since the only time they laid eyes on him was when a woman was being placed. He gleaned that useful piece of information from one of his clients who lived there.

"Kon'nichiwa," a soft voice spoke as a woman with long dark hair, carrying a white plastic bag with a smiley face on the side, crossed paths with them.

"Good evening, Reina," Reno greeted, his eyes wandering down to her hands.

As if she could read his mind, she said, "I am on my way in. I ordered noodles from the Chinese restaurant, and I went to pick it up."

"Whatever you need, Reina, we can get for you," Skyler chimed in.

"Just call."

"I know," she replied. "I did not want to be a bother for something so simple."

"Your safety comes first," Reno reminded her.

"It will not happen again, Mr. DeLuca."

Reina Hamasaki was another client who lived in the adjacent building from Zuri and Olga. She was the lone witness to the arson of her family's Japanese restaurant fire in Arlington Heights. Her parents, aunts, and six siblings all died in the blaze set by Reina's boyfriend; a disgruntled ex-employee who was terminated for theft. Now, he was on the hunt for her before the case went to trial. Little did he know, she was right under his nose on the other side of the tracks.

Once Reina entered the brown brick building she was assigned, they went into an identical one next to it and climbed to the second story. The furnished two-bedroom apartment was equipped with stainless steel appliances and a pantry and refrigerator stocked with food and plenty of dishes at her disposal.

Zuri ventured into the bedroom.

"I think she'll like it here," Reno whispered to Skyler and Kaleb.

"Dude," Kaleb said, pressing a few fingers into the plush loveseat, then sofa bed. "This is nicer than my first apartment. The furniture selection and warm color scheme have a feminine touch." Kaleb shot him a side-eye glance. "I know you didn't pick this out."

"I'll take credit for that," Skyler chimed in, rubbing her hand along the back of the sofa. "I know what we like. My goal is to make this temporary place feel as much as their own home as possible."

"I knew it," Kaleb replied, smiling. "You did a great job."

Skyler blushed.

Zuri entered the living room. This was the first time she wasn't clutching her duffel bag. "This is too much. There are linens and fancy towels and two big flat screens. I do not need all of this." She walked into the kitchen and pulled open the drawers one by one, then examined the contents of the pantry. "Is it food in there, too?" she asked, pointing to the refrigerator.

"Yes," Reno said, moving closer. "If there's anything specific you want, let Skyler know, and she'll order the items for you."

"I do not want to be a bother."

"This is what we do," Reno countered, resisting the natural urge to slide his hand in hers or swipe the loose strands of hair behind her ear. "This drawer right here," he said, pointing, then extracting a key from his pocket. "Has our contact information. There's a credit card, five-hundred dollars, a prepaid phone, and the keys to this apartment. The only persons who have access to this unit while you're staying here are you and me. I have a master key that stays with me at all times. I will never come here without your permission. The management company does not have access to your apartment. If you encounter a problem with anything in your unit, contact them, and they will contact me. Do you understand?"

"I got it."

"I'm very particular about who I let enter these four buildings. Even the management company isn't aware of the delicate circumstances. I need to vet everyone, down to the toilet repair guy."

Zuri's lips turned upward, and she flashed the most beautiful smile that Reno had ever seen. "Thank you so much for this."

"You're welcome."

Reno's hands flanked to his midsection as he tried to muffle the abrupt growl of hunger.

Kaleb and Skyler laughed. Zuri did her best to hold back a snicker, but her giggle broke through, and the melody of her voice was joyous. Reno caught a glimpse of what she sounded like when stress wasn't a dominant factor, and he liked that very much.

"Someone is hungry," Zuri teased, patting her stomach. "Let me cook you dinner? All of you. That is the least I can do for everything you have done for me today."

"I'd love a home-cooked meal that I didn't have to prepare," Skyler replied, checking her watch. "But I have to get home and relieve the sitter. I'll grab a bite on the way." She turned to Kaleb. "Could you take me back to my car?"

"Sure thing."

"At least let me buy you guys dinner, as promised." Reno peeled off a one-hundred-dollar bill.

"I got her," Kaleb shot back, placing a hand over Reno's wallet and pushing it down to his side. He extended his arm, and Skyler slid her fingers around his bicep. "I'll call you later." Then Kaleb turned to Zuri and said, "It was a pleasure meeting you."

"You take care of her," Reno warned.

Kaleb continued walking to the front door, and with his back to Reno, he flung his arm above his head and flashed the peace sign, then closed the door behind them.

Reno crossed his arms and shook his head. Unspoken sparks flew, and Reno hoped Skyler knew what she was in for. *I wonder if those were the same sparks that Skyler saw between Zuri and me.*

The sound of running water snapped Reno from his thoughts. Gracing the kitchen entryway, Reno stood and watched Zuri slide a silk scarf from around her neck and wrap her thick coils in an updo. Her long mahogany neck glistened under the ceiling light. He had an instant sweet tooth for chocolate.

"Thanks for the offer, but I better get going."

"Are you sure?" Zuri asked, pumping the liquid soap dispenser and lathering her hands. "I do not mind. I love to cook."

"Yeah, it's getting late. I'm going to let you get settled in, and I'll be in touch tomorrow."

Reno hurried out of there. Not only did he want dinner, but he wanted dessert, too.

The forbidden fruit was always the most tempting.

CHAPTER 11

The following morning, Reno left his lakefront condo on South Shore Drive and headed to the Near West Side UIC campus. He was determined to help Zuri in every way possible. Strolling the campus amongst bright-eyed and hopeful college students, Reno noticed the area had changed quite a bit since he graduated ten years ago. Reno reveled at the role he played in part of that development, admiring the new Chemical Engineering Building he designed.

Utilizing his resources, Reno spoke with the Dean of the International Relations Department and informed her that Zuri Okusanya had extenuating circumstances, without disclosing her personal business. He asked if she would be allowed to take her finals via satellite. Also, Reno implored that her records be sealed to everyone, including her family and anyone claiming to be her fiancé. Thankfully, because of who Reno was and his lineage, along with the contributions and various scholarships he provided to architectural students—— and *now*, international relations students, the Dean obliged.

Reno couldn't wait to share the news with Zuri, but first, he had to check-in with Skyler. He dialed the number to the shelter.

"Second Chance at Life Women's Shelter, Skyler speaking. How may I be of service to you?"

"Someone sounds chipper this morning," Reno teased, walking across campus to his car.

Skyler had always been full of personality, but he hoped the extra bubbliness didn't have anything to do with Kaleb. As much as Reno wanted to know, he wouldn't dare ask—— at least not Skyler.

"I'm going to contact the window people again and see how fast they can come out."

"I just got off the phone with them," Skyler countered. "Someone will be out later today to assess the damage. They already have the window measurements and specialty glass on file from the initial installment."

Reno found himself smiling as he slid into the driver's seat. Good workers were plentiful, but exceptional ones were hard to come by, and he'd found a jewel in Skyler.

"Thanks for following up."

"No problem," Skyler replied in that perky tone she'd been exuding ever since she answered the phone. "How's Zuri?"

"I was just about to call her. I haven't spoken with Zuri this morning, but she seemed alright last night," Reno said, pulling the seatbelt across his shoulder and fastening the buckle.

"Let me know if she needs anything. I'll swing by after I leave here."

"Will do," he replied, pressing a button on the compartment above the rearview mirror and retrieved his sunglasses. "How are the rest of the women? Did they have a pleasant night? I know it's weird staying in an unfamiliar place, no matter how nice it may be."

"Overall, the ladies are fine," Skyler said with hesitation. "Some are on edge about the way everything went down yesterday. They're concerned about their jobs and want to know when they'd be able to return to the shelter."

"I'll answer all of their questions when I head out there later today," he replied. "Call me if you need anything. Talk to you later."

"Will do," Skyler replied, ending the call.

Reno started the car and adjusted the air conditioning. He put in a call to Zuri.

"Hello," she answered, sounding unsure.

"It's Reno——Mariano," he corrected because she wasn't accustomed to hearing the nickname that his boys gave him when they first met at Macro. They said, he looked to smooth to be called Mariano, so he'd been Reno ever since. "I wanted to let you know I'm heading your way. Did you need anything before I get there?"

"That is really nice of you, but no, I am fine."

The shakiness in her voice had subsided.

"I'll see you in about thirty minutes," he replied, disconnecting the call.

The journey from the near west side to the far south side was an uneventful one since he was traveling between the morning and afternoon rush. He took in the familiar sights and enjoyed the calmness up until the moment he pulled along the curb in front of the apartments.

Parking, he left the car running and opened up a web browser. He typed *Godfrey Okusanya* in the search engine and began reading about the man who'd brought significant positive change in the Tanzanian government, who the people praised and respected. Then he paged down to the subtitle, *Early Life*, and learned that Godfrey was a cattle farmer in Musa, a Ward of 66 rural district where arranged marriages were both common and illegal.

"Whoa," Reno blurted out loud.

The phone rang, closing out the current screen he'd been reading. *Apt203* danced across the top of the display. The burner phone assigned to Zuri's unit.

"Hey," Reno answered, turning off the car. "I'll be right up."

He moved across the quad with stealth. No one was out; not even a bird chirping or a stray cat. By the time he made it to the second landing, Zuri had opened the door wearing a pair of shorts and an oversized t-shirt that exposed one shoulder.

"Why were you sitting in the car so long?" she demanded. "I saw you park about ten minutes ago."

"I was doing some research on your father," Reno admitted, walking to the picture window and glancing toward his vehicle. "I needed to know what we were up against."

"Godfrey Okusanya is amazing on Wikipedia," Zuri murmured. "But the man behind the name is another story best left untold."

An awkward silence filled the room. That one sentence said enough, and Reno wouldn't pressure Zuri to explain further.

"You hungry? I made beef stew, and I am boiling water for the ugali."

"I—— nah, I have to——"

Zuri approached Reno and grasped his hand. She led him into the kitchen. "You would not let me cook for you last night, but you will have lunch with me. I insist."

"Well, since I don't have a choice." He grinned, pulling out a barstool. "I've never had ugali before." He inhaled a pleasant aroma.

"It is a Tanzanian specialty. You will love it."

She washed her hands, then took a bag of white cornmeal from the cabinet and grabbed a fist full. Zuri held her hand over the boiling water and let the grainy substance fall through her delicate fingers into the pot as she slowly stirred.

"My Baba used to mean everything to me, even though I did not see him much. He was a cattle farmer and spent most of his time on the ranch. My Mama was a circular migration worker. I saw her even less, but when I did see her, we had such an amazing time."

"Why's that?" Reno asked, happy that she was opening up on her own and sharing personal details about her life and family.

"My Mama came to the States to work for six months at a time. I am not sure why because her family was wealthy. Baba made her so he could manipulate me in her absence, but I did not know that at the time," Zuri admitted. "Mama sent half of her paycheck back to the home community every time she got paid to help support the family. Four hundred and fifty dollars every two weeks may not seem like a lot here, but it was life-changing for the tribe back home. She lived here in Chicago with another migrant family," Zuri explained as she continuously stirred the contents in the pot and kept her focus on the contents. "That is how I learned about UIC. Mama worked as a custodian. She boasted about how beautiful the campus was and how she prayed, I would someday be able to attend a university like that."

"Your mother's wish came true." Reno smiled, resting his elbows on the counter.

"They did," she whispered, tossing her head back and sniffling. "But at what cost?"

He frowned, searching her face for understanding.

"Mama knew I did not want to get married. Not like that. I wanted free will to fall in love and choose my forever mate," she said, pursing her lips. "Long ago, when I was just eleven, I overheard my parents arguing during one of Mama's visits home. Baba had already received large dowries from prospective suitors for me. I cried and cried. I had just completed my seventh year of primary school and could test to go to the secondary level—— which is equivalent to high school here in the States," Zuri clarified, scraping the sides of the pot and removing it from the heat. "Baba tried to trick me into failing my test by drawing a line through the circle instead of darkening the whole circle with my pencil when I answer the questions. That way, it would read invalid, and I would not qualify to the next level of education, but Mama told me to mark the answers the way I had always done, and she would protect me. I passed my exams with a perfect score."

Reno listened in awe.

"When I finished testing, a lady I had never seen before ushered me and ten other girls into the back of a wagon and hauled us off to a special children center. She promised no harm would come to us and that she was only there to help girls further their education. I did not see my parents for three years. I thought Mama had abandoned me and did not keep her word." Zuri's eyes pooled, and tears swam down her cheeks. "It was not until we were reunited that I learned she had sent me away for my protection. And in return, Baba treated her worse than a lady of the night."

"Don't cry." Reno vacated the bar stool and yanked a paper towel from its holder. He rushed to her side and tenderly dabbed Zuri's eyes.

She glanced up at him, her fingertips brushing against Reno's wrist, sending tingling sensations up his arm. Zuri placed a hand over his, slowly wrapping her fingers around the towel. "Thank you."

Reno nodded and smiled, hoping the kind gesture offered Zuri comfort. He gazed in silence, taking in her vulnerability, understanding that what she shared wasn't easy and feeling honored that she trusted him with such information.

Balling the paper towel in her fist, Zuri let out a deep sigh before she continued. "There was a bounty on my head because Baba accepted monies and had not delivered me to the Aku family." She paused, biting her bottom lip. "He found me right before I took the Advanced Certificate exam. That was the final test to see if I qualified to attend college. But it did not matter." A smile split her face. "My teacher, Mama Winnie, had me take a mock exam three weeks prior, and I aced it. She submitted that as my final. I did not know at the time that Mama Winnie had been secretly in touch with my Mama. She helped her apply for a student visa for me to enter the States and attend UIC. I was never supposed to return to the family home."

"Your mom was a warrior."

"My real-life superhero," Zuri added, moving around Reno, tossing the used paper towel in the trash, then washing her hands. She transferred the ugali into a large serving bowl, re-wet her hands with water, then scooped sizeable amounts and rolled the cornmeal mush into several balls. She spooned beef stew into ceramic bowls and placed them on the center of a plate, then sat the ugali on the side with a tablespoon. "Mama was scheduled to come back to Chicago. Baba usually took her to the airport, but he wanted to find the Aku family as soon as possible. He was too paranoid about leaving me alone, so he shackled me to a tree. She begged for one last moment to speak with me, and Baba allowed it." Zuri shrugged, and a world of hurt was in that gesture. "Maybe he figured nothing could go wrong since he had me chained like an animal. Soon as he was out of earshot, Mama kissed my forehead and whispered, "Do not worry. Mama Winnie's coming for you. I may never see you again, but at least I know you will be alive and safe.""

Reno's heart thumped, but she signaled for him to lift both plates and carry them to the table. He pulled out a chair for her to sit.

Appearing lost, Zuri stood frozen, not uttering a sound. Reno didn't know what to say or if he should say anything at all. She'd divulged a part of her past to him that he assumed no one else knew existed, other than Godfrey. He was having a hard time digesting what he just heard, so Zuri had to be struggling as well.

Blinking as she inhaled a large intake of air, Zuri muttered, "This feels like déjà vu—— Baba trying to sabotage my graduation. I do not have that invisible safety net protecting me anymore. I miss my Mama," Zuri said, lowering into the seat.

"History will not repeat itself." Reno caressed her damp cheek; his heartstrings were being tugged to the max. "You will graduate with your class. I promise."

Zuri turned her face into his hand, closed her eyes, and kissed his palm. "When you say it, I believe it—— but I do not know how that is possible."

Reno squatted at her side until they were eye level. "Because I spoke with the Dean of International Relations this morning. She emailed your professors, instructing them to allow you to take your finals via satellite. I have the verified emails and exam schedule right here." He patted his breast pocket.

"Whaaat?" Zuri's eyes glistened as she swung her legs from underneath the table and pulled Reno into a tight embrace, making him lose his balance. He fell backward, and she landed on top of him. "I'm sooooo sorry."

The savory scent of Zuri's breath and the full pressure of her soft body gave Reno intense pleasure, even if it only lasted for a second.

Zuri quickly rolled over and knelt beside him. "Are you okay?"

"Yes." He simpered, pushing up on his elbows, gazing at the beautiful woman who was off-limits.

She stood, then extended her hand. "Seems like one of us is always on the ground."

Reno was enjoying the view from the floor as he admired her heavenliness, although the close proximity had his mind fuddled. He needed clarity before he did something stupid.

"I'm good," he said, getting to his feet. Reno pulled the document from his pocket and handed the schedule to Zuri.

"Thanks for this." She lifted the folded paper to her lips and kissed it. "I do not know how I will ever repay you."

"Lunch is all the payment I need."

He could think of several other ways if the circumstances were different.

CHAPTER 12

Leaving Zuri's unit, Reno hopped in the car and released a breath he wasn't aware he'd been holding all that time. She hadn't been in his life a full forty-eight hours, and he was smitten. How? He didn't have the answer to that question. What Reno did know was that after Zuri's graduation, he was going to keep a healthy distance.

Checking the time, he started the engine. The drive to the family's estate in Rockford was a two-hour drive. Reno figured he could make it out there, check on the women, and get back in enough time to visit Khalil.

Reno uploaded a playlist and cranked the volume, 'causing 90's Hip-Hop to boom from the speakers as he opened-up his Porsche on the Dan Ryan expressway. Midday traffic in the opposite direction flowed with an enviable effortlessness.

An hour into the drive, Reno's music was interrupted by an incoming call. He pinched the bridge of his nose when his father's picture came across the screen. He'd missed the monthly family meeting. Nothing was worse than that in his parent's opinion. Although, Reno had a good reason and they knew why he was sure this phone call would be more of a tongue lashing than a pleasant conversation.

"Hey, Papà."

"What happened to you?" Giacomo questioned. "You skipped out on our gathering. This is the second one in a row."

"Papà, you know I had an emergency," Reno protested, aiming the car into the express lanes.

"I'm aware. Your emergencies are all over the grounds of my property. That's not the *problema*. You were supposed to come back," Giacomo grunted a sign of displeasure. "Your *fratello e sorella* are always here."

Because they still live at home.

Reno hated being compared to his siblings. He had gone against the grain and moved out of the family home right after his twenty-fourth birthday, breaking the tradition of offspring living with their parents until marriage. Reno's business was a twenty-four hour, seven days a week affair that required him to be nearby and available. He couldn't stay in Rockford. His brother and sister had challenging lines of work that consisted of long hours, but they clocked out at the end of their day and parked their feet under the DeLuca family table.

"How's Mamma?"

"Upset that you graced the doors of her home and didn't have the decency to say hello."

Again, Reno wanted to shout *emergency* but thought better of it. The family meeting was the only time he made it out to see his parents and siblings. Reno missed them too. Why couldn't his dad cut him some slack? He could think of the many times his father was absent during the teenage years due to mandatory work engagements. He should understand—— but what Giacomo DeLuca wants, he gets.

"I'm headed that way now, Papà."

"To work or spend some time with la famiglia?"

Reno clamped down, covered the phone, and inhaled so deeply that it felt as if his chest would explode.

"Mariano Francesco DeLuca."

The air spilled out of Reno's lungs. That loud commanding tone still had the same effect on him. Not nary another man had the ability to shake his core; not even the most ruthless businessmen he encountered. "I'm gonna check on the women, then head to the house with you and Mamma."

"Fantastico! I'll tell Emma to prepare the risotto and make some fresh focaccia. Arrivederci'."

The call disconnected.

Reno shook his head. Giacomo DeLuca wasn't an easy man to please unless he was getting his way. It was just as well. He wanted to talk to his father bout Zuri and her predicament. Reno valued his input.

He arrived at the property situated on 330 acres of land and was surprised to see Kaleb carrying cases of gourmet coffee and tea boxes to the cabin. Reno parked alongside his car. "Hey, man. What are you doing here?"

"What's up." Kaleb placed the boxes on the edge of his trunk and balanced them with a hip. Kaleb gave Reno a fist pump through the open window. "Skyler asked me to bring these to the women."

"She did?" Reno cocked his head, peering at Kaleb with suspicion.

"Skyler didn't want to leave the shelter. She said something about the glass people coming out and needing to be there in case a client wandered in."

"And you just happened to be available?"

"What can I say—— I'm a sucker for a pretty lady." Kaleb grinned, then hoisted the boxes into his arms. "Are you gonna help me or what?"

Reno climbed out of the car and grabbed the two additional cases in Kaleb's trunk. "Skyler's special, you know. Whatever your intentions are, you better be good to her; she's been through a lot."

"Is this your roundabout way of asking if anything happened last night?" Kaleb questioned, glaring at Reno. "A gentlemen never tells."

Reno's jaw clenched.

"Seriously, bro. I hear you," Kaleb said as they carried the heavy boxes toward the cabin. "We ordered take-out for her and the kids, then I took Skyler back to the shelter to retrieve her car and trailed her home to assure her safety. You know," Kaleb huffed, shifting the boxes in his arms. "MeMe messed up my whole concept of marriage with her *special incentive method* for male clients to close business deals, but Skyler could be Mrs. Valentine based on her conversation alone. Stimulating, sarcastic, and funny. Let's not forget she's fine as hell. "A smile split Kaleb's face. "That's a recipe for a good wife. My life right now isn't conducive to a relationship with a ready-made family—— but maybe one day. We exchanged numbers, that's all."

Reno trusted Kaleb more than anyone else he'd been close to. No matter the nature of he and Skyler's budding friendship, he knew that Kaleb would do right by her.

Pushing the gate open with his foot, Reno said, "You know the women aren't used to men coming in and out, except for me. Be cool if they seem on edge."

"They're expecting me," Kaleb countered, maneuvering through the gate. "Skyler called ahead so they wouldn't be startled."

She's thought of everything.

Once Kaleb had left, Reno spoke with the women.

"Ladies, I know we had to move abruptly, but rest assured, I'm doing everything I can to make you as comfortable as possible until we're able to return to Second Chance," Reno said, pulling a retractable utility knife from his back pocket and cutting the box seal with caution. "It may be a couple of weeks until everything's properly secured and back to normal, but in the meantime, you'll have all the comforts that you're accustomed to, from laundry service to the gourmet caffeinated drinks that Skyler had sent over. Whatever you need, we will provide."

"What about our jobs?" one fair-skinned lady with blonde hair asked. "I'm still on the ninety-day probation period. I can't miss work."

"Most of the employment placement programs that most of you work for are part of my organization," Reno explained, halting his movement to give the women his full attention. "It won't be a problem. I'll speak with them."

"I have to be at court tomorrow morning at nine," another woman with freckles on her nose like the actress, Rashida Jones, mentioned.

"I already have transportation in place for you," Reno countered, wearing a slight smile. "So, you don't need to worry."

He answered a few more questions, putting the women's concerns at ease before heading out.

Reno left his car by the cabins and strolled the twenty-minute stretch across the ranch-style scenery leading to the main house. He reached the cobblestone walkway that was lined with beautiful rose bushes. He got ready to stick his key in the lock when the door swung open.

"It's about damn time," his older sister, Sofia, shouted, grabbing his face and kissing his right cheek, then the left one. "Mamma's in the parlor and Papà is where he's always is."

"His office," they said in unison, chuckling, their voices echoed throughout the vestibule.

"I wasn't expecting to see you," Reno said, "But I'm glad you're here."

"Papà called and said you were coming by. I didn't have any surgeries scheduled this afternoon, and I pushed my non-emergency patient's appointments back an hour. I've missed you, little brother." Sofia tapped his cheek with the palm of her hand. "I couldn't pass up the chance to see you."

"The prodigal son's home," a masculine voice belonging to Vicente hollered. He and Reno exchanged a crafty handshake they had made up as kids, that consisted of slaps, snaps, fist bumps, and ended with a salute. Then they gave each other a brotherly hug. "Two months is too long not to talk or hang out. We gotta do better."

"Agreed." Reno nodded, taking in the tannish skin-tone, muscular build, dark-spiked hair, and penny-loafer colored eyes of his younger brother who could pass for his twin.

The only thing distinguishing them apart was their style of dress. Reno's attire was more business casual, and Vincente wore jeans and fitted tees. He got off on showcasing his buff physique.

"What are you smiling at?" Reno asked Sofia, who was leaning against the grand staircase railing with one hand in the pocket of a pair of tailored black trousers.

"Just you two big heads," she replied. "Now, let's move it 'cause I'm starving, and Mamma wouldn't let us touch lunch until you got here."

"I'm her favorite. That's why."

"You wish," Vicente smirked and shoved Reno as they traipsed through the living room, then entered the parlor.

The antique chandelier sparkled over the forged iron coffee table. Emma DeLuca stood in front of an elaborate white fireplace, gazing out of the Cathedral window covered in custom-made floral damask drapes.

"My love." Emma turned and opened her arms to her firstborn son.

Reno exchanged cheek to cheek kisses with his Mamma, then the four-foot-eleven woman with dark-hair and boisterous personality pulled him into her bosom. Releasing Reno, her sharp brown eyes scanned him from head to toe.

"You look a little thin. Are you eating enough?" she asked, opening the blazer and squeezing the sides of his stomach. "When's the last time you had a homecooked meal?"

A couple of hours ago was what he wanted to say, thinking of Zuri, but he'd never tell his Italian mother that he came to her house with a full belly. Emma wasn't happy unless she was plying the people she held sacred with food. That had always been her love language.

"I'm fine, Mamma."

"Well, I'm not," Sofia chimed in, tucking her shoulder-blade length hair behind her ears. "Let's eat. I have to get back to the hospital soon."

The three members of The DeLuca Clan walked the expansive hallway illuminated by rustic lighting and multi arches, passing several rooms on their way to the kitchen. Reno caught a glimpse of his father through the cracked door of his office with his feet propped on the desk, throwing back a Heineken.

"I'll catch up with y'all in a minute," he said to the others, stopping outside the door and knocking.

"Ma. Ri. Aaaaaa. No," Sofia called his name in that annoying way that only his big sister could get away with, accompanied by an evil glare. He'd swear they were eleven, nine, and five, instead of thirty-six, thirty-four, and thirty.

"Start without me. I wanna speak with Papà for a minute." Reno pushed the door open, "Hey, Papà."

Giacomo lowered his legs, stood, and affectionately slapped Reno's face. "Here's my boy." The robust, white-haired man with bushy brows grinned, pointing a weathered finger at Reno. "Don't come home again and not speak. I don't care what's going on, ya hear?"

Both duly chastised and frustrated, Reno sighed. "Yes, Papà. It won't happen again."

"Great." Giacomo kissed his cheek, then reclaimed his seat.

"I'll have the women out of here as soon as possible. "

"Ehhhh." He gave a dismissive wave of the hand. "You know I don't care about that. They can stay as long as you need. We have enough room and then some."

"Thanks," Reno said, relief filling his mind, then he perched on the edge of the oak desk. "I need your advice about something."

Giacomo grabbed another beer from the small refrigerator behind his desk, popped the cap off, and handed the cold brew to Reno. "What's troubling you, son?"

CHAPTER 13

"What I'm about to say can't leave these four walls," Reno expressed to his dad, closing the door to his office and didn't miss the shadowy figure that inched away. His sister was ever the nosey one, and he wouldn't put it past her to eavesdrop.

"Very well."

"I have a new client whose life's in danger," Reno said, leaning on Giacomo's desk. "She needs protection from an outside source—— I may have to get my hands dirty."

"How dirty?" Giacomo's bushy gray eyebrow shot straight up, almost touching the furrowed lines in his forehead. "Nothing that'll land you behind bars, is it? You know your mother couldn't handle that."

"I don't know. I've never had to deal with a problem of this magnitude before."

"What makes her situation different from the other women?" Giacomo asked, taking a swig of his beer. "Is she at the shelter or with those other women you brought here?"

"Neither. The apartment complex."

"I see. So, this woman's circumstances are delicate." Giacomo leaned forward and extended the green bottle to Reno. He took a lengthy guzzle, then handed the Heineken back to his dad.

"Zuri's being forced to marry."

"What do you mean *forced?* he growled in that raspy voice that had struck fear in the hearts of the most seasoned criminal. "This is America."

"She's from Tanzania."

Giacomo rocked back in the executive chair, wearing an unpleasant expression that hardened with each passing second. "I still don't see the problem. They do that all the time, and from my understanding, it's legal."

"Who's they?"

"Africans," he replied with a dismissive shrug. "Muslims."

"No, Papà," Reno countered, sitting on the edge of Giacomo's desk. "Arranged marriages are legal where *both* people consent. Forced marriages mean there's no consent. Zuri's father received money, basically auctioning his daughter to the highest bidder. When she disappeared, a bounty was placed on her head. Delivery or death."

Giacomo flinched. "But how does this——"

Several hard knocks on the door silenced their conversation. Emma entered without invitation.

"Amore," she said, gripping a wooden serving spoon with a long handle. She placed a hand over her heart, glancing at Giacomo. "I want to spend time with my son. You're not going to monopolize him. Let's go," Emma ordered, pointing the spoon toward the hallway.

End of discussion. When Mamma gave a command, everyone listened and obeyed.

They gathered around the antique dining table that had been handed down from Reno's great-great-great-grandmother. Boisterous laughter, spirited conversation, stick to the ribs food, and lots of wine was part of a typical meal at the DeLuca home. The only thing missing was the aunts, uncles, and tons of cousins who assembled for the once-a-month family gathering. He enjoyed the more intimate setting with his immediate relatives.

Reno moaned with delight, biting into one his Mamma's tube-shaped, deep-fried cannoli, filled with creamy ricotta cheese with just the right amount of sweetness. The traditional dessert had won Emma several awards in pastry contests, and with Papà's help in manufacturing, they have a permanent spot in Mariano's Supermarket, Chicago's number one Italian grocery store. She was envied by her sisters for that accomplishment since they were the ones considered the "better" cooks; in their own mind, of course.

He grabbed a fourth cannoli when Giacomo snatched the pastry from his hand, biting over half of it, then bellowed around the food in his mouth, "Tell your Mamma about this arranged, forced marriage stuff."

Reno's pressure boiled. Apparently, Papà didn't understand how sensitive Zuri's situation was or else he wouldn't have blabbed with such carelessness. The fewer people who knew, the better. Although Reno trusted his family, he didn't want anything to slip out in regular conversation with the wrong person.

"What was that, amore?" Emma asked, wiping her hands on a cloth napkin.

"Papà mumbled something about an arranged marriage," Sofia repeated, locking a steady gaze on Reno.

Reno shot Giacomo a glance accompanied by a frown. "That was private."

"What's he talking about?" Vicente teased, snatching up the last cannoli. "Is some unlucky girl being forced to marry the prodigal son?"

Reno kicked his younger brother under the table.

"Ouch."

"Some African woman's at the shelter and is in *danger* from her big bad father who sold her like a whore," Giacomo dismissed Reno's concern with the wave of a hand. "I still don't see how this is your problem."

"Papà," Reno shouted, outraged at his father's comment and that he still didn't get the fact he'd betrayed a confidence. Now, he may be forced to move Zuri—— yet again.

"You've always had a weakness for them black girls."

Reno banged his fist on the table, causing the nearest wine glass to tip over. Sofia squeezed his thigh, and Vicente glared at Papà. The tension in the room was picante spicy, but Giacomo failed to notice.

"Who was that girl that died—— Evonee——, Imani." Giacomo's arms flailed. "It was something with an *eee* at the end."

"Ehhh," Emma slammed her hand against the table, snatched a spoon, and threw it in her husband's direction. "That's enough!"

"Her name was Ebony Stanton, and she was my friend," Reno roared. "Why are you so damn insensitive?"

"Watch your tone," Giacomo cautioned, eyes narrowing to slits.

"Reno, your phone's vibrating," Sofia alerted, tapping his shoulder.

The pulsating sensation hadn't registered, probably since his nerves were shaking at his core. By the time Reno reached behind his back and plucked the phone from his back pocket, the vibration had ceased. He checked the missed call and saw it was from Vikkas, but before he could redial the number, the phone vibrated a second time.

"Whoever that is can wait," Giacomo barked, his face turning a bright shade of pink. "We're in the middle of lunch for crying out loud."

"You've got to be kidding me right now, Papà." Reno pushed back the chair with such force that it tipped over. "Scusami, Mamma."

Reno hadn't cleared the threshold into the hallway before Emma started ripping Giacomo a new one. He deserved every ounce of Mamma's wrath. Betraying a confidence was a huge disgrace in the DeLuca family. His father was the one to lay down that rule. The fact that he would break it because Zuri was black and brought Ebony to mind made Reno see red. Walking several feet away, Reno slid the icon across the screen to answer Vikkas' second call.

"Hey, Is everything good with Papa K?"

"He's doing alright. Twenty-four hours out of surgery, and he's already bossing folks around."

"That sounds about right." Reno smiled and propped against the wall.

"What's all that commotion in the background?"

"Lunch with my family." Reno sighed, shoving a hand in his pocket, grateful that he wasn't within striking distance of his father. "You couldn't have called at a better time. I need to get out of here before I say something to that man I can't take back."

"We're all at the hospital with my dad," Vikkas replied. "I'm taking the guys to The Castle for a tour after our visit."

"Vikkas, I'm not even sure I can do what Khalil asked or even if I want to at this point."

"You don't have to make a decision today. I know it's a huge undertaking but come with us anyway."

The tones of voices coming from the dining room became shrewder and angrier by the second.

Reno tilted his head back and closed his eyes. "I'm on my way."

He ended the call and made his way down the hall with a purpose. The dissension that erupted was too much to handle. It would be a long time before he'd stepped foot inside this house again when Giacomo was present. What he had done was an affront on so many levels. The majority of the women housed on the DeLuca property were Black. Would he have a problem with them, too?

"Wait up," Vicente yelled, jogging down the hall with Sofia's heels clicking close behind. "Papà was out of line. You good?"

"Yeah," he replied, glancing toward the front door. "I'm good for getting the hell up out of here."

"I'm sorry he brought up Ebony the way he did," Vicente said, placing a hand on Reno's shoulder.

"We know how much you cared about her," Sofia added in a soft tone, embracing Reno. "Papà wants what's best for us, but he can be a real asshole sometimes."

"That's the understatement of the century."

The siblings shared a knowing glance and a quiet laugh.

"Mariano," Emma's voice called from a distance. "Mariano, baby. Thank goodness you're still here," she said rushing down the hall, stopping a few inches in front of him, and grabbing both sides of his face. "Ignore your father. He's an idiot. You do whatever you can to help that young lady, you hear?"

"Yes, ma'am. I love you, Mamma." Reno wrapped his fingers around Emma's hands, removing them from his face and holding them to his chest. "I have to go."

"Me too," Sofia added, smoothing the collar on her crisp white shirt. "I have to get back to the clinic." Sofia bumped her hip against Reno's. "See you later."

"I'll walk you out," Reno replied.

"Ehhh. Don't be a stranger, now," Emma said, casting an evil eye on him. "I don't care about all that mess with your Papà. I'd better see you at the next gathering. If not, you'll have me to deal with."

Reno nodded and kissed her cheek. "Yes, Mamma."

CHAPTER 14

Reno walked into Khalil's hospital room. He was greeted with a warm welcome from his Macro brothers—— a stark difference from twenty-four hours earlier.

"Glad you could make it," Khalil said with a warm smile that contradicted the pain he must be feeling.

"Me too."

Reno slid through the men until he was standing alongside Khalil's bed. He leaned in and hugged his mentor, being careful not to apply too much pressure. Besides the bags resting beneath Khalil's eyes, he looked good. The hospital was the last place to get rest with the nurses barging in every twenty minutes, but Reno would take this version of Khalil over yesterday's any day of the week.

"Have you thought about my offer?"

"I'm still weighing the pros and cons," Reno said, forgetting how direct Khalil could be. In school, this was a tactic used to engage the students in healthy debates.

"Well, don't take too long," Khalil shot back. "Every day that passes, another injustice happens at The Castle. That place was part of my life's work. I sacrificed so much to bring it into existence."

Reno took in Khalil's words. He was honored to be considered, yet, confused on how the Macro brothers could make a difference in overturning the underhanded Castle affairs, especially when the members in question were politically and globally connected.

"You see the state I'm in——, this was no accident. Someone wanted me out of the way, and with the failed assassination attempt, things are going to be more dangerous than ever."

"Don't' worry, Dad. I'm sure *everyone* will do what's right," Vikkas added, glancing at each of the men. "You focus on your recovery and let us do the rest."

A slight corner of Khalil's lip turned upward.

"Good afternoon." The nurse entered the room through the sea of men. "Every time I check on Mr. Germaine, there's an extra set of bodies in here," she teased, approaching Khalil. "You've been quiet and respectful, so I let it slide, but the shift changes in fifteen minutes. The next nurse may not be so lenient."

"I appreciate you letting my boys stay, Maggie," Khalil said with a smile that reached his eyes.

"I have to change your bandages, Mr. Germaine. It'll take ten minutes or so. Everyone's going to have to step out. I need the room to be as sterile as possible for less risk of infection. This is probably a good time to say your goodbyes."

"It's fine, Dad. We're about to head to The Castle anyway." Vikkas gave Khalil's leg a reassuring pat.

"See you later, Papa K," Reno said, giving him some dap and chuckling when Khalil returned the gesture.

Daron, Jai, Grant, Kaleb, Dro, Shaz, and Dwayne all followed suit, and then they filed out of the room under Maggie's watchful stare.

* * *

Arriving at The Castle, Reno had a flashback of the day Khalil was shot.

Wilmette Police were crawling all over the place like a crime scene off of *Chicago PD*, questioning why he was on the property grounds.

One officer even had a hand over his service weapon as if Reno were a threat or worse—— the gunman. Had Vikkas not come from behind the yellow caution tape and rushed into the parking lot when he did, Reno might be in the hospital bed next to Khalil or in the morgue.

The beautiful estate had lost much of its luster since the shooting. The eighteen-hole golf course, the horse stables, the tennis courts, and the lake were all reminders of a time Reno took for granted. Would things had been different if he wasn't so distant and all about work? Would Khalil never had been shot if he and the others read the letters that were sent and acted on them?

"Hey, man. You good?" Kaleb snapped his long, tapered fingers in Reno's face.

Reno blinked until he was able to focus. Everyone had gotten out of their cars and were walking toward the entrance.

"Yeah, man." Reno killed the engine and climbed out of his Porsche.

"I know it's weird being here after everything that happened," Kaleb soothed, falling in step beside him. "Imagine how I feel being the first person on the scene."

"We hadn't talked about that," Reno whispered, not fully understanding what Kaleb meant. "You said you were on your way to Chicago when you called about Khalil."

"Technically, I was," Kaleb replied. "I had made it in from Detroit early. I was going to surprise you, but I had time to spare, so I drove out here to Wilmette to see The Castle. I hadn't been here in ages," Kaleb explained as they took their time to catch up with the others. "I heard the gunshots, and I saw a man flee through the woods. I immediately called the police, then went to see if anyone was hurt or needed help. That's when I saw Khalil laying in an expanding pool of blood and Vikkas with a graze wound to his arm."

Reno halted his movements and glared at Kaleb. "Damn, KV. Why didn't you say anything?"

"I'm not even supposed to be back in Illinois."

"Why not?"

"We'll discuss that later," Kaleb countered. "I'm the one who called the police. I offered to stay with them until help arrived."

"Wait a minute." Reno put a hand out to keep Kaleb in place. "Vikkas knew you were here?"

"He's the one who insisted that I leave before the police came. How else would I know that he wanted you to meet him at The Castle?"

Reno thought that over for a moment. What Kaleb had shared had to remain a secret. If the others knew, they'd feel some kind of way.

"So, why was Vikkas acting the way he was at the hospital?" Reno asked, halting in his tracks.

"I don't know." Kaleb shrugged, stopping beside Reno on their journey to the front entrance. "If I hadn't arrived when I did, Khalil may not be alive."

"Come on you two," Vikkas shouted, waving them forward.

They entered the grand foyer of The Castle. Breathtaking would be the word to describe the entrance best. Reno felt like he stepped off the canvas and into a 3-D version of Michelangelo's Sistine Chapel painting. He marveled at the vaulted Cathedral ceilings with gold crown molding, encompassed two grand staircases lined with red velvet carpeting down the middle with gold-post lamps on each side. Rich. Regal. Royal.

Reno's gaze lowered to the not-so-immaculate red carpet on the other side of the threshold. The outline of the darker bloodstain pattern was etched in the fibers.

"Don't worry about that," Vikkas said, walking over to Reno. "I just got the green light to rip it up. Forensics got everything they need."

Vikkas escorted the men throughout The Castle. Every room was spectacular. The pool looked more like a river, with an expansive fire pit, and rock waterfall. The kitchen was large with dark wood cabinets and professional-grade stainless steel appliances. The bed, bath, and entertainment rooms were exquisite with original fixtures mixed with a modern flair. The décor was a surprising blend of English, French, India, and African artifacts that worked well together despite the distinct differences.

"What's behind this large door?" Daron asked, examining the heavy copper hinges.

"I don't know," Vikkas muttered in a low voice. "And that's the problem. There are several rooms that I don't have access to *in my own damn home*."

"That needs to be rectified sooner than later," Reno said to no one in particular.

Vikkas ended the tour at the circular state-of-the-art conference room. "This is the place where the big decisions are made. If——" He paused and inhaled. "*Once* you accept your appointment, you'll see exactly what I mean."

Reno slid his palm across the semi-circular wooden table, then walked over to a metal stand in the middle of the table opening and examined the black Polycom sound-station.

"We use that for conference calls," Vikkas said, pressing a button, and a loud dial tone resonated in the room. He then pressed another button, and a seventy-foot movie screen monitor descended from the ceiling along the wall. "That's for the international face-to-face meetings with our partners in China, India, Switzerland, and Europe, just to name a few."

"You know I like this high-tech stuff," Daron beamed, checking out the control panel.

"Vikkas," a brawny middle-aged man with a full salt and pepper beard, tanned skin, and a thick accent spoke, eyeing everyone in the room. "Sorry to hear about Khalil. Who are your *friends?*" he asked, walking over and pushing the button to rescind the screen.

Reno didn't miss the shade for one second, and by the expressions on the other guy's faces, they hadn't either.

"They're my high school classmates my father once mentored," Vikkas answered slowly. "They were concerned about him as well."

"And you picked the conference room to have a reunion?" the man said, his expression repulsive. "There are plenty of spare rooms that aren't being used at the moment."

"I'm sorry, did you need something?" Vikkas snapped, folding his hands in front of him. "Last I checked, I had more right to be here than you do."

Frowning, the man gave each of them a dirty-look, mumbling something under his breath, then vacated the room.

The Macro brothers gathered in a tight huddle around Vikkas.

"Something is definitely amiss," Grant said in a hushed tone.

"Agreed," Shaz added, glancing toward the door.

"This is your home," Reno commented. "He doesn't have a right to question who you bring in and what you show them."

"Unless he has something to hide," Daron countered, lifting an index finger. "Which brings me to something I've wanted to discuss with you guys."

"What's up?" Kaleb inquired.

"Remember, I've developed tracking tattoos for each of us," Daron explained. "It's a tatt of a gold crown with the name of the neighborhood that each of us would be King over in the center of it. If we find ourselves in a tight spot and need help, just press the name and the GPS will activate, alerting all of us."

"Ingenious, Daron," Vikkas said. "No one would suspect a tattoo as a tracking device."

"I think that's a great idea, especially with us venturing into the unknown," Dwayne countered. "We don't know what these guys are capable of."

"Count me in." Shaz nodded, giving Daron a fist bump.

"Me too," Grant said, followed by the rest of the men, except for Reno.

Reno liked the concept, but he didn't want to agree until he was sure if he'd accept the appointment.

"I just might take Khalil up on his offer to live here," Kaleb said. "I can be an extra set of eyes and ears."

"Thanks, bro." Vikkas held out his fist, and Kaleb gave him some dap. "I'll take all the help I can get."

"We," Jai corrected. "Not I, we."

A group of eight men darkened the doorway to the conference room in quiet conversation, pausing long enough to steal a glance. Each one of them held a countenance that would strike a chord in men who were weak and insecure. The Macro crew were not those men.

Vikkas walked over, smiled, and said, "Good day, gentleman." He grabbed the oversized double doors and shut them.

"Who are they?" Dwayne asked.

"Let me guess," Reno said with a smirk. "Castle Board Members."

CHAPTER 15

In the last several days, Reno intentionally hadn't been by the transitional apartments or kept in touch with Zuri. Skyler handled the day-to-day functions for the women unless something needed his specific attention. He made a point not to treat Zuri any different than any other client. Reno had to take extra precautions. She stirred up something unexplainable inside of him.

"No news is good news, right?" Reno asked Skyler as he entered the office, scanning the bulletproof door and window replacements.

"Everything's been quiet here," Skyler replied, grabbing two file folders and handing them to Reno. "I had two intakes last night."

"Shelter or extenuating circumstances?"

"Here. You know if it required placement at the apartments, I would've called you immediately."

Reno skimmed through the files on both women. One lady needed temporary shelter due to her landlord not paying the taxes on the apartment building. The bank sold the property, and after several notices to vacate, she was evicted by the Cook County Sheriff.

"Maybe Kaleb can help this woman." Reno placed the folder in front of Skyler. "He has rental property. I'll see if he have any units available."

The other woman's file indicated she had been in a scuffle. The photo of her with a black eye and discolored cheek showed evidence of such. "Did she accept medical care?"

"She refused to go to the hospital, but she did let our nurse check her out. Nothing was broken, just bruised. It'll probably look worse than it is during the healing process. You know—the normal stuff."

"Did Nurse Jewel come here?"

"No. I took them to the Rockford Estate, and she examined her there. It was late, and I didn't want Jewel making that two-hour trip alone."

"That was thoughtful." Reno smiled, handing the files back to Skyler. "But don't forget about *your* safety in the process. You shouldn't be out that late by yourself, either."

"Aren't you sweet—— always worrying about me," Skyler teased, reclaiming the seat behind her desk. "But there's no need. I drove back this morning, and this was waiting for you when I returned."

Skyler lifted a white envelope with bold red letters in the upper left-hand corner that read, *Priority Mail*.

"Who's it from?" he queried, flipping it over before opening the package. "University of Illinois at Chicago."

Reno had requested that Zuri's finals be mailed under his name to the shelter. He'd take it over to the apartment and set up the laptop so she could Skype with her professor while taking the exam. At least, that was the original plan.

"Could you do me a favor, please?" he asked, stuffing the contents back inside the envelope, realizing he would need to go with Plan B. "Deliver this to Zuri and take one of the spare laptops. Make sure the internet connection is working."

"No problem. I'll finish placing the orders for the toiletries and towels when I get back. I just need to grab the keys to the cabinet," Skyler said, reaching into the bottom drawer, pulling out a janitors-style ring of keys. "I'll be right back."

Skyler's heels faded into the background.

With his back turned to the door, Reno shuffled through the mail sitting on Skyler's desk. Nothing stood out, only the standard light, gas, and water bill, along with flyers of the latest chicken shack and discount store opening down the street. The neighborhood had plenty of those and didn't need another. A rec center with afterschool programs or an adult daycare that supported health, social, and daily living needs would serve the community better. But the alderman wasn't hearing any of those suggestions.

The stuffy air that whirled through the lobby made Reno turn toward the entrance.

"Good morning, welcome to——" Reno hesitated, taking in the man dressed in a white robe, a European-style black suit jacket, and a gold cylindrical cap with a flat middle embroidered in diamonds. Besides appearing older than the images gleaned from the internet search, Godfrey Okusanya looked as he seemed in print. "How may I help you, sir?"

"I am looking for someone," the deep, heavily accented voice said, handing Reno a picture. "This is my daughter, Zuri Okusanya. She is missing. Have you seen her?"

Reno prayed his expression wouldn't betray the lie he was about to tell. This wouldn't be the first time someone had sought out a client and landed in the right place but were asking the wrong people to divulge these secrets.

"Mister …"

"Godfrey." He drew a hand adorned with gold rings to his chest. "Godfrey Okusanya."

"Mr. Okusanya. We are not supposed to give out any client's information—— but I can tell you for a fact, that she's not a client here," Reno said, passing the photo back to him.

"That is not what I heard."

The hair on the back of Reno's neck was spikier than a porcupine. The only people that knew Zuri was there, were Kaleb, Skyler, himself, and his family, who he was certain would not have contacted this man.

"Look again," Godfrey commanded, the bass in his voice became even deeper. "She's in danger. I need to find her as soon as possible."

Skyler's laughter snapped Godfrey's attention to the area of the sound. He took off running, further into the lobby.

"Excuse me," Reno cut him off. "You can't walk through here."

"Zuri," he called out, nudging Reno.

"Hey," Reno shouted, lifting his hands. "Let's not do this. The woman you hear is my assistant. You can see for yourself when she comes up here, but you *will not* be all up and through my place of business."

"Mariano." Skyler giggled, the echo of her clicking heels getting closer and closer. "Look at this crazy video Tru sent me. I swear she turned thirteen and has lost her complete mind."

Skyler rounded the corner and froze. She had to clutch the laptop as it almost slipped from under her arm.

"Miss, have you seen my daughter." Godfrey whipped in front of Reno and shoved the picture in Skyler's face, forcing her to step backward. "Her name is Zuri Okusanya. I need to find her right away."

His angst was quite convincing for a man who meant his own flesh and blood a significant amount of harm.

"No, sir, I've haven't seen your daughter," Skyler said in a voice that even convinced Reno. "I do the intake of the women who come into the shelter, and I've never seen her before. She's beautiful. I hope you find her soon," Skyler said, rubbing Godfrey's hand in a comforting fashion. The man flinched at the contact, but gave Skyler an appreciative once-over, before forming that grim expression again. "You may want to check the shelters on the north side. They have several facilities. I can give you a list if you like?"

Damn, she's good.

Godfrey handed Skyler and Reno a rectangular card. "I am staying at the Hyatt Regency on Wacker Drive. You can reach me at the number listed any time. I am not leaving Chicago until I find my daughter."

"Why would you think she'd come here?" Skyler asked in an innocent tone. "This place is for women in abusive relationships. You are not her husband or boyfriend, right?"

A sliver of doubt flashed on Godfrey's face.

"If we hear anything, I'll be sure to call," Reno said, escorting Godfrey toward the front door. "Best of luck."

A man garbed in an African dashiki stand-up collar onyx and gold-colored shirt was posted by a tinted black Suburban in front of the building. He opened the rear passenger door as soon as Godfrey stepped onto the sidewalk. Reno didn't miss the unnatural bulge along the man's side.

Soon as the SUV pulled off, Reno said, "Something's going on. Godfrey made a comment about hearing that Zuri was here. Now either somebody's talking or fishing, but he's too close for comfort."

"Who would say anything?" Skyler shrugged with a bleak expression. "Not me. Not Kaleb."

Giacomo. Emma. Sofia. Vicente.

"I don't know," Reno whispered, pacing the area in front of Skyler's desk.

"That leaves the staff, but they're all in Rockford, so it couldn't be them. They didn't know enough about Zuri anyway." Skyler pursed her lips. "She had just arrived before the shootout. It was chaotic."

"That means the outside help. Maybe the detectives or the bus driver," Reno commented, tapping the tip of his chin with his index finger. "They couldn't have done it either."

"Do you still want me to take this stuff to Zuri?"

"No. No. No. I'll do it," Reno insisted, extracting the laptop and envelope from her hands. "Matter of fact, you can ride with me. Leave your car here just in case they run your plates."

"My plates are registered to the shelter's location," she reminded him.

He'd forgotten, but still ...

During the two years, Skyler and her kids were residents at Second Chance at Life; they didn't have a permanent address. Her husband violated the sanctity of their marriage and kicked his pregnant wife and child out of their home as if they had done something wrong. While getting back on her feet, Reno allowed Skyler to use the shelter's address to receive mail, enroll her daughter in the neighborhood magnet school, and to register her City and State car tags.

"That's right, but I don't want you being followed," he said, setting the alarm. "We're going to close down for the rest of the day."

"It's too early——"

"Skyler," Reno called her name in a tone reserved for zero negotiation.

"Yes, sir."

CHAPTER 16

Reno and Skyler drove around for thirty minutes, making sure they weren't followed. He didn't see anything out of the ordinary, but Reno still parked a few blocks away from the transitional apartment buildings and took an alternative path that was more like a maze. They walked side-by-side, and to the naked-eye, Skyler and Reno looked more like a couple, than CEO and trusty assistant.

Entering the building, Reno paused. "Do you smell bleach?"

"Yes, lots of it."

"That's strange," Reno said, scanning the hallway, stairs, and utility closet. "The janitor isn't scheduled to come out until tomorrow."

"Maybe someone got a little heavy-handed while doing laundry," Skyler countered, following him.

"I suppose that's possible." He frowned, but the uncertainty he felt did not subside.

"Who's there," a female voice called out from behind the door of the first-floor unit where Olga Smirnov had been placed nine months ago with her infant son.

"Olga, it's Mariano and Skyler," he answered.

She opened the door with the baby on her chest. "Mr. DeLuca, is everything alright?" she asked with wide blue eyes while patting Yvengy's bottom. "I heard loud voices. I didn't know it was you."

"My apologies," he said, moving closer. "We didn't mean to startle you."

"Hello, Ms. Skyler," Olga said, stepping into the vestibule.

"Hi." Skyler smiled, glancing at her son, who was wearing one of the outfits donated by Catholic Charities. "How are you adjusting?"

"Good. Thanks for setting me up with Ms. Yolanda's Daycare. She said once my immigration status is verified, I'll have a job waiting for me." Olga smiled, bouncing the chubby little guy who gave a healthy burb as her reward. "No matter what I feed him," she said, waving a hand in front of her nose. "It always smells like bologna."

Skyler chuckled. "I remember those days when my girls were little."

Olga's lips turned upward for a moment. "My online status says I'm a citizen; I'm just waiting to receive the official documents."

"That's wonderful. In the meantime, keep a low profile," Reno cautioned. "You can never be too careful. Whatever you need outside of these walls, Skyler and I will get for you."

"Thanks."

"If you hear a man's voice out here, *do not* open that door. Call me on my cell," he instructed, lifting a brow while giving direct eye contact. "Go on inside and take care of that baby." He rubbed Yvengy's head, then waited while Olga entered the apartment and locked the door.

They ascended the stairs to the second landing. Reno handed Skyler the laptop so he could unlock the door to Zuri's unit.

"Hey, Zu——, whoa." He fell back into the door, dropping the envelope and grabbed his bleeding hand.

"No, Zuri. Stop," Skyler screamed, barely moving out of the way of the thrashing blade.

Reno grabbed her wrist and squeezed the inside, right below the palm of her hand, pressing his thumb into her pressure point. The knife clattered to the floor with a resounding clunk.

Thankfully, he'd learned that move in martial arts class at Macro.

"Zuri, it's me—— Mariano."

Her chest heaved with a rapid flair. Reno held both of Zuri's wrists until her breathing steadied. Her eyes softened after a few minutes, and they were filled with regret.

"What are you doing here?" Zuri screeched. "You said you'll never come by without calling first. I didn't know who was coming in here."

"You're right," he admitted, gazing into her eyes. "I'm sorry. It's been a day."

"Mariano. You're bleeding." Skyler entered the apartment and placed the laptop on the kitchen island. She flipped the faucet handle, snatched paper towels from the holder, and soaked them in water.

Blood dripped from a single slash across the back of Reno's hand. He hadn't felt any pain until Skyler called attention to the superficial wound.

"I didn't mean to hurt you."

"I know," Reno said, holding his hand up by the wrist, red streaks trickled down the front of his wrist and arm.

"Bring him over here," Skyler ordered from the kitchen.

Zuri guided Reno to the sink, and Skyler cleaned his wound. After she had the bleeding under control, Skyler retrieved one of the first-aid kits that they supplied in all of the units, from the cabinet above the sink, and bandaged his hand.

"Thank you." Reno smiled down at Skyler. "One way or another, you're always looking out for me."

"I can't have anything happen to the best boss I've ever had," Skyler smirked and winked, replacing the first-aid kit in its designated spot.

"I'm so sorry," Zuri apologized a second time, tossing the gauze packaging and adhesive medical tape scraps in the garbage.

"It was an accident," he replied, examining Skyler's handy work. She could double as a nursing assistant. "I'm the one at fault."

Skyler's head whipped around, and Zuri's eyes widened.

"You're right. I came by unannounced; something I promised never to do," Reno said, leaving the kitchen, and retrieved the bloodstained envelope near the front door. "Hell … I'm glad to know you're able to protect yourself."

"I may get hurt, but I am not going to be the only one."

"My girl." Skyler lifted a hand in the air, and seconds later, Zuri gave her a high-five.

"This is for you." Reno passed the package to Zuri.

"What is it?" she asked, snatching a paper towel from the counter and wiping the drops of blood.

"Your finals."

Zuri grinned and twirled in a small circle doing a dance where her head bent, and her arms stretched back and forth. "Thank you so very much. You do not know how much this means to me. It feels like Mama is smiling down on me from heaven."

"You're welcome," he nodded, massaging his injured hand.

Skyler sauntered to the window and peered out from the side of the blinds. She glanced back at Reno and nodded. He returned the gesture.

"What is that all about?" Zuri frowned while pulling the contents from the envelope.

Reno plucked the papers from her hand and placed them on the counter that separated the kitchen from the living room. Skyler came over and stood beside Zuri.

"What is it?" Zuri's focus darted from one to the other. "You all are scaring me."

Reno closed the gap, creating a right triangle formation. "Your father's in Chicago."

"No." She shook her head with a twisted expression. "It is too soon. I did not expect to have to deal with him for another week. Are you sure?"

Reno swallowed past the lump in his throat. "He came by the shelter looking for you."

"I cannot go back there. I refuse," Zuri protested with trembling lips. "No woman deserves to live that way. I won't." She stumbled backward.

Reno shifted to catch her if she fell.

"We're gonna make sure that you're safe," Skyler reassured, wrapping her arm around Zuri's shoulder. "We sent him on a search and find mission. By the time he realizes what's happening, we'll have you placed somewhere else."

"I will not leave Chicago before my graduation. Mama sacrificed her life for me to have an education. I am certain things for her were not pleasant after she helped me escape, so no," Zuri cried, swiping the tears from her face. "No matter how frightened I am … death before dishonor."

Reno nodded, taking in her last statement.

"Am I still safe here?"

"Yes. No one knows about this place except for me, Skyler, Kaleb, and the women who've resided here in the past. Trust me," Reno said, clasping his hands together. "They aren't going to say anything. They know how important it is to keep this location confidential." After a brief pause, Reno added, "My family knows of the transitional apartments, but they've never been here."

Zuri sighed with relief.

"It's not going to be easy to focus on my finals with this looming over me." Zuri eased down on the couch, pulling her knees to her chest and wrapping her arms around them. "On top of the men hanging around here at night. How do I know they aren't spies hired by my Baba?"

"What men?" Reno's voice hitched, and this time, he rushed over and peeked out of the blinds, scanning the quad. Nothing seemed amiss.

"I haven't seen them, but Olga has. She said they drink and smoke in front of her living room window and hang in the hallway outside of her door."

Reno shot a glare at Skyler, who had the same astounded expression. He'd never heard of anything like this happening before in the complex.

"We just spoke with Olga. She didn't say anything about that," Reno looked at Skyler, then back to Zuri. The women here were the second line of defense in making the place safe. "Why didn't you call me?"

"I just learned of it this morning when Olga asked me to watch Yvengy. She brought him upstairs so she could get a couple of uninterrupted hours of sleep. She said all of the loud talking late at night was keeping her up."

"Excuse me." Reno walked with a purpose to the door, but Skyler caught him before he left.

"Call her, first," Skyler advised, handing Reno her phone. "We can't have a repeat of what happened earlier. Olga took those self-defense classes at the School of Wing Chun, and she'll put you in the hospital."

"What am I? A weakling?"

"Zuri caught you off guard," Skyler shot back.

She did have a point.

He called Olga and asked her to come upstairs. Within five minutes, she was knocking on Zuri's door.

"Please come in," Reno said, tickling the baby's feet. The little guy giggled and reached for him. "May I?"

"Sure," Olga replied, stroking the long thick braid that rested over her left shoulder that extended to her waistline. When she arrived, it was only sweeping her shoulders. "Hey, Zuri. Thanks for your help."

"Anytime," Zuri responded, closing the door behind Olga.

"Am I in trouble?" the Russian beauty asked, her porcelain cheeks flushing scarlet the moment she laid eyes on Skyler. "Did my citizenship paperwork get denied?"

"No, Olga. Nothing like that," Reno reassured, sitting on the arm of the couch. "I wanna talk to you about what's going on around here at night. I hear there's riffraff lurking in and around the building, and that's not supposed to happen."

Olga fiddled with the rosary beads around her neck. "They have been coming about eleven-thirty the past three nights and stay until four in the morning, talking vulgar and smoking hash. The hallway smells like urine and stinky bodies in the morning." She shuddered.

"Why didn't you call me or the police?" Reno asked.

"I didn't want to bring attention to myself," she said, lowering her head. "The police aren't kind to women like me. And I was afraid the men would know I called since I'm the only person on the first floor. I didn't know what they would do to me."

Skyler sat beside Olga and lifted the woman's chin. "You don't have a reason to be ashamed. We understand."

"I don't know why they're here," Olga mumbled, sliding her arms around her middle. "I used to feel safe, but now——"

"I'm going to get to the bottom of this," Reno promised. "The unit across from Zuri's vacant. I'll get someone over here, and we're going to move you upstairs. I know it's a temporary solution, but at least you won't be downstairs alone if or when they come back."

"Thank you," Olga said, reclaiming her baby and holding him close to her chest. "Can I go now? It's time for Yevgeny's feeding."

"Of course," Reno replied.

"I'll walk you down." Skyler bounded to her feet and headed toward the door.

Once Skyler and Olga left the apartment, Zuri whispered, "This is unnerving. It poses a greater risk than my Baba. What if these men want more than to use the building as a hideout for whatever they're doing?" she inquired, picking her fingernails. "What do we do if they knock on our doors or force their way inside?"

"That's not going to happen," Reno assured. "I'll have someone looking into this tonight."

"Can't you stay here with me?" Zuri asked as Skyler entered the apartment again. "I'm scared to be here by myself."

"I—— that's not—— I can't, Zuri," Reno stammered, rubbing his chin.

"Then I can no longer live here and be at the mercy of these unknown men. I will find my own way." She rose from the couch and stormed into the bedroom. "Life does not have to be fair, but it has to be better than this. Why am I unable to escape this kind of hell?"

Reno whipped around to face Skyler, stunned. "What am I supposed to do?"

She rushed to his side and whispered, "We'll figure something out, but you *can't* stay here."

"Zuri," Reno called after her as he and Skyler walked into her bedroom.

"No, Mariano. I appreciate all of your help, but this isn't working," she fussed, stuffing the few belongings she had into a duffel bag. "I'd rather take my chances elsewhere. I refuse to lie in wait to be mistreated, abused, or maybe even raped by some strange man."

"What if I stay the evening with you?" Skyler offered, closing the space between them. "I'll ask my mom to keep the kids for the night. You won't be here alone, and it'll give Mariano a chance to look into things."

Zuri gave her a half-smile. "That's kind of you, but you're a woman. If those men barge into this apartment——" Zuri paused, holding a Kente scarf. "There's not much you can do either."

"I'll stay."

"Mariano," Skyler snapped, slapping her thigh and giving him a lethal side-eye.

Zuri gasped, extending open arms toward Reno, but retracting them before she made contact.

"Mariano." Skyler's brow arched, intensifying the glare she had fixated on Reno.

"It'll be fine. After we get Olga moved upstairs, I'll spend the evening in the first-floor unit. I'll set up video and audio surveillance. Those men will never know I'm listening."

CHAPTER 17

"Thanks for always coming through when I need you," Reno said, stepping aside to allow Kaleb to enter the condo."

"Well we're moving on up—— to the east side—— to a deluxe apartment in the sky-y-y." Kaleb sang, doing the George Jefferson walk with his arms swaying from side to side.

Reno needed that laugh after what he had just learned. He grabbed Kaleb by the arm and yanked him all the way inside. "Man, get in here."

"What's up? It sounded urgent." Kaleb leaned-in for a brotherly hug as he entered the living room, then plopped down on the chocolate leather sofa.

"The past three nights, I'd been staying in one of the transitional apartments——"

"Do tell? Sounds like a woman's involved." Kaleb grinned, leaning back and crossing one leg over the other. "Where's the popcorn?"

"Get your mind out of the gutter," Reno shot back, grabbing his phone from the coffee table and parking his rear-end there. "I stayed in the first-floor unit—— *not* with Zuri."

"Talk about a downer," Kaleb teased, shaking his head. "I thought at least one of us had got some action."

"I have, but not that kind," Reno countered, activating a video app on his phone, then leaning forward to show Kaleb. "There's been gang and drug activity in and around the building after midnight. These assholes are stashing drugs in the hall, drinking, and outright being uncouth, pissing at the bottom of the stairs and in the corners."

Kaleb rubbed the back of his head. "Those are Sovereign King colors."

"That's what I presumed when I saw that black and gold," Reno said, shifting his focus to Kaleb. "Do you recognize any of these guys?"

"It's been years," Kaleb replied, scooting to the edge of the sofa and staring at the screen. "Nah, these are young cats. They weren't even a twinkle in their mother's eye when I was banging." Kaleb snickered. "And unless the boundaries have changed, they're in the wrong territory. How'd you get this footage?"

"I replaced the floodlight motion-activated sensor with a Ring floodlight two-way camera." He swiped his screen to a design. "The devices are identical, and it picks up everything within thirty feet. All I have to do is tap on the app, and I can check the time, the day, I can zoom in——, the whole shebang."

"Ingenious."

"Thanks, but it doesn't do me any good if I don't know who these guys are and why they're in this area." Reno sighed, closing the app. "Can you contact some of your old buddies from the neighborhood—— The ones you're still cool with."

"I'm not cool with any of those guys. Not anymore." Kaleb wiped his hands on a pair of True Religion jeans; something Reno's brother highly coveted. "It's time you knew the real reason my family moved to Detroit."

"Your mother got a great job offer with better pay was what you told me."

Kaleb stood and moved to the sliding glass door that separated the living room from the private rooftop swimming pool and hot tub. The spot had a view of Lake Michigan and the South Shore Cultural Center. "To protect my mother, I turned State's evidence against the leader of the Sovereign Kings. In return, I was granted immunity from prosecution and relocated. This is the first time I've set foot in Chicago in fifteen years." Kaleb paused, cracking his knuckles. "Ain't no love for a snitch in the hood, but there are long memories."

Reno closed the distance between them. "Damn, KV. I didn't know."

"I couldn't say anything," Kaleb replied, turning to face Reno. "I wasn't supposed to keep in touch with anyone from my past. I saved your number in my new phone under the name Mariah and shuffled the area code around, so my mother didn't recognize that it was a Chicago number."

"That's extreme, but I understand." Reno eyed Kaleb with a clearer appreciation of the value of their continued, but secret friendship. "I'll find another way."

"Nah, man. Your girl needs help," Kaleb shot back, bumping Reno's shoulder with his fist. "The kind a straight-laced pretty boy can't provide."

"Zuri isn't my girl." Reno protested, biting his bottom lip. "She's just a client."

Kaleb gave him the side-eye and a half-smile. "But you care about her, right?"

"Anyway." Reno walked into the kitchen and grabbed an apple from the refrigerator. "Download the Ring app. I'm going to give you access to my account so you can see what I see."

"Cool." Kaleb held his hand in the air and curved his fingers. Reno tossed him an apple.

"Don't bring any attention to yourself," Reno warned. "If it gets too dangerous, walk away."

"I may not be in the streets anymore, but I still know how to navigate them."

* * *

Later that day, Reno went back to the transitional apartments to check on Zuri and Olga before he hunkered down for the night in the first-floor unit. Even though he had surveillance at his fingertips, he knew it would put the women at ease if he were in the building.

Reno dialed Olga's number, and she answered on the fourth ring.

"Good evening, Mr. DeLuca."

"Hey, Olga. Is everything okay?" Reno asked, scooting to the edge of the sofa. "It took you a while to get to the phone?"

"We're good," Mr. DeLuca, she said in a breathy voice. "The phone was in the other room. I'm feeding Yvengy."

"My apologies. I'll let you get back to it."

Reno ended the call and dialed Zuri. He hadn't seen her in seventy-two hours, which helped keep his feelings in check.

"Hi, Mariano, guess what?" she said with an airiness in her voice. "I have completed my exams and received my final grades. Three A's and one B. I finished with a 4.2 GPA. That means I will be graduating summa cum laude."

"Congratulations. That's an amazing accomplishment."

"Thank you." Zuri giggled, and he could feel her happiness through the phone.

He placed the call on handsfree so he could hear Zuri while navigating the Uber Eats app. Reno was going to order take-out from his favorite sushi spot, then thought better of that plan. He didn't want anyone who wasn't affiliated with Second Chance coming to the building. Not even the delivery guy.

"I swear I don't remember getting my grades back that fast," he commented, maneuvering to the kitchen, opening the freezer, and retrieving a Lean Cuisine. He popped the frozen dinner in the microwave, then grabbed a bottle of water from the refrigerator.

"It had better been—— graduation is in two days," she said, "Oh, I have to pick up my cap and gown, and the tickets tomorrow at nine.

"I'll grab them for you."

"Thanks, Mariano. I do not know how I would have got through all of this without you," Zuri expressed her gratitude. "Are you here? I mean, downstairs."

"Yes."

"Good—— I'll be right down."

Before he could object, she had disconnected the call.

Reno ran to the bathroom and glanced at himself in the mirror. He worked his fingers through his hair, checked his teeth for foreign particles, and cupped a hand over his mouth and exhaled, making sure his breath wasn't ripe. He gargled with the travel-sized mouthwash he kept in a toiletry bag for good measure.

He moseyed to the door, pulling in a deliberate intake of air as he unlocked the deadbolt and turned the knob, offering Zuri entry.

"Hey." She grinned, entering the apartment with a small sack in her hand.

Her tight coils were loose and damp, hanging over her shoulders, sweeping the valley of her breasts in a flesh-toned camisole. The feelings that laid dormant for the past couple of days were ever-present.

"This is for you. My mother gave it to me as a little girl," she explained, unwrapping the cloth and handing the necklace to Reno.

"Thanks," he said, admiring the intricate carvings of the dark-wood elephant necklace with bamboo beads. "I can't accept this."

"You can and you will," Zuri insisted, pushing his hand away. "This handcrafted trumpeting elephant represents good luck, protection, and wisdom. I think it is time I passed it on to someone who is worthy of such good fortune."

Reno couldn't take his eyes away. "I don't know what to say."

Zuri lifted the necklace and tied the pliable black cords with beads around Reno's neck. He adjusted the pendant center mass, and it laid right beneath his collarbone.

"I like this very much. Thank you."

"I did not believe in the elephant's power at the time my mother gave it to me, but when I look at my life and all that I have been through," Zuri reflected, standing in front of Reno and placing a finger on the pendant, causing a flood of feelings to flow through him. "And all that I have overcome—— what else could it be?" She rested her hands on each of Reno's shoulders. "You are taking on a battle that I brought to your doorstep and others that you could not have foreseen. Let the wisdom and good fortune of the African elephant protect you."

Reno gazed into her compassionate orbs. No woman he'd ever loved showed him the kind of thoughtfulness that Zuri had. Her caring nature validated his strong attraction, and the feelings coursing through him were more than physical.

The beeping microwave interrupted the moment.

"Excuse me for a second," he said, stepping backward and going into the kitchen.

Reno grabbed the steaming plastic container with his fingertips.

"Is that your dinner?" she asked, leaning on the counter and fanning the hot mist away from her face.

"Yep. Something quick and easy."

"Let me cook you a decent meal?" she offered, twitching her nose at the contents of the pre-packaged meal.

Reno laughed. "Why are you always trying to feed me?"

"That is how we show the people we love—— *care about,*" Zuri corrected, sliding a finger across the counter. "How much they are appreciated."

"You and my Mamma would get along great," Reno said with a smile that he felt in the pit of his stomach. "She loves to feed me. Every time I visit, she checks me out as if I'm a picky toddler who doesn't eat his vegetables."

Zuri stifled a giggle with the palm of her hand.

"It's not funny," he said, stifling a laugh. He rifled through the kitchen drawers until he found a large serving spoon, then went to the pantry and grabbed a white apron, slipped it over his neck, and tied the strings behind his back. "Mariano, are you eating enough?" he said in the best imitation of Emma DeLuca. "You're looking thin, baby. Who's cooking for you?" He patted his own stomach with the oversized spoon. "When are you gonna find you a wife so she can cook for you?"

Zuri reared back with uncontrollable laughter. "Then that settles it." She took the Lean Cuisine, then tossed it in the trash. "At least for tonight, your mother will not have to worry if you are eating a hearty meal."

"If you insist," Reno surrendered, remembering the last delicious meal they had shared. "We can cook together."

Smiling, Zuri nodded. "Let me see what you are working with." She inspected the cabinets, pantry, and refrigerator, her expression registering approval.

An hour later, they sat on the living room couch, enjoying Titanic on the television while eating spaghetti, fried catfish, broccoli, and garlic bread. Two hours into the film and Titanic was watching them.

Loud voices jarred Reno out of his sleep. Groggy and disoriented, he attempted to lift from the couch, but something kept him rooted. He glanced down, and Zuri's head was in his lap. His gaze followed the outline of her body. She was fully dressed, curled in the fetal position, sleeping soundly. Reno never intended for Zuri to be in the apartment so late, and she definitely couldn't leave now.

Reno lifted Zuri's head and was easing from underneath her when an explosive crash slammed into the apartment door. Zuri jerked upward, eyes wide with terror. Reno put his index finger to her lips and whispered, "Go into the bedroom."

He snatched the phone from the end table, opened the app, pulled a handgun from under the couch cushion, and tip-toed to the door in less than sixty seconds. Unlocking the safety, he held the pistol at his side and stared through the peephole.

"One more kick and this door should cave in," the thug boasted, turning his black cap with the gold SK to the back.

"I bet you fitty bucks that it won't," another guy said, pulling money out of his pocket and sitting the bills on the stairs.

Reno unbolted the locks as quietly as he could and waited. Soon as the degenerate ran with his foot flying toward the door, Reno swung it open, and the young man flew inside and landed on his ass with his legs twisted in an awkward position. Reno aimed his weapon.

The four other guys took off running.

Reno stomped the thug in his chest, followed by a bone-cracking kick to his ribs, then stood on the man's mangled knee. The culprit dressed in gold and black shrieked like a newborn baby protesting its entry into the world.

He cocked the gun, and pointed the barrel in his face, "Let this be the last time I see you on this property." Reno squeezed the trigger and let off one round into the floor, mere inches away from the left side of his face.

The man relieved himself where he laid. His hand trembled as it traveled and covered the ear closest to a shell casing.

"I know you probably can't hear all that well right now," Reno said, bending toward his right ear. "So, I'll come a little closer."

The man flinched, unable to mask his fear or pain.

"Next time, it'll hit between the eyes."

Reno patted him down but didn't find a weapon or any identification.

Digging in his own back pants pocket, Reno pulled out his wallet, extracted a business card, and dialed the number written on the flip side.

"Detective Carter, this is Mariano DeLuca from Second Chance at Life Women's Shelter," he said, sitting down on the couch, watching the broken man who struggled but couldn't get to his feet.

"Hi, Mariano," Detective Carter replied. "I remember. Is there a problem?"

"You said if I ever needed anything to call. Well … I have a situation."

CHAPTER 18

"After the hurting, you put on that boy," Detective Carter said, as the EMT hauled Michael Sampson, known as Li'l Smoke on the streets and by law enforcement away on a gurney. "I don't foresee you having any more problems. I doubt there'll be any retaliation. These are the young foot soldiers in training. They may look like grown men, but not one of them in that video is over seventeen."

Reno shook his head, looking down at the urine stain on the carpet. He would have to replace the entire thing.

"I've seen it before. Coming face-to-face with death can do that," Detective Carter commented. "I'm surprised he didn't shat himself, too. Well, don't let it sit too long; it's hard to get that smell out of the carpet."

"Maintenance will take care of it when they arrive later today. Right now, all I want to do is get some rest."

"I'll have a couple of uniforms stationed out front and others patrolling the area for the next several days, so that you and your tenants can have some peace of mind."

"I appreciate that," Reno shook Detective Carter's hand. "Thanks for the quick response."

"Anytime you need me," he said, holding his thumb and pinky fingers out and placing them to his ear. "I'm just a phone call away."

Soon as the detective left, Zuri emerged from the bedroom, with her arms wrapped around her body as if she were cold. "Is this really over?"

"That's what the police say, but I have someone looking further into the situation. I can't fathom anyone coming back here tonight— well, this morning," Reno moved around the couch and lifted her shoes from the floor. "I'll walk you upstairs."

Zuri pulled away. "I do not want to be alone tonight. Can I stay? I will sleep on the sofa. Please."

After the fiasco that took place, he wasn't going to deny Zuri that comfort. He would sleep on the couch.

"Sure," Reno agreed, walking to the linen closet to grab a sheet and throw blanket. "Take the bedroom. I just need to get one of the pillows off the bed."

Later that morning, Reno left the apartment to pick up Zuri's graduation tickets, cap, and gown. He'd left a note on the bathroom mirror letting her know where he went, so she wouldn't be frightened. That's the one place he was certain she'd visit after waking.

The bright sunlight greeted Reno soon as he stepped a foot onto the pavement, causing him to lift an arm to shield his eyes. As he made his way across the quad, the trees blocked the direct beam of the sun and he was able to catch a glimpse of a uniformed officer alongside the building and another one in a Chicago Police cruiser. That gave him some comfort.

Soon as he slid behind the wheel, a thought hit him, he texted Kaleb. *I need you to move like supersonic. These little punks tried to kick in the door to the first-floor unit. If I hadn't moved Olga upstairs four days ago, this could've been tragic.*

Thirty seconds later, Kaleb replied, *I'm on it.*

Reno returned to the apartment two hours later. He opened the door and saw Zuri on her hands and knees scrubbing the carpet with a brush and a bucket of sudsy water.

"You don't have to do that."

"It is the least I could do. I am almost done anyway," she replied, glancing up and smiling at the black garment bag in Reno's hands. "Is that my stuff?"

"What do you think?" he teased.

She climbed off the floor, running to the kitchen sink, washing and drying her hands. She darted back to the living room just as fast, unzipping the garment bag while Reno held it up.

"Without your help, none of this would have been possible," Zuri said, admiring the black graduation cap, silky robe, and triple honor cords. "Thank you."

"No need to thank me. You did the hard work," he dismissed, handing her the white envelope with the tickets inside.

"You know what I mean," she shot back with a smirk. "Will you come to my graduation tomorrow? I want you there."

"I'd be honored."

"Skyler and Kaleb, too."

He leaned back against the counter. "I'm sure they'd love to come but let me check with them first."

"That leaves me with one ticket remaining," Zuri said, removing the rectangular stub from the envelope. "It was reserved for my Baba before all of this mess happened. Two weeks here and you all have been more like a family to me than my blood relatives." She marched to the kitchen, turned the stovetop pilot on, and held the ticket in the flames.

"Invitation or not, you know he's going to be there," Reno reminded her, turning off the burner, taking the charred paper from her hands, then flipping on the cold water to douse the fire. "But I'll have a security team in place. The only thing you have to be concerned with is walking across the stage to get your degree."

Zuri pressed a lingering kiss on his cheek.

Her soft mouth on Reno's skin ignited another kind of flame. He rotated his head until he was gazing into his reflection in her eyes. Touching Zuri's soft hair, he tried to push down the heat rising within. It took all of his might not to envelope her full cherry lips.

Blinking, Reno removed his hand from her hair and stepped backward. "I need to make some calls. I'll pick you up tomorrow at noon."

"I cannot wait. I am so excited."

Zuri gathered her things and he escorted her upstairs. Once she closed and locked the door, he ran down the stairs, two at a time and let out a loud sigh when he made it to the bottom landing, clasping the African elephant in his fist.

Collecting himself, he grabbed his belongings from the first-floor unit, examined the wooden and steel frame door for damages. Since there wasn't any, Reno locked up.

He needed to go home first, then visit the shelter. The women would be moving back in tomorrow and he wanted to go over the checklist with Skyler to make sure everything was in place.

Reno left the building and strutted on an angle across the quad, pulling a phone from his pocket and dialed Daron Kincaid. He owned Crossroads Security; one of the best security firms in the business.

The phone barely completed one full ring before it was answered.

"Kincaid."

"Daron. It's Reno. I need a favor."

* * *

The following morning, the special car Reno requested was parked outside of his condo with an armed driver dressed in a black, three-piece suit, and shades.

"Good morning, Mr. DeLuca," the man with short-curly hair said, opening the rear door. "Bryson Kale with Crossroads Security."

"Nice to meet you." Reno shook his hand, then climbed into the backseat and called Zuri.

"Hello," she answered on the third ring; sounding out of breath.

"It's Mariano. Is everything okay?" he asked; his posture rigid.

Reno tapped the back of the seat and Bryson glanced at him through the review mirror. He covered the receiver and said, "Let's go."

Nodding, Bryson fired-up the engine.

"Everything's fine," Zuri assured in an uneven tone. "I'm running a little behind, that's all."

The alarming tension eased, reversing that galloping jolt that had sent his heart racing a second ago. "I'm on the way."

"I will just need a few extra minutes," she explained. "Please, let yourself in."

Within fifteen minutes, he arrived at the transitional apartments. Reno knocked on Zuri's door as he inserted the key into the deadbolt.

"Zuri. It's Mariano," he announced, shutting the door and securing the lock. He paced around the living room before perching on the arm of the sofa.

"I will be right out," she hollered from one of the back rooms.

A text message notification from Daron, pinged from Reno's phone.

Everything's in place. Bryson will be at your disposal for as long as you need him. You owe me LOL.

Reno snickered at the last comment. He was more than grateful for Daron's ability to provide top-notch security with less than a twenty-four-hour notice. Even though Reno didn't know all the details, he was sure that Daron had him covered. He responded.

Whatever you need. Anytime. Any place. I got you.

"Sorry for keeping you waiting," Zuri said, sauntering into the living room looking every bit of the African Princess she was, in an orange dashiki print overlay V-neck jumpsuit, trimmed in gold and blue accents. The vibrant colors were radiant against her glowing skin. Sexiness draped across her feet in strappy gold sandals and Zuri's hair bounced on her shoulders with every step she took.

Reno couldn't peel his eyes away.

"You're beautiful."

With a smile bright enough to outshine her ensemble, Zuri said, "Thank you."

"Are you nervous?"

She shook her head.

A berry fragrance wafted from her hair. Reno was in heaven on earth all over again, remembering how that same scent infused his senses when they first met.

"I have worked too hard for this to be nervous."

He stood as Zuri came forward.

"You promised to protect me, and I believe you." She grabbed a gold clutch off the loveseat. "I am ready."

Reno tapped a code into his wrist watch. "We're on the way down."

They slid into the backseat of a black Adali XLS that Reno borrowed from Cadence for the day. The vehicle had been fitted with international license plates. The windows appeared normal, but they were reflective; passengers could see out, but no one could see in. The car was equipped with hidden cameras in the headlights, taillights, and side mirrors. If anyone followed them, Reno would know it immediately. And if someone ran his plates, it would lead them to a warehouse in Germany.

"Where is Skyler and Kaleb?"

"Skyler's at the shelter. With all the transitioning going on, she wanted to be available to the women there——, give them some sense of normalcy upon returning and getting back to a regular routine. She sends her blessing. And Kaleb, had some business that required his attendance."

"I understand," but there was no mistaking the disappointment in her voice.

Thirty minutes later, they arrived at the expansive UIC Forum. An armed guard was at every entrance. Scanning each of their faces and uniform, Reno couldn't tell the difference between the campus security guards and Daron's men.

People were lined-up at all five doors waiting to gain entry, even though the ceremony didn't start for another two hours.

He remembered his parents dropping him off early for his graduation and the stories his mother told of them standing in line to get the closest seat to the stage so they could get great pictures and video. Mamma faked a heat stroke an hour into waiting, and the guard allowed the family early entry until the ambulance arrived. But she convinced them that all she needed was to get out of the sun, sit, and steady her breathing. Dad made several trips to the bathroom to soak a facecloth in cold water to apply compresses on her forehead. The maintenance guy amped up the air conditioning as she sucked in air from an empty oxygen tank.

By the time the ceremony began, she was fine … and they all had front row seats.

"I have to gather with my class in Meeting Room G upstairs."

"Okay," Reno responded, following Zuri to the glass door.

"Only the graduates are allowed to enter at this time," the guard said, granting Zuri and Reno access.

He had to be one of Daron's men. He didn't scan me with the wand or he honestly thinks I'm a graduate.

As he crossed the threshold, Reno flinched as a program booklet was shoved into his hands by an usher. The pamphlet was unnaturally weighted. Reno glanced at the woman and she tapped her ear, then walked away.

Reno followed Zuri up two flights of stairs. The hall was flanked with young men and women in blue gowns and decorated graduation caps.

"I will see you after the ceremony." Zuri smiled at Reno, kissing his cheek, then disappeared behind the door to Meeting Room G.

He grabbed the handle to peek in the room when a broad-shouldered man in graduation attire bumped into him, dropping his phone.

"Sorry," Reno said, clutching the program booklet.

They both bent downward to retrieve the device.

"Meeting Room G and all the rooms upstairs are secure," the baritone voice whispered, grasping the phone. "Check the contents of your program and have a seat in the auditorium."

The man stood, straightened his gown, then vanished into the same room Zuri just entered.

Damn. Daron's good.

Reno hurried downstairs to the auditorium and sat in the far-left corner; hidden from direct view. He opened the program booklet to find a class of 2019 silver pin, diamond studded earring, hearing aid, and a keychain were attached with Velcro to the center page. Above the items, a handwritten note was stapled explaining how each gadget functioned. Reno fastened the camera to his lapel, slipped the flesh-toned hearing device in his ear, then pushed the post of the earring through his pierced lobe, securing the back and rotating the diamond clockwise until he heard it click and a robotic voice say, "*You're connected.*" Lastly, he stuffed the taser keychain in his pants pocket.

Now he felt more like an undercover CIA agent than a civilian. Reno slid his hand across the concealed gun resting in the holster under his suit jacket. He'd be an assassin if it came down to that, with a secret weapon of his own.

CHAPTER 19

The live orchestra hit the first chord of the familiar pomp and circumstance song, and the entire audience shifted their bodies one-hundred and eighty degrees, facing the rear of the auditorium, except Reno. He was looking for anyone who stood out from the rest. Unfortunately, with the size of the crowd, he'd have a better chance of finding a single strand of hair on the floor.

Reno situated in an end seat to have the best mobility if he had to make a sudden move. Turning to check the side closest to him, he spotted Zuri marching down the aisle. She smiled as she passed by, applying a slight pinch to his forearm. Any time, Zuri touched Reno it gave him the feels, but he couldn't bask in them, he had to focus on his surroundings.

One-fourth of the way through the ceremony, six men in black suits stood strategically in even intervals in the aisles and on the sides of the stage. The pulsing in Reno's heart, shifted into his throat. He placed a foot in the aisle and rested a hand on the bulge under his jacket.

A click in his ear made him shudder.

"Stand-down," the robotic voice commanded through the device. "These men are here to protect Michelle Obama, she's the commencement speaker."

Reno eased back in the seat, allowing his alert level to return to normal.

He'd never seen the former First Lady in person, so this was a treat. Reno eyed the lifelong Secret Service detail, a perk that President Richard Nixon relinquished in 1985. The Herculean men were clad in the same attire as his driver, Bryson Kale. If she wasn't in attendance, Reno would've thought they were contracted with Crossroad Security.

Reno's vibrating phone pulled him from his thoughts. He'd received a text message from Kaleb. Meet me at The Burger Joint after Zuri's graduation. It's important. Like a sixteen-alarm fire, tsunami, volcano erupting important. I'll be there at three.

He texted back, *I'll be there.*

Applause roared like thunder after Mrs. Obama's speech. Secret Service flanked the front of the auditorium and escorted her down the aisle, tucked inside a human sphere of muscle and weapons. She waved to the audience until they disappeared behind the exit doors.

The remainder of the ceremony was uneventful. Reno was curious to know who would cheer for Zuri when her name was called to walk across the stage. All of her family was supposed to be in Tanzania. If Godfrey was in the audience, Reno didn't want to give away his position just in case he needed to make a move, although he wanted to jump out of the rafters to celebrate her accomplishment. No one other than her graduating class, and the faculty on stage clapped for Zuri.

Something isn't right.

Standing as the graduates descended down the aisles, Reno leaned in Zuri's direction as she came close. "I'll be waiting out front by the car with Bryson. Be careful."

She nodded and continued to march toward the exit.

Reno blended into the sea of people, following the last graduate walking out of the auditorium and into the lobby. He weaved his way through the crowd, apologizing along the way until the sun's bright rays hit his face. The surrounding noise was loud, and his vision was obscured with several bouquets of congratulatory balloons floating in the air and groups of people hugging and screaming with excitement.

"Bryson," Reno called out, finally making it to the car. "This crowd is out of control. Keep your eyes open. I don't know who's who."

"Will do. Where's Zuri?"

"What do you mean? She's not in the backseat?" Reno asked, snatching the rear door open. "Shit!"

"I thought she was with you."

"No." He scanned the crowd as best as he could with all of the obstructions in the way. Reno tapped a button on his watch. "Does anyone have eyes on Zuri?"

He ran along the curb to the corner, tripping over a little girl who zig-zagged in his path.

"Hey, slow the hell down," a woman shouted as the child released a piercing scream.

Reno's body whipped from one side to the other, his upper limbs favoring those of a rag doll. He saw nothing. His pulse raced and he could taste the bile in the back of his throat. He knew something wasn't right. How could Zuri vanish so fast?

The device clicked, then robotic voices reported: "CS4 responding. Auditorium. No visual, CS2 responding. 700 block of Roosevelt Rd. No visual, CS5 responding. 400 block of Halsted. No visual, CS1 responding. Entrance ramp southbound Dan Ryan Expressway. Roosevelt Rd. Visual, I repeat visual, black Suburban with tint, license plate YPP638. CS1, CS3, and CS6 in pursuit."

Reno catapulted as he turned to dash back to the car, but Bryson was already in place with the engine roaring. He hopped in and Bryson took off.

"I heard them," Bryson said, burning rubber as he turned the corner.

"No wonder the ceremony flowed without incident." Reno huffed, securing his seatbelt. "They must've been waiting outside the entire time."

"True, but where? No one was sitting out front but me, thanks to the parking pass Daron received from the City Clerk's office 'cause that's a tow zone," Bryson remarked, flying down the southbound ramp at Roosevelt Rd. "We'll get to her. That Suburban is no match an Adali."

The third click in Reno's ear seven minutes later had been anticipated. Report: "CS1 update. Suburban exited the Dan Ryan Expressway at Thirty-fifth Street. CS1, CS3 and CS6 have vehicle surrounded in Guaranteed Rate parking lot."

That lot belonged to the Chicago White Sox baseball team on the south side.

"Yes," Reno shouted, gripping the handle above the door for stability.

Within three minutes, the Adali was soaring off the ramp and making a hard-right into the Guaranteed Rate parking lot. Reno climbed out of the car and approached with caution. The security detail that apprehended the Suburban had their guns drawn.

"Watch yourself," one of the men cautioned, with a sharp-shooter aimed at the front passenger's window. "He may be armed."

Reno acknowledged the warning with a nod. "No one needs to get hurt," he said in a raised voice. "All I want is Zuri. I need to make sure she's okay."

After several minutes, the back window lowered to the halfway mark. Reno still couldn't see inside because the elevation of the oversized SUV.

"Mariano," Zuri called out. "Open my door. It won't unlock from the inside."

He glanced toward the security detail and they gave him a nonverbal okay as they moved in closer.

A fourth click in the device caused Reno to stumble.

"Report: CS2 update. CS2, CS4, and CS5, exiting the ramp at Thirty-fifth Street."

Before the robotic transcription could finish relaying the message, three vehicles entered the parking lot and filled in the empty spaces forming a circle around the Suburban. The men darted out of their cars with guns drawn.

Reno swallowed hard; one wrong move and he might end up on the ten o'clock news as another victim of gun violence. He'd be alright with that as long as Zuri was safe.

Creeping at a steady pace to the rear door, he pulled the handle.

Zuri sat razor straight with a knife pointed through the opening between the headrest and the seat in front of her, the tip puncturing the back of the driver's neck and a small caliber gun, aimed at the ear of the man in the front passenger's seat.

Reno was familiar with the kitchen knife, he had the battle scar to prove it, but where did the gun come from? She didn't walk out of the house with one. His eyes traveled down to the gold clutch laying open, faced down on the floor at her feet. *Or did she?*

Mascara discolored Zuri's cheeks and her lipstick looked as if a toddler had painted the entire bottom-half of her face. Her gown was ripped, and her hair tussled, proof that she'd been in a scuffle.

"Did they hurt you?" Reno asked, balancing a hand underneath Zuri's arm closest to him, the one balancing the knife.

"I would never hurt my daughter," spoke the husky voice belonging to Godfrey from the front passenger's seat, resting his hands on the dashboard. "Zuri—— you have to know that."

"No, Baba. You just want me to be your cash cow," she spat, twisting the knife in a slow circle. "I am not marrying him."

Reno's eyes darted to the jagged line of red fluid, trickling down Djimon's neck.

"I love you, Zuri," Djimon professed with a shaky voice. "I just want you to have a better life."

"Djimon. You do not even know me. Not the way a man should know a woman he is supposed to marry. I know you are only doing what you were bred to do, and that is fine, but you cannot do it with me."

Reno grabbed Zuri's forearm and drew her hand toward him. "Let it go, Zuri. You're safe. All of these men out there are here to help me protect you."

The hand pointing the pistol at her father shook. "I am never going back to Tanzania. You fooled me once, but it will not happen again."

"What do you propose we do?" Godfrey asked. "You're slated to marry Djimon. It's no longer up to me. If you don't come back. The Aku family will come after you for humiliating them and kill you."

"No, they will come after *you*, Baba," Zuri shot back. "*You* took their money and did not make good on your promise to deliver me. But guess what, I am not a possession. I am a human being who did not give consent. This was not an arranged marriage, it was a *forced* marriage, which is illegal," she said through clenched teeth, eyes glassy with unshed tears. "I am well over twenty-one, you cannot make me do anything."

Godfrey turned, facing Zuri. The barrel of the gun pointing at his left eyeball. "You don't have the right to say no."

"What did you say to me?" her voice hitched with every word spoken.

"Zuri. No," Reno said, after observing her index finger twitch over the trigger. He turned her face toward him. "Give me the gun. I can't help you if you shoot him in cold blood, at least, not with half a dozen witnesses present."

The device clicked: "Reno. Is everything alright. Does the assailant have a weapon? If I don't get a response in two minutes, we're moving in."

Reno glanced through the back, front, and rearview windows, all the assault rifles were still aimed at them.

"So, here's what's going to happen," Reno said to Godfrey looking him square in the eyes. "Zuri's going to get out of this SUV and you're going to let her without causing a scene. I'm sure the cavalry would love to pump you full of hot ones."

"You lied to me," Godfrey growled. "What kind of man are you?"

"The kind that will protect his woman at all cost."

Djimon flinched and so did Godfrey.

Reno realized the slip of the tongue, but there was no taking anything back. Maybe if Godfrey thought they were a couple, he might back down. Somehow Reno doubted that would happen.

"You need to be on the first thing smoking back to Tanzania," Reno said, guiding Zuri out of the backseat, removing the gun from her hand with caution, and sliding it inside the front waistband of his pants.

"My love, you have one of two choices," Godfrey countered. "You can leave with me now or I will have you deported."

"Djimon. This is the kind of man you have aligned yourself with.

Wake-up, brother." Zuri glared at her father. "So much for never hurting me. Goodbye, Godfrey."

Zuri swiped a tear from the corner of her eye, then walked away.

Godfrey appeared broken, but Reno wouldn't believe that façade for one second.

"Next time, the authorities will be involved. They don't take too kindly to foreigners throwing their weight around on American soil," Reno scowled, retrieving Zuri's phone and empty purse from the floor. "So, make sure *this* is the last time."

Reno closed the door, then gave the all clear to the security team while jogging to catch up with Zuri. She had almost made it to Bryson's car when he called out, "Hey, are you alright?"

She wrapped her arms around his neck and whispered in his ear, "Not really, but I will be."

Zuri's heart was thumping so hard that he felt it hammering against his chest. He held onto her and for the first time, Reno didn't care if it was inappropriate. He just wanted to be there for her.

From the corner of his eye, Reno peeped the three security cars that had the front of the SUV blocked in, back away. The Suburban sped off, leaving a heap of gray exhaust in its wake.

"You know this is not over," Zuri said, resting her head on Reno's shoulder.

"We'll see what happens," Reno replied, thinking about the ultimatum he had given Godfrey. "Just know that you won't have to face him alone, if he comes back."

"Thanks." She smiled through the tears, ending their embrace.

Bryson held the rear door open and Zuri slid into the backseat and Reno followed.

"Where did the gun come from?"

"My duffel bag," she replied. "Mama Winnie sewed it into the seam with a special formulated material drug smugglers use that would go undetected by airport security systems or any metal demodulator. I never thought I would have to use it against——"

"It's alright," he soothed, wrapping his fingers around her hand.

"Where to, Mr. DeLuca?" Bryson asked, starting the engine.

"Your place," Zuri blurted out, squeezing Reno's arm. "I do not want to stay alone."

"Okay," he said without hesitation. "But I have some business to take care of first, so we'll go to the condo so you can freshen up, then I'll take you to my parent's house until I get done."

CHAPTER 20

"Sorry, it took longer than expected," Reno said, sitting in the chair across from Kaleb on the outside patio of The Burger Joint. "I took Zuri to my parent's home. Papà turned up his nose when we walked in, but I ignored him. He may not like Zuri being there, but he would never do anything to jeopardize her safety. Besides, Mamma assured me she'd be fine. Sofia didn't have any patients, so they were going to have a girl's day—— indoors, of course, and celebrate her graduation."

"Ms. Emma has always been cool like that," Kaleb remarked, biting into one of the infamous cheeseburgers. "She made me feel like one of the family every time I was at your house. I don't know what your Dad's problem is with Black people."

"It's not that," Reno countered as the waitress brought him a menu and a glass of water.

"Let me know when you're ready to order," she said before moving to the next table.

"Papà has a problem with me dating Black women, although I've never dated a Black woman." Reno shrugged at the irony. "He always assumed me and Ebony were in a relationship since we were so close. He didn't understand that male and females could be platonic friends. The real problem is, Papà has that old antiquated way of thinking. He doesn't want our *gene pool* to mix, he wants to keep the Italian bloodline *pure*," Reno dismissed with the wave of a hand. "Hell, Papà's so worried about me that he doesn't even realize that Sofia's a lesbian and Vicente's been dating a Jamaican woman for the last two years."

"Wow. He's gonna shit hella bricks when he finds out."

"Without a doubt he will. Anyway, back to Zuri," Reno said, scanning the lunch menu. "It's a temporary fix. She wanted to stay at my place, but I'm not comfortable leaving her alone. Not after what I witnessed today. Although, she had things under control."

"Self-preservation will make a person do things they never thought they were capable of. Ask me how I know? Which brings me to why I asked you here," Kaleb said, sipping a fountain drink from a Styrofoam cup with a lid. "I found out who's behind the Sovereign Kings setting up shop in Chatham. His name is Frank Maddox and he frequents that place every Friday at noon," he said, pointing to Soul Nia Café across the street.

"That name doesn't sound familiar."

"I bet his face does," Kaleb countered, taking the last bite of his cheeseburger before scrolling through his phone and shoving it in Reno's face.

"I can't place him," he commented, taking the phone out of Kaleb's hand, pinching and spreading the screen with his fingers to enlarge the image. "Should I know this man?"

"Not officially, but yes. He's The Castle board member who Vikkas confronted the day of the tour."

After a slight pause, Reno's mouth fell open. "That's right. He questioned why we were in the conference room," he recalled, stealing a french-fry from Kaleb's basket. "But what does this Frank Maddox guy have to do with the gangs at the transitional apartments?"

Kaleb parted his lips to respond just as four waitresses marched by clapping and singing the happy birthday song to the table right next to them. They placed an ice cream dessert with a single candle on the table in front of an adolescent girl with a bright peach ribbon in her hair.

Once the song was over, everyone, including Reno and Kaleb clapped as the girl blew out the candle.

Kaleb smiled, then stood and moved his seat next to Reno. Leaning forward, he explained, "Frank Maddox is behind the sex trafficking of foreign girls. He's also the new leader of the Sovereign Kings."

"What?" Reno closed his eyes and shook his head. "Come again?"

"You heard me right the first time," Kaleb countered. "You know how the mafia has a connect that everyone's heard of, got mad respect for, but nobody's ever seen. *That's* Frank Maddox. How a white man is over a notorious street gang is beyond my understanding."

Reno fell back in the plastic patio chair so hard that the front legs lifted off the ground, it's a wonder he didn't flip over backward.

"I don't know why he has soldiers in the Chatham area. They typically respect each other's territory, unless they're trying to take it over, then they'll have a blood-bath."

"But why there?" Reno questioned, pointing an index finger into the table. "Chatham's corrupted with gang and drugs and the hardworking citizens are held hostage, but there's no activity where the transitional apartments are—— *none*. It doesn't make sense."

"That's what we need to figure out," Kaleb said, taking the last bite of his cheeseburger.

"Do you think he's trying to lure the women so he could traffic them?" Reno asked, lowering his voice. "Most of the clients in the apartments are foreigners. I have a Russian woman here. Do you think he's after her?"

"I don't know what his motives are. What I do know, is that he'll be at Soul Nia Café tomorrow around this time."

The waitress graced the table. "Sir, what can I get for you today?"

"Nothing, thank you," Reno responded with a courteous smile.

"How about you, sir?" she asked, giving Kaleb a winning smile. "Did you leave room for dessert?"

"I'm good. Thank you," Kaleb replied, handing her the empty basket. "Could you bring the check, please."

She dug into her green waist apron pocket, produced the bill, laying it face down on the table. "You can take care of that whenever you're ready."

"Thank you." Reno scooped up the tab and pulled a fifty-dollar bill from his wallet.

"Whatcha doing, man?" Kaleb inquired, reaching for the check.

"I got it," Reno said, handing the waitress the bill. "Keep the change."

"Thank you so very much, sir."

She finished gathering the empty glass and used napkins, then disappeared behind a swinging wooden door.

"Thanks for copping lunch," Kaleb said, shifting in the seat. "You're feeling generous today."

"You earned your keep," Reno teased, laughing out loud. "But on a serious note, thank you. I knew it was a big ask, more so now that I know the history behind you leaving Chicago and your severed affiliation with the Sovereign Kings. You risked a lot for me—— for Zuri. The least I can do is pay for your lunch."

"I'll always have your back," Kaleb said, giving Reno a fist bump.

"Speaking of watching my back. It's time that I paid Frank Maddox a visit."

* * *

Kaleb slid into the basket-weave cushioned chair at a corner table of Soul Nia Café outdoor patio, where he could see everyone who entered or exited, even though his seating position was camouflaged by the patrons dining at the table in front of him.

There was no way possible that Kaleb would allow Reno to meet with Frank Maddox alone, no matter how much Reno insisted he could handle him on his own. He knew the type. Men like Frank always rode around with a crew to handle the dirty work. And with his new position as the leader of the Sovereign Kings and the unlimited resources of The Castle, Kaleb would bet his last breath that Frank was packing heat.

The tantalizing aroma of warm frosting and caramelized brown sugar swirled in the air, tickling Kaleb's taste buds for something sweet.

"Excuse me," Kaleb said, flagging down the waitress. "Could you bring me a cinnamon roll with icing and a caramel iced coffee, please."

"Sure thing," she replied, jotting down the order. "Coming right up."

At least, this way, if Frank caught a glimpse of Kaleb, he wouldn't look so out of place amongst the patrons enjoying afternoon desserts.

The waitress came back with his order. Kaleb whirled a straw in the tannish-colored liquid, stirring the contents before taking a sip. The divine sugary scent of Kaleb's pastry and drink were overtaken by the stench of cigar smoke. Kaleb frowned.

Frank's here.

The large man whose muscles looked as if they would burst out of the powder blue shirt sleeves at any moment, leaned against the red brick under the *smoking prohibited* sign, puffing a Black & Mild. Women and small children were present in the family friendly establishment, but it was apparent that Frank didn't care.

Kaleb was just about to text Reno when he swept in, bypassing him. Reno's six-foot frame was clad in an expensive suit, Wall Street front-cover fresh, as always. He pushed the desserts to the side, shifting his body to the perfect angle to zoom in, and record their exchange with his phone.

The disrespect had already begun as Reno stood with his hand extended and Frank looked at him as if Reno was gum stuck to the bottom of his Wingtip Stacy Adams shoe.

This meeting is going nowhere fast.

Reno's lips moved, but Kaleb couldn't hear or make-out what he had said, but whatever words spilled out of his mouth must had pissed him off. Anger flashed across Frank's face as he stood to his full height, taking a final pull from the cigar, then flicking it across the pavement like a savage.

"Do you know who you're fucking with?" Frank growled, his right hand disappearing behind his back.

Mother's clutched their children at the loud outburst. Some covered the kid's ears, while others rushed to the exit. It was then, that Kaleb caught a glimpse of the gun tucked in Frank's waistband. Either Reno didn't know, or he had one hell of a poker face. Reno hadn't flinched. In fact, he stood even taller, closing the distance between him and Frank.

Kaleb scanned the area for Frank's flunkies as he moved a few tables forward just in case he needed to get the jump on him. It was never a good idea to provoke the enemy and Reno's lack of fear was doing just that, a sign of disrespect to a man in Frank's position.

"Excuse me, sir," the waitress said loud enough to get Reno and Frank's attention as she approached Kaleb's table with a tall man wearing a white polo and a manager's name badge. "You forgot to pay your bill?"

Damn. My presence has been exposed.

Reno and Kaleb exchanged a glance while Frank glowered at the both of them.

Kaleb peeled off a twenty-dollar bill and handed it to the waitress. "My apologies," he said, never breaking eye contact with Reno.

"Thank you," she replied gliding past, but the manager stayed behind. He moved toward Reno and Frank. "I need the two of you to leave. Now."

Flipping over a chair, Frank's brows knitted. "Watch yourself, DeLuca," he warned, pointing his index finger at Reno, then tilting his head, closing one eye, and bending his thumb as if shooting Reno between the eyes. "No one threatens my family and lives to see another day."

Kaleb hopped to his feet, then maneuvered between the chairs and tables, nearly knocking the manager down.

Frank stalked off before Kaleb had a chance to pummel him. Two other men sitting among the remaining patrons followed behind Frank to an awaiting SUV with black tinted windows. Frank scowled at them right before he stepped into the vehicle and peeled away from the curb as though fleeing the scene of a bank robbery.

"What just happened?" Kaleb asked, shifting his weight on both feet.

"I put Frank on notice," Reno said, running a hand through his dark-spiked hair.

Kaleb looped his fingers in the belt loops of the khaki linen pants he wore, eyeing Reno. He said a mouthful without saying much of anything at all. "What exactly does that mean?"

The manager steadied on his feet, clearing his throat.

"My bad, Parker," Kaleb said, reading the name on the manager's badge. "Are you okay?"

"I'm fine," he shot back, smoothing the uniform shirt. "But, I need you all to leave as well."

"Can we have a minute?" Kaleb asked, turning the chair upright and sliding it under the table. "I promise there won't be any more disturbances."

"You have our word," Reno added as they waited for Parker's response.

Parker stood in silence for a moment, staring at them, then he glanced around the entire patio area. A few patrons remained, giving them, their undivided attention while others carried on as if nothing had just taken place.

"Another outburst and I'm calling the police," Parker warned before walking away.

"Thank you," Kaleb called out as he and Reno claimed the seats at the nearest table. Giving Reno a thorough onceover, Kaleb asked, "What did Frank mean when he said you threatened his family?"

"I didn't," Reno said, waving him off. "I want to know what are you doing here? I saw you sitting in the cut."

"Why do you think?" Kaleb smirked, leaning back in the chair and crossing one leg over the other. "There's no way I was going to let you meet with that man alone. I've seen too much in these streets. Frank isn't your average businessman. I knew you would need backup," Kaleb explained, folding his arms across his chest. "Stop deflecting and answer my question."

"You sound like Khalil." Reno chuckled. "Straight to the point."

"No chaser," Kaleb completed his sentence.

Leaning forward and placing elbows on the table, Reno stated, "Frank said he knew who I was, then told me to tell my parents and siblings he said hello. He called them by their full names."

Kaleb's relaxed demeanor changed to stiffness as he dropped his leg and pulled the seat closer. He interlocked his fingers atop of the table.

"My parent's names are common knowledge, but when Frank rattled off Sofia and Vicente's names, I'd be lying if I said that didn't surprise me more than a little bit. But Frank wasn't the only one who had done his homework."

Kaleb tilted his head.

"I told that asshole to send my best regards to his wife, Tina and daughter, Ava."

"Checkmate." Kaleb slapped the wrought iron patio table. "That explains the hostility. Well played," he said, pointing an index finger of approval at Reno.

Reno lifted a hand and gave Kaleb a fist bump. "A man who doesn't have impulse control is dangerous."

"He's also inclined to make mistakes. Especially, if he let emotions dictate his actions. You knocked him off his square." Kaleb nodded as he spoke. "A man like Frank Maddox doesn't get to the position he's in by being distracted. We need to capitalize on this weakness."

"Definitely. Now I'm sure more than ever that I'm going to accept my appointment at The Castle," Reno said with certainty. "First, as a way to pay homage to Khalil for all that he's done for me, for us. Second, for the unlimited resources." Reno paused, rubbing his hands together.

"What's your little mastermind cooking up over there?" Kaleb asked, giving Reno the side-eye. "Does it have anything to do with Zuri?"

A smile split Reno's face. "Yes, but not the way you're thinking."

"I'm listening, lover boy," Kaleb teased.

"It's about keeping Zuri and all of the women safe, then maybe we—
—"

"I knew you were into her."

Shaking his head, Reno grinned. "I'll admit, she does it for me, but first things first. We're going to meet with the rest of our brothers and formulate a plan to exterminate the thorn threatening the women's safety amongst the roses.

"Frank Maddox?" Kaleb asked, glancing to the spot the SUV had vacated.

"Most definitely."

CHAPTER 21

Reno had spoken to the fellas and they arranged to meet at The Castle on Monday at four in the morning. Besides a few grunts and moans about the early hour, everyone agreed that was doable. The likeliness of bumping into a Castle Member at that time was next to none. Also as an extra precaution, Daron had installed motion sensors that picked up sound and movement within a hundred-yard distance outside the board room and the surrounding windows.

"I can't believe you got us up at this time," Jai grumbled, as the seven men congregated outside, waiting on Vikkas and Kaleb to open the back entrance that led to a tunnel and directly into the conference room.

"Sorry to interrupt your beauty sleep, Mr. Holistic Medicine," Reno teased, flicking Jai's hair.

They all muffled a laugh until the vibration of Reno's phone rendered them silent.

He glanced down at the text message and informed the guys, "Vikkas said step back."

The lower outer bailey opened, granting them access.

"Where's Kaleb?" Reno asked.

"Already inside," Vikkas replied, stepping aside, letting everyone enter. "Use the flashlight on your phone to see. Once I close this door, it's going to be pitch black. Be careful and stay close. This tunnel branches off to different parts of The Castle."

"I bet this is how they're doing their dirty work undetected," Dro countered. "We need to look into this."

"Absolutely," Grant agreed, turning on the flashlight, his brown eyes glowing under the light.

"I didn't notice another door in the conference room," Dwayne chimed in, rubbing his full beard.

"Because there isn't one. I discovered this passageway as a child by accident. I was left with the nanny who gave me a little too much freedom. Boredom had set in, so I climbed the bookshelf, pretending to be Cesar from Planet of the Apes."

"Really, Vikkas," Grant commented with a hint of sarcasm in his tone.

"So, anyway, I knocked all the books down because——, you know——, I was destroying the city and all. When I lost my balance, I grabbed onto the shelf and my hand hit that back panel. The entire bookcase slid over like something in a horror movie."

"Did you investigate?" Dro inquired.

"Heck no. I ran out of there so fast. I was only five or six at the time."

"I bet that was a way to sneak chicks in back in the day," Reno added, walking close behind Vikkas.

"You better know it," he concurred, causing the others to chuckle.

"Shhhhh," Vikkas said, continuing to move forward. "This is supposed to be a covert operation. It won't be if y'all keep laughing like that."

Ten minutes later, they arrived at the conference room. Vikkas angled to shine a light on the concrete wall, then pushed a red button.

A motorized hum echoed in the tunnel. Reno shielded his eyes from the light that appeared brighter for its illumination after they'd come out of the darkness. Kaleb, dressed in plaid lounge pants and a t-shirt gave everyone some dap as they filtered into the room one by one.

Settling at their designated places around a semi-circular wooden table, Reno brought everyone up to speed on The Castle member known as Frank Maddox.

"I don't know why Frank is focused on the Chatham Village Cooperative community as a place to do his dirty work. That area has been deemed a sacred ground as it's known for its magnet schools and filled with family-oriented people. There aren't any corner or liquor stores in the immediate area. No place for passersby to casually hang out——, that's why I chose that location for the transitional homes. It's in the hood, but it doesn't have a 'hood' feel and the women are safe. Frank's all the way out here in Wilmette. I know you're not supposed to shit where you eat," Reno said, splaying his hands in the air. "But why there and why now?" Reno walked around the table, staring at each of his former classmates. "This feels personal."

"What do you need us to do?" Jai asked, folding his hands atop of the table.

"Daron, I need top of the line security at the apartment complex and shelter." Reno placed his palms on the table and leaned forward. "See if you can tap into Frank's phone."

"I'll do you one better." A devilish grin crossed Daron's lips. "I'll clone that bad boy. You'll have audio recordings and the numbers of every incoming and outgoing call that's made."

"Is that even legal?" Reno asked with a slight tilt of the head. "Don't you need a warrant or something?"

"Not even a little bit," Shaz countered. He and Vikkas, the two lawyers in the room shared a glance.

"But it does flout the boundaries of ethics," Vikkas added.

"Let me worry about the particulars." Daron gave them a conspirator's wink. "Sometimes you have to do a little dirt to catch the wicked."

"What you need from me, Reno? You know I live for this kind of action," Dro asked, perching at the edge of his seat.

"I need you and Shaz to work together," Reno replied. "I heard that Frank had been housing women from Russia and Europe at The Castle for sex trafficking. He only cleared them out when he received wind that we were coming on the scene. We need to find these girls. I can set them up at the shelter and with your immigration expertise," Reno said, gesturing to Shaz, "You can see how to go about making these women American citizens without fear of deportation since they were brought here and held captive against their will. A lot of women, the majority in the hood and Latino areas around Chicago are coming up missing."

Reno shifted his focus to Dro. "I need you to use your Mexican connects to set up an opportunity for Frank to traffic girls from Mexico. They'll look underage but the girls must be eighteen and will work with a couple of detectives, so they'll actually be undercover cops. Make him an offer he can't refuse. And Shaz, I need you to find a way to protect these women from ICE, as well."

"Okay." Dro nodded, looking at Reno, then to Shaz.

"We got you," Shaz added, jotting down a few notes on a legal pad.

"Shaz, I also need you to do something else for me," Reno said, placing a hand on his shoulder, causing Shaz to glance up at him. "Check on Zuri Okusanya's green card status. Make sure it's still current. She has a student visa, but just graduated. I'm not sure what she needs to do next to stay in the country."

"Say no more," he replied, scribbling a few more notes. "I'm on it."

"Thanks." Reno released a sigh of relief, turning his attention to Jai. "Mr. Holistic Medicine, I need you to find a secluded area where you can have a pop-up treatment center for these women we're about to encounter. Grant, can you can help him with this?"

Grant nodded. "Sure thing."

"The women are going to need a place where they can heal and be integrated into a normal society once their immigration status goes through. That's the kind of healing that Jai provides."

"I'll start searching for properties. Maybe ones that have been foreclosed and forgotten about. Like old warehouses that won't draw any attention," Grant said, facing Jai. "You come with me. Let me know what works; how much space you need and so forth. Purchasing the land and fixing it up won't be a problem."

Jai extended a hand to Grant and gave it a hearty shake. "Let's do it."

"Great." Reno smiled, happy that his plans were coming together and that his brothers were more than willing to help. When they reunited at the hospital, he didn't believe they would come together quite the way things had worked out. "Dwayne, I'm not sure how old the women or girls are. Some may need academic enrichment. Can you put together a lesson plan? Hire tutors for specific grade levels if needed."

"Absolutely."

"Together, we're going to put a stop to Frank Maddox's reign." Reno pumped his fist in the air, scanning the faces of his former classmates. "Destroying his network —— "

Daron shot straight up from his seat and placed a finger over his mouth. His thumbs danced a fierce tangle across his phone screen. All the men looked from one to the other, then back at Daron, who stood still. A second later, he held his index finger in the air and whipped it in a fast circle.

Movement had been detected on the motion sensor Daron installed several feet outside of the conference room. Their secret meeting would have been exposed if they didn't move quickly.

Synchronized, all nine men vacated their seats and rushed to the tunnel. Once inside, Vikkas pressed a button to close the bookshelf. They turned on the phone flashlights and fled. The ten-minute trip took five.

Gathering inside the lower bailey before exiting, Reno informed his brothers, "I *will* be taking the appointed seat on The Castle Board. These things can't continue to happen. Look at how we came together and orchestrated a plan to get rid of one of The Castle's enemies in less than an hour. With us at the helm, our skill sets, plus The Castle's unlimited resources—— , we'll have this place restored to its original premise and better," Reno exclaimed, taking a deep breath and squaring his shoulders. I am, King of Chatham."

Reno turned to Daron, "I am ready for my tracking tattoo."

CHAPTER 22

Reno returned to his condo a quarter after seven and eased the door closed. It was still early, and he didn't want to wake Zuri. She insisted on sleeping on the couch, even though he offered her his bedroom. Reno wasn't going for that. So, after a lengthy debate, she said they'd alternate so no one would be uncomfortable for too long. He had to honor a woman who took his welfare into consideration. Though he did not like the arrangement one bit.

Dropping his keys in a crystal dish by the front door, Reno bypassed the lump of covers on the couch and tip-toed to the bedroom.

The aroma of Zuri's berry scented hair swirled in his room like fresh baked blueberry pie. It was potent and he loved every inhale. Reno didn't recall the scent being that powerful before he'd left. Disrobing in the darkness that the blackout drapes provided, he slid off a pair of grey sweatpants and pulled a white t-shirt over his head, tossing both on the floor. With only a pair of fitted Calvin Klein boxers on, Reno slipped under the covers.

Snuggling into his pillow, the fragrance grew stronger. Zuri had slept in the bed the previous night, but the scent didn't linger the way it did, right now. Reno flipped over to inhale the other pillow and grabbed a handful of soft hair.

Pushing himself upright and flicking on the bedside lamp, Reno took in the full view of the angel sleeping in his bed. "What." His mouth fell open, but no further sound came forth.

He gazed openly like an artist, admiring his subject. Zuri was stretched out peacefully in a golden spaghetti strap pajama top, that made her chocolate skin glow more than it already had. She took long even breaths as if she didn't have a care in the world. No wonder her scent was everywhere.

Reno's heart did a few cartwheels and summersaults. It had been a minute since he shared a bed with a woman he cared for.

"This can't happen," he whispered, cuffing the pillow in his arms, then bending to pick-up his sweatpants.

"Heyyy," a sleepy voice groaned, halting his movements. "How did it go?"

Reno slowly turned. Zuri had stretched, then propped on one elbow. The spaghetti strap had slipped off of her shoulder, exposing an ample part of her breast. "Go back to sleep. We can talk about that in the morning." He stood, sliding into his pants.

"It is morning," she countered, pulling back the covers. Zuri's long chocolate legs were on full display. "I was not expecting you back so soon. I should not have taken over your personal space like this—— it is not my night anyway."

"You don't have to get up," he insisted. "I'll sleep on the couch."

"No you will not," she said in a voice so sultry an erection almost sprang to life.

This is not a good idea.

"Come on." Zuri snatched Reno's pillow and placed it back at the head of the bed, then laid down under the covers.

Although hesitant, Reno slid in the bed, but he did not remove his pants.

"I just need a cat nap," he admitted and rolled on his side with his back to Zuri.

For a while, they both remained silent. Reno thought she was asleep. Time ticked by and his every thought was filled with her. Every inhale was that wonderful scent. Another thought was the mother whose regal bearing came to mind, and her parting words. *My daughter may come to you one day and need your help. I am trusting you to do right by my girl if she ever graces your door.* He was certain Suby Okusanya did not mean in this way. When he finally started to drift off, she rubbed his back. Her soft hands on his bare skin were magnetic.

"Are you awake?"

"Yeah," he mumbled.

"Thanks for everything. It has been a long time since someone has done anything nice for me." She paused, letting out a soft breath that swept across his back. The combination of her touch and the faint breeze on his skin was enough to send his hormones into overdrive. "This is the first time a man has ever made me a priority who did not want something in return."

Reno absorbed that statement for a moment before turning to face her.

"You're welcome. But you shouldn't have to thank any man for being a stand-up guy. That's who we're supposed to be."

"Not where I come from."

"Yeah, I know, but maybe one day things will change. You deserve to be loved and cherished for the beautiful woman—— person—— you are, and nothing more."

"You make me feel special," Zuri purred, inching closer to Reno. "And not because it is your job to protect me. I feel like you see me and truly care about me."

Her breath danced in whispers on his face. Reno was intoxicated on her pheromones.

"I see the way you look at me when I talk to you." Zuri moved even closer, her breast resting against his chest. "We have a connection. Please tell me I am not alone in this."

"You're not," he whispered, pushing Zuri's hair out of her face and caressing her baby-smooth skin. "But I can't act on my feelings. It's unethical for me to get involved with a client."

"Not if I want the same thing." She moaned and traced his lips with her tongue, then pressed her mouth against them with a slow precision that unsettled his soul.

Reno was losing this battle to stay on the right side of morality. His body betrayed the words that came out of his mouth seconds ago. His erection pulsed until it ached with a hunger and passion that had to be unleashed and fed, but only by her. Taking a deep breath, he teased her lips in a sensual kiss. Zuri worked her way out of the shirt and tossed it off to the side.

She gave a low, throaty chuckle as his tongue traveled down her long neck, then traced the smooth skin along her collarbone. He gently massaged her breasts in a circular motion, pushing them together and feasting on both nipples at once. Zuri moaned and ran her fingers through his hair, holding him in place as she glided her thigh over his erection.

Drifting down, Reno nibbled at her belly-button, removing her blue lace panties and slipping a finger inside her tight center. She was moister than the creamy filling inside a cannoli shell and he had to have a sample.

"I have a confession," Zuri said as her breath came out in gasps. "I have never been with a white man before."

"Well that makes two of us." He burst out in laughter, then lowered his nose to the neatly trimmed patch of hair right above her pearl.

Zuri ruffled his hair. "You think you are funny, huh?"

"You think I am too," he teased, inhaling her sweetness, then opening his mouth to taste her.

"This will be my first time with *any man*," she admitted.

The tip of Reno's tongue paused before making contact, taking in the meaning of her words. He removed his fingers and climbed along the side of Zuri. "First time? Are you sure you want to do this?"

She gazed into his eyes. "I have never been more sure about anything in my life than I am in this moment right now."

Reno stroked her face in admiration. "You want your first experience to be special and with someone you love."

Zuri placed a finger to his lips, cutting off any further speech. "That is why I am giving myself to you," she admitted, removing the finger and resting her hand on his chest. "You have proven that you are worthy of my love, my heart, and my body. I want to be with you in a way that I have never been with anyone else, because *I do love you.*"

Reno lifted her hand to his mouth and pressed a kiss to the back of her fingers ever so softly. "I didn't mean for it to happen. I've fallen in love with you, too. I've never felt this deeply connected to a person in such a short period of time," Reno said, swallowing the nerves of his admission as he pulled her closer. "I'm not sure where this leads, but I promise to do right by you."

"I could not ask for anything more," she replied, gazing at him, her eyes dreamy.

He cupped her face, then kissed Zuri with such tenderness. Reno's passion grew stronger with every moan, squirm she made. "I'll go slow," he promised as his tongue swirled in and out of her steamy mouth.

Without breaking the kiss, Zuri shimmied Reno's sweatpants down to his knees, leaving him in a pair of Calvin Klein boxers. He worked them the rest of the way down, gathered beneath his feet.

Reno maneuvered Zuri onto her back, then took that same journey as before down her neck, to the collarbone, visiting her breasts for a while before traveling to her navel. Zuri's back arched, causing the perfect dip as his tongue slid to her midsection. He gently inserted his fingers and played with her G-spot as he flicked her pearl with his tongue.

She tasted even sweeter than she smelled.

"Mmmmm," she moaned, damn near lifting her bottom off the mattress.

He extended an arm to her breasts and rotated a nipple with the palm of his hand, alternating with a light pinch between his fingers.

"Mariano," she whispered amidst breaths, quivering from every touch.

The more aroused she became, the more pleasure he wanted to give. His erection stiffened to the point that it was damn near painful, but he came up for air to get his hormones in check. Reno didn't want to have his own pleasure before he had a chance to feel Zuri's wrapped around him.

He leaned back into a kneeling position, lifting Zuri's legs. Reno placed one on his shoulder and sucked her toes on the other.

She whispered something in her native tongue that Reno couldn't understand as he dipped her big toe in his mouth. That was the first time he heard Zuri speak in Swahili.

Once the intensity of his arousal settled to a level where he wouldn't have a spontaneous combustion, Reno switched positions, parting Zuri's thighs, and gently sucked her pearl.

Zuri flinched so fiercely that she exploded on his mouth and chin. Reno's tongue continued to tease and taste until she climaxed, and her legs went limp.

He moved back onto his knees and smiled down at her. She was even more beautiful after reaching her pinnacle of pleasure. This was only the beginning. He had much more in store for her. "You good," he teased, gliding a finger from her thigh down to the top of her foot.

"Mmmm hmmm," she responded, pushing her once tamed hair away from her face.

Reno climbed out of bed, glancing down at a smiling Zuri. Keeping his gaze squarely on her, he slid his fingers inside the elastic band of the boxers and guided them over his erection. Her eyes grew wide. He stepped out of them as they dropped to the floor.

Reaching to grab a gold square foil package from the drawer, Reno knocked the phone to the floor causing the home screen to illuminate the darkness. Narrowing his eyes, Reno retrieved the device. He had several missed calls from Daron, Kaleb, *and* Vikkas. *What was that about?*

Reno glanced over at Zuri and sighed. As much as he wanted to stay in the moment, his intuition gnawed at him. There was no way he could put off returning the unanswered calls until later. The Kings wouldn't reach out to him repeatedly, unless it was an emergency. "My love," Reno whispered, perching alongside the bed. "Give me a minute. I need to make a call."

"Okay," she responded, rolling onto her side, gliding the tips of her fingers along Reno's thigh, causing him to flinch as tingling sensations danced beneath his skin.

What am I doing? He dialed Kaleb's number, then smiled down at Zuri. He had a beautiful woman in his bed. Nothing else should matter.

The line was answered before a full ring echoed on his end.

"Where the hell have you been?" Kaleb barked through the phone not even saying hello. "We've been trying to reach you for the last three hours."

"What's the 9-1-1?"

"Daron was able to clone Frank's phone much sooner than expected. And there's a recorded three-way conversation between Frank, Godfrey, and—— " Kaleb's voice trailed to a halt.

"And who?"

"Reno, I don't know how to tell you this—— "

"Just tell me, already," he demanded. "This ain't how we work. Maybe some of the others, but not us."

Zuri stood in front of Reno with narrowed eyes and a frown, she whispered, "What's going on?"

"That's what I would like to find out," Reno said exasperated, and loud enough for Kaleb to hear. "Just tell me, man."

"Don't do anything stupid until we learn more."

"Whatever," Reno remarked, slapping his thigh. "Who is it?"

"Promise me," Kaleb yelled, his loud voice booming through the receiver, causing Zuri to wince.

"Okay," Reno conceded, rubbing Zuri's arm in an effort to sooth her. "I promise. I'll be cool."

"It's your father."

CHAPTER 23

It's your father.

"That can't be true," Reno countered, jumping to his feet. "Papà doesn't know Frank. Hell, they wouldn't even be associated with the same kind of folks, let alone hold a conversation. And there's no way he knows Godfrey. He can be an asshole at times, but there's no way … that has to be a mistake."

Zuri flinched at the mention of her father's name, and Reno kicked himself for alarming her unnecessarily.

"I'm telling you what I heard," Kaleb reaffirmed, clearing his throat. "It's been years since I've been in your dad's presence, but Giacomo's voice, I could never forget."

Reno's brain swirled, bringing on a spell of discomfort. What could his father possibly have in common with those two men? They were everything he wasn't.

Giacomo had a bone-crushing work ethic. He sacrificed the happiness of his home life to provide for his family, sometimes being away on business for weeks at a time, securing the DeLuca's future. Frank was a ruthless businessman who degraded women. And Godfrey … that was a whole other beast.

"Zuri, I have to go." Reno tossed the phone on the bed, somehow switching the audio to speakerphone.

"Are you there? Reno—— Hey man, answer me," the voice echoed in the bedroom.

"Kaleb, is that you?" Zuri asked, picking up the phone.

"Zuri."

"Yes," she responded, grabbing Reno by the arm. "Where are you going?"

"Don't leave this apartment," he warned, searching under the covers for the sweatpants Zuri helped him out of moments ago. He tossed them over his shoulder and grabbed the boxers that laid at his feet, then slid both of them on.

"You are scaring me." She sat upright and pulled the sheet over her breast.

"I'm sorry. I didn't mean to," he said, stepping into a pair of sneakers. "I'll be back." Reno waltzed out of the bedroom, plucked his keys from the crystal dish, then dashed out of the condo, slamming the door behind him.

He jabbed the down button for the elevator several times. This was one of the few instances Reno wished he lived in a house or regular apartment building. His penthouse was on the thirtieth floor. By the time he ran down the stairs, the elevator would have been there and back.

"Screw this." Reno hit the wall, knocking a painting down. He caught the artwork before it crashed to the floor and hung it back in place, then Reno stormed toward the stairwell at the other end of the hall.

"Reno. Wait," Zuri yelled, her voice traveling down the corridor.

He turned around just in time to see her running toward him barefoot in a pair of shorts and the gold pajama top that hugged her breasts. "You forgot your phone."

Reno backpedaled and met Zuri halfway. No matter how distraught he'd become, he couldn't let his emotions affect Zuri's safety, although nothing out of the ordinary should be happening at his residence. Having his phone was imperative; there was no such thing as being too precautious.

"Here." She smacked the cellular device in his hand.

"Is Kaleb still on the line?"

"Yeah. I'm here," Kaleb announced. "Come to Daron's house. Don't make any other stops."

"Alright," Reno agreed, ending the call, but a certain disappointment filled him. He wanted to spend the entire day loving on Zuri. He searched Zuri's sad eyes. "Everything's going to be fine, my love. I'm going to get to the bottom of this."

"My father's dangerous."

Reno kissed her forehead and whispered in a tone that only surfaced when beckoned. "So. Am. I."

He waited for Zuri to go back inside. Once Reno heard the deadbolt engage, he rushed to the stairwell and pushed the door open and flew down thirty flights of stairs. Adrenaline was a powerful endorphin. He wasn't tired at all.

Speed-walking to his car in the indoor parking garage in the basement, he called Bryson.

"Hey, this is Mariano DeLuca. Are you available?"

"Um—— sure, Mr. DeLuca. When did you need me?"

"Now. My place."

"I'll have to speak with Mr. Kincaid, but it shouldn't be a problem."

"I'm on my way to Daron's house," Reno informed him as he pulled out of the garage. "I can guarantee you that he'll sign-off on it. I'll text you the address."

Daron lived in the Morgan Park neighborhood, so it only took Reno twenty minutes to arrive at his residence. The beautiful mansion sat perched at the peak of a hill with a long driveway. Taking in the immaculate landscaping, he drove the concrete path, passing through an open black fence that led to the rear of the house where he parked his vehicle. Reno couldn't see any cameras, but he was sure a state-of-the-art security-system was in place. He wouldn't have expected anything less.

Reno reached the back entryway and the door opened before he rang the bell.

"Hey, man," Daron said, stepping aside. "Come on in. Kaleb and Vikkas are in the media room.

"Nice digs," Reno commented, admiring the simple, yet modern décor of Daron's home as they walked the open-floor plan past the eat-in kitchen, formal dining room, and study. "Giving you a heads up—— I asked Bryson to go by the condo until I got back."

"I know. He called me."

"You have loyal employees. I can respect that." Reno nodded, knowing that Skyler would've done the same thing had anyone other than him asked her to do something that might not meet with his approval. "Whatever you normally pay him, I'll double it. I appreciate Bryson doing this for me on such short notice—— hell, no notice."

"And he'd be more than happy to receive it, I promise you. His daughter was just accepted into Howard University." Daron chuckled as they entered the media room with eight leather reclining chairs, a theater-sized movie screen, a bar well stocked, and an old-school red and white popcorn popper.

"You good?" Kaleb asked with a raised brow and a voice laced with concern.

"It depends on what I'm about to hear," he responded, glancing in Vikkas' direction. "What's up, Vik?"

"Anything but this," he replied, giving Reno a quick hug.

Daron pressed a button and a twenty-one-inch computer screen, keyboard, and a Polycom sound-station appeared from behind the wall.

Reno's mouth fell open. "This is some real-life Inspector Gadget type of shit."

"I know, right." Kaleb grinned, putting a hand under Reno's chin and pushing upward. "Don't worry, me and Vikkas had the same facial expressions earlier."

"You can never be too careful," Daron chimed in, sounding very matter-of-fact. "No one else has ever seen this."

"Understood," Reno responded, acknowledging the level of trust that Daron had placed in the three Kings who differed greatly by their professions.

"Once I hit this button——"

"Wait a minute," Vikkas said, pointing to the device Daron had just mentioned. "Isn't this the same Polycom sound-station that's in The Castle's conference room?"

"Yes. I'd never seen that model before, so I committed it to memory, did some research, and upgraded my system," Daron admitted. "And it's a good thing I did. The clarity on this is impeccable."

Kaleb placed a hand on Reno's shoulder. "That's why I'm certain I heard who I heard."

"Play the recording," Reno demanded, crossing his arms before shifting his weight on one foot.

Daron pressed a square play-back button, then glanced over at Reno. A low-rolling hum filtered into the room before the audio chimed in.

Is this Godfrey Okusanya?

Soon as Reno heard Giacomo's voice, the room swam out of focus and his heart sank.

Who is this? Came the gruff reply from a familiar voice.

That's not your concern. I hear you're looking for someone named, Zuri.

"Son of a bitch," Reno mumbled under his breath, having a hard time swallowing his Papà's disloyalty.

Do you know where my daughter is?

The Second Chance at Life Women's Shelter and—— "

"I've heard enough. Cut it off," Reno said, plucking the car keys from his pocket, and taking purposeful strides toward the door. "I'm out."

"There's more when Frank entered the conversation," Daron added, forcing Reno to halt his movements.

Reno gripped the edge of the bar. "If I hear anything else with my Papà betraying me, someone's gonna have to bail me out of jail."

CHAPTER 24

"Where is he? Reno belted, storming in his family's home unannounced.

Although he had a key, Reno would always give his parents the courtesy of a phone call, unless it was an emergency. That was his self-imposed rule. But this time, things were different.

"Mariano," Emma called out from the parlor as he stalked by the opened door. "Is that you?"

He didn't answer for fear that the fury boiling over would be directed at the wrong person.

"How could you?" Reno barked, pushing Giacomo's office door open with more force than needed.

The awkward silence of the darkroom wasn't the response he expected. With his internal temperature rising, Reno whipped around to leave the office and ran smack into his mother's petite frame.

"Sorry," he said, attempting to side-step her.

"Ehhh." She gestured with her arms spread out to both sides, resting hands on the door frame creating a human barrier. "What's the matter? Why are you so upset?"

"Not now. I need to find——"

"Wait. One. Damn. Minute," Emma countered, placing a firm hand on his chest.

"My apologies," Reno said, recognizing he had messed up by the menacing tone of voice and scowl on her face. Mamma did not tolerate disrespect.

"He's in a meeting with a business associate on the veranda."

"Scusami."

"Oh, no. You're not going back there until you tell me what has you in this state," she demanded, with a flourish of her hand that extended from Reno's head to his toes.

Huffing, then turning around in a full-circle, Reno blurted, "Papà told Zuri's father that she's been staying at the shelter. He put her life in danger, and he *knew* what was at stake."

Emma's hand splayed across her ample bosom. "He wouldn't—— "

"I didn't think so either until I heard it with my own ears."

Emma frowned at Reno as the corners of her mouth turned downward. She stepped to the side, giving him access to the exit.

Reno kissed her on the cheek, then rushed down the hall, past the kitchen, and through the dining room to the opened glass-paneled French doors. Cigar smoke greeted him as he stepped from the carpeted floor to the warmth of the wooden deck.

Giacomo and his guest sat at the bar-height table with a laptop and two whiskey tumblers between them, engrossed in conversation at the far end of the veranda with their backs to Reno.

"I need to talk to you. Alone," Reno commanded, approaching the table.

Giacomo glanced over his shoulder, but the other man didn't shift his focus from the computer screen.

We were just chatting about you," Giacomo said with a bewildered expression. "I want you to meet someone." He slid off the barstool and placed a hand on Reno's shoulder.

He shrugged him off.

Giacomo flinched, glaring at Reno with narrowed eyes. "Frank Maddox, this is my son, Mariano."

Reno's chest lurched forward as Frank swiveled in the seat and faced him. "Nice to meet you." He grinned, extending his hand, but Reno stood with defiance filling every corner of his mind, ignoring the gesture.

"What is he doing here?"

"Frank is going to make us lots of money," Giacomo commented, pressing a few keys on the laptop. "We're going to tear down those dilapidated buildings in Chatham along Seventy-Ninth Street and build a shopping center, creating a business district for mom-and-pop shops."

"What?"

"I'd love your input on the architectural design," Frank interjected, ignoring the tension building around him. "Giacomo's told me all about your particular skill set. We'll make great partners."

"Stop talking," Reno ordered.

"Please excuse my son," Giacomo said to Frank, quickly ushering Reno off to the side. "Why are you being so rude?"

"We'll pick this up at a later time," Frank said, tossing back the last of his drink, then cuffing the laptop under his arm.

"I'll walk you out," Reno offered, waiting for several minutes while the two men said their goodbyes. "After you."

Frank crossed the threshold into the dining room with Reno hot on his heels.

Soon as they passed the last of the opened rooms and made it further down the corridor, Reno spoke in a hushed voice, "I don't know what you're really up to, but I'm going to make it my mission to find out what it is. In the meantime, lose my dad's number and let this be the last time you set foot in my parent's home."

"You have such a lovely family," Frank said with a lopsided grin. "I'd hate for *anything* to happen to them, especially Emma. She's a foxy old dame."

Refusing to take the bait, Reno opened the front door. "You've been warned. Get out."

Reno slammed the door so hard that the glass vase sitting on the stand in the hallway rattled.

"What the hell was that?" Giacomo growled, standing off to the side.

"Oh, no. You don't get to question me. Not after what you've done," Reno spat, pointing a finger as he stormed past.

He grabbed Reno by the arm. "You've been disrespectful from the moment you opened your pie hole, and I wanna know why?"

Once again, he jerked out of his father's grasp. "Don't touch me."

"Hey. What's going on down there?" Vicente asked from the top of the stairs.

"Your Papà's a traitor and can't be trusted," Reno spat in Giacomo's face. "You told Godfrey where Zuri was after I told you he was a threat to her safety."

Giacomo flexed. "So, what if I did?"

"Amore," Emma called out from behind them. "How could you?"

"That girl brings nothing but trouble to this family."

"Regardless of what you may think." Emma wagged a finger in her husband's face. "She was in distress, and Mariano went out of his way to help her. That should've been enough for you to keep your trap shut." Emma planted her hands on her hips. "What if that were Sofia? Would you want her ratted out because someone who wasn't even involved in her situation felt she was unworthy?"

"That's different. She's White."

"Did you really just say that," Reno shrieked, pacing the floor to keep from punching his father in the mouth.

"Papà, you know Italian immigrants, such as ourselves, weren't considered White and acceptable for a long time," Vicente added, rounding the bottom of the staircase.

"I don't need a history lesson," Giacomo growled. "I said what I meant, and I meant what I said. "First, you tell me ..." Giacomo shot his eyes in Reno's direction. "That her father is forcing her to marry. Then you bring her to my home without my permission——"

"I gave the okay," Emma corrected him.

Giacomo angled to scowl at his wife, then turned his focus back on Reno. "You love this girl. I've never seen you bend over backward the way that you have for her. Not for any other client, *ever*. Next thing I know, you'll be talking about marriage and making babies."

"Are you delusional?" Reno grasped his hair and pulled. "There's nothing going on between Zuri and me."

"I know better," Giacomo countered. "Maybe not now, but there will be, and she's better off gone back to backward ass Africa."

As much as Reno wanted to have a comeback for that last statement, he couldn't. Things *had* changed between them, but that didn't excuse what his father had done.

"She'll bring nothing but bad fortune our way."

"No, Papà," Reno chimed in, poking a finger in his chest. "That's what you've done by having Frank Maddox is this house."

The front door creaked, drawing everyone's attention in that direction.

"Hey," Sofia spoke with slight hesitation. "I just saw the weirdest thing; my patient's father was sitting at the bottom of the stairs, smoking a cigar."

Reno charged the front door and snatched it open. He stepped on the landing and scanned the immediate area, the heavy stench of cigar smoke lingered in the air, but no physical sighting of Frank.

"You're not a pediatrician," Reno said, shutting the door behind him.

"I know that," she countered. "What's going on here?"

"Your patient's father's name? Does his name happen to be Frank Maddox?" Reno asked, standing in front of his sister.

Squinting, as though her blue contacts didn't give her 20/20 vision, Sofia asked, "How did you know that?"

Reno turned around and glared at Giacomo. "Because he just left here. Frank has an eleven-year-old daughter, named Ava, and there's no way possible you examined his daughter."

Sofia moved forward, closing the gap between everyone. "I'm breaking doctor-patient confidentiality," Sofia said, eyeing each of her family members who were gazing at her expectantly. "What I'm about to say, stays here."

"You may want to be careful disclosing anything private in front of

Papà," Reno shot Giacomo a dirty side-eye. "He doesn't know what that word means."

Giacomo opened his mouth to respond, but Emma held up a hand, and he closed it just as fast.

"My patient is eighteen years old. She speaks very little English, but I found it odd that her *father* accompanies her to every appointment." Sofia's lips turned downward. "I've always wondered why not her mother or sister? I checked her file, and everything on paper was legit, so I had no grounds to dig deeper."

Reno mulled a few things over in his mind. "Is she Russian?"

"Now that you mentioned it, yes. Why is that important?"

The Castle meeting where Vikkas explained some of the backhanded dealings with the mafia, dirty politicians, missing girls, and women came to the forefront.

Reno's jaw clenched. "We believe that Frank Maddox is smuggling undocumented Russian and European women to the U.S. for sex trafficking."

"Noooooo." Vicente shook his head and lowered his bottom onto the stairs with a loud thud.

Emma's hand flew to her mouth.

"And this is the kind of man you're in cahoots with, Papà." Reno reprimanded. "He, who is more lily White than you, me, and all of us put together, managed to become the new leader of the Sovereign Kings gang. He's sent his foot-soldiers to sling dope in the transitional apartments. But I've solved that problem."

Sofia lowered to the long beige tufted bench along the wall in the foyer.

"I didn't know," Giacomo said, stepping toward Reno, who backed away.

"The only reason he'd reached out to you was to let *me* know that he could get to my family," Reno admitted, releasing a deep sigh. "And you let him walk right in without vetting him first. And gave him the ammunition he needed to buy up those properties through back-door channels."

Walking away before Giacomo came close enough to touch him, Reno stood next to the place Sofia was seated.

"I may need your help, sis."

"Whatever it is, you can count on me," Sofia responded, hugging him.

"How can I fix this?" Giacomo asked, his eyes pleading with everyone to understand.

"Take care of them." Reno gestured to Emma, Vicente, and Sofia. "Don't talk to Frank or Godfrey ever again if you know what's good for you and this family and stay the hell away from me."

CHAPTER 25

The two-hour drive back to the city did nothing for Reno's peace of mind. He wanted to choke Giacomo for the role he played in this mess, making things worse than they had to be. His misguided way of thinking could've cost Zuri her life. He'd never forgive him for that betrayal. At least no time soon.

Reno pulled into the garage of the condo, parked, and hopped on the elevator, taking the time to mellow his thoughts on the ride to the penthouse suite. He didn't want to bring that negative energy to Zuri; he'd already left her earlier on a sour note.

He was fiddling with the apartment keys when the elevator chimed. The steel panels separated, and Reno took a step forward. The base of his foot never touched the landing. Bryson's six-foot-seven frame darkened the opening.

"It's me," Reno announced, standing face to face with the barrel of Bryson's gun pointed between his eyes.

"Sorry, Mr. DeLuca," Bryson said, retracting the weapon. "I stay ready."

"Indeed."

"How've things been around here?" Reno asked before sticking a key in the lock.

"Quiet," he responded, returning the gun to its holster. "Besides the background noise from the television. It has been an uneventful afternoon and evening. And in my line of work, that's the best kind of day to have."

"No doubt," Reno said, extending his hand. "I appreciate your service, especially on such short notice. Your money, plus a little something extra, has already been deposited into your account."

"Thank you," Bryson replied, shaking his hand. "It's been a pleasure working for you."

"I'll take it from here."

Bryson nodded, moving toward the elevator, pressing the square-shaped down button.

Reno entered the condo. Zuri was sprawled out on the sofa, wearing an orange tank top and high-waisted African print skirt, sleeping with one of his favorite novels, *Great Expectations,* laid face down on her chest. Smiling, Reno glanced in the direction of the bookshelf to see if it was the one he owned or if she brought it with her. The empty slot confirmed it was his copy.

"Hey, sleeping beauty." Reno lifted the book and placed it on the end table, sliding a receipt from his pocket and using it as a bookmark to hold the page. "I'm back."

He didn't want to disturb her, but Reno also didn't want Zuri to wake up to the unexpected movement in the background. Last time Zuri was caught off guard, she nearly sliced his hand in half.

Squatting in front of her, Reno called out again, "Zuri." He tapped her shoulder, then gave her a slight nudge. She began to stir after a few seconds.

Yawning, extending her arms above her head, she asked, "When did you get back?"

"Just now," he answered, gazing into her beautiful russet orbs.

"Do you want to talk about it?" she asked, shifting into an upright position. "I can see the worry etched in your face."

The corners of his lip turned upward.

"Do not try to hide behind that charming smile of yours," Zuri countered, scooting over, giving Reno room to sit. "I see something is bothering you."

He parted his lips to protest but opted to claim the seat next to Zuri instead. How could he argue knowing she was right? Reno pulled her legs onto his lap, resting a hand on her knee. "I'm sorry."

"For what?" she inquired, peering through slits; her expression perplexed.

Reno dropped his head as he tried to find the words to explain what had happened. It wasn't his fault, but that didn't keep him from feeling responsible for Giacomo's betrayal.

"My father," Reno whispered, shaking his head in disbelief, then looked Zuri square in the eye. "He was the one who told Godfrey you were at the shelter. He is the reason——"

"Shhhh." Zuri placed an index finger to his lips. "None of that matters now. I am secure as long as I am with you."

Reno puckered his lips, gently kissing her finger. "That doesn't change what he did. How can I ever trust him again? He intentionally put your safety at risk."

Zuri caressed his face. Her soft hands on his skin made him feel a little better. "It seems both of our fathers are a piece of work."

"That's the understatement of the century," Reno remarked, causing them both to chuckle.

"I know he did a bad thing, but at least you have your mother to help you figure things out and get through it," she added, moving in closer. Whispers of her breath swept across his neck.

Her last comment made him think. Zuri was alone in her new life. Although Reno's father was a complete waste of space, he did have Emma, and she would do anything to protect her children, even go to war with Giacomo. Zuri's mom was snuffed out, and here she was, giving him words of encouragement.

"With everything you've been through," Reno said, twirling loose strands of her hair. "Your continuous positive spirit is amazing."

Zuri didn't utter a word. Instead, she kissed his cheek, peeling off of the couch, then reached a hand down to Reno. He glanced upward, locking a pointed gaze at Zuri, sliding a hand in hers. She guided him toward the bedroom, and he followed like an obedient child.

Going up on her tippy-toes, Zuri whispered, "I think we should finish what we started."

Pausing for a second, Reno raised her chin as he lowered his head until their eyes met. "Are you sure?"

"Yes," she replied in a sensual tone, slipping her arms around the back of his neck.

Inhaling her scent, Reno eased Zuri's skirt over her ample bottom, letting the flowing fabric fall to the floor. Then, he lifted her into his arms, firmly holding her backside as she wrapped her legs around his back. They kissed like passionate lovers who hadn't seen one another in years. Reno trailed kisses down her neck, sliding the thin tank top strap over her shoulder with his teeth. She squirmed in response.

"That tickles," she said, releasing the gripping hold of her legs and standing. Glancing up at him, Zuri rested her hand on the waistband of his pants. After a moment, she eased them *and* his boxers down to Reno's ankles, then gazed at him expectantly.

His erection throbbed under her intense stare. Working Zuri's tank top over her head, Reno lowered his lips to her firm nipples, giving them all of his attention before Zuri pulled away with a throaty moan, backing to the bed and sitting.

He smiled, reaching into the nightstand drawer for a gold square foil. Reno grabbed the ends with his fingertips to open the contraceptive, but Zuri took it from his hands before he plucked the sheath from the package. "Not yet," she purred.

"Do you want me to stop?" he asked, searching her eyes. Maybe she was having second thoughts, but her sensual tone said otherwise. "It's okay if you do."

Reno reached to guide Zuri to a standing position, but she pulled him down onto the bed and rolled him onto his back. Reno chuckled as she laid on his chest and kissed him with such a force that he almost forgot she didn't have any experience. "Turnabout is fair play." She grinned, licking his chin, and planting kisses on his Adam's apple that jumped every time she touched it. He moaned in pleasure as Zuri kneaded his nipples and massaged his testicles at the same time.

This has to be what heaven feels like.

She gave him the ultimate hand job, and when she wrapped her soft lips around his shaft, he convulsed as hard as she had, and then some, growling in ecstasy.

"You left me earlier in a state of bliss that I did not know how to handle, but now we are even," Zuri teased with a satisfying smile that split her face.

Reno couldn't help but grin at her playful banter. She was in full control of her sexuality, wielding a power that he wasn't sure Zuri realized she had. The seasoned partners he had in the past weren't this comfortable in their sensuality.

Zuri sat upright, grabbing the foil packet from the bed. Reno held out his hand, but she pulled away. "Let me do it," she said, carefully removing the condom from the package and placing it on the tip. He watched in pure amazement. For a novice, she mastered rolling the rubber over his shaft on the first attempt.

She glanced up at him and said, "Cucumber practice. There is an app for that." Zuri climbed on top of Reno as he roared with laughter.

"No, sweetheart," he warned, holding her in place as the head of his erection pressed against her midsection. "I'll take it from here."

Zuri would be in a world of hurt if she tried to lower onto him, not knowing what to expect. That's the last thing he wanted. Reno lifted her petite frame and laid her body down next to him. Rolling over, he plucked a bottle of flavored lubricant from the drawer and coated his shaft and Zuri's vaginal lips. Placing his body over hers, he spread her thighs open. "There's going to be a little pain. Just a little, but I promise to bring you such pleasure, you'll forget that part."

She nodded.

"If you want me to stop—— at any time—— say so. You're in control," Reno reminded her. "Just say the word."

"Okay," Zuri replied, stroking the side of his face.

Reno eased inside of her, a little bit at a time. She gasped, clutching the muscles in his upper arms with her eyes tightly shut. He held his position for a moment.

"Zuri, look at me," Reno demanded, his voice just above a whisper.

Blowing short spurts of breath between her lips, her eyes fluttered open.

"Do you want me to stop?"

She shook her head in protest. "Keep going. I am alright."

Reno smiled at the beautiful woman lying beneath him. "Eyes on me," he instructed, holding her gaze.

He eased into her a bit more, this time moving past the precious tissue that blocked full entry. They both groaned as his girth expanded, filling her insides. Zuri took in a slow intake of air, digging her nails deep into his arms, continuing to hold Reno's gaze. He didn't move an inch, giving Zuri time to adjust. The warmth of her walls snuggly enveloped him, and Reno savored every moment.

"Breathe baby," he said with a fixed look at Zuri.

As the intensity of the nails eased in his skin and Zuri's breathing steadied, Reno began a slow and deliberate stroke, paying close attention to her reactions.

Silent tears slid down the sides of Zuri's face as she moved into him, causing their movements to take on a synchronized rhythm. He cupped both sides of her face, pulling her lips to his, exploring her mouth with a passionate kiss after yet another orgasm. She wrapped her arms around his neck, and he grunted in Zuri's ear as he plunged into her deeper, releasing the climax he'd been holding back. Reno had wanted to make sure she was completely satisfied first, before letting himself go.

Reno rolled over, pulling Zuri on top of him. She rested her head in the crook of his neck, and he cradled Zuri in his arms until they both fell asleep, still connected in every way.

* * *

Three hours later, Reno was pleasantly awakened to the rhythmic motion of Zuri riding him. He stiffened with every stroke. Sliding his hands around her curvy hips, Reno made love to Zuri, filling her with as much of *him* as she could handle.

Finally, leaving the bedroom at seven in the evening, they hopped in the shower. Reno lathered his hands and washed Zuri's body, paying careful attention to those spots he'd been relishing all morning.

"This feels great," she said, angling her head backward under the streaming water, letting it flow on her hair. "Almost as good as." Zuri glanced down at his neither regions, then grinned. "Almost."

"Now, who's trying to be funny?" Reno smirked, retrieving the shampoo from the shower caddy. "Will this do?" he asked, showing Zuri the bottle. "It doesn't smell like berries, but I think you'll like the scent."

"Whatever you have will be fine," she replied, pecking his lips as the water tap-danced on her back.

Reno poured a generous amount of shampoo in his hand. Zuri closed her eyes, letting a slight moan escape every time Reno kneaded her scalp. The pleasure she felt was evident, and Reno's heart swelled. He lifted her chin, angling her head under the water, rinsing away the sudsy residue from her hair. Kissing the skin along Zuri's graceful neck, she squirmed, lifting her head upright. They gazed into each other's eyes as the flowing water cascaded on their faces.

"I've never been with a woman as amazing as you," Reno said, sliding his arms around her waist. "We've had a shared *first* experience, and I must say, I liked it very much."

"Me too."

Reno handed Zuri a gray Wing-Chun Kung Fu t-shirt, then slid on a fresh pair of boxers and a white undershirt. She slipped the cotton material over her head and let the loose-fitting garment fall. She lifted the collar to her nose and inhaled. "You smell so good."

He smiled. "Not half as good as you," Reno countered, loving the way the fabric fell right below Zuri's round backside, tempting and teasing him with a sneak peek of the part of her that he'd gotten familiar with all evening.

"Are you hungry?" Reno asked, tugging the t-shirt as they ventured into the kitchen.

"Yes," she said, opening the pantry. "I'll fix us a quick bite to eat."

"Oh, no," Reno replied, sliding up from behind, wrapping a hand around her waist, then whispering in her ear. "I'm going to cook for you for a change, so be prepared to get pampered for the rest of the evening."

Zuri twisted around in his arms and smiled.

"Turnabout is fair play, right?" he asked, kissing the tip of her nose. "Isn't that what you said earlier?"

Laughing, she replied, "You are turning my words around."

"Maybe I am," Reno shrugged, guiding Zuri out of the kitchen leading her to the sofa. He lifted the book and the remote control from the end table, placing them both in her lap. "Relax while I cook us an *Emma specialty.*"

"You know it is nine o'clock at night, right," she teased, glancing up at him. "It will be midnight before you are finished."

"I'm not new to this," he smirked, leaning back, giving Zuri a playful side-eye. "My last name is DeLuca. Cooking is only *one* of the things I do well."

CHAPTER 26

"It's been a week," Reno said, nuzzling his nose in Zuri's hair. "I have to go to the office. I don't know how much longer I can get away with operating remotely before Skyler starts asking questions." He chuckled. "I'm shocked she hasn't made an appearance over here yet."

Shifting under the covers, then turning to face Reno with an inquisitive stare, Zuri asked, "Does that mean I have to go back to my apartment?"

"Never," he said, kissing the tip of her nose. "You can stay here as long as you want."

She wrapped her arms around Reno, squeezing him like a teddy bear. "Can I go with you?"

"You'll be safer here at the condo," he replied, returning the embrace. "I can have Bryson stand guard while I'm out."

"I will be safe wherever you are," Zuri countered, pulling away and sitting upright. "I know my father is still out there, but I do not want to live as a prisoner. I need to be productive. Let me help at the shelter."

Reno gazed at Zuri for a moment, admiring the tenacity of the woman he'd fallen so hard for. He wasn't sure where their relationship was headed. What he did know was that this beautiful woman had given herself to him in the most sacred way, and he would cherish her always.

"As you wish," he said, tossing the covers back. "I'll start the shower."

* * *

An hour later, Skyler buzzed the front door, granting Reno and Zuri entry to the shelter.

"Good morning, Skyler," Reno greeted, moving toward the front desk where she was stationed with Zuri by his side. She slipped her arm in Reno's and laid her head against his arm as they moseyed forward in sync.

Skyler blinked several times, crossed her arms, then leaned back in the chair. Reno was trying to get mentally prepared. She reminded him of Emma right before the verbal arsenal was released.

"Hello, Skyler." Zuri smiled, seemingly unaware of the tension in the room.

"Good morning," she replied, a tiny voice taking her attention away from Reno and Zuri for a moment.

"Slow down, Kiley," a woman shouted, chasing after a toddler in a purple shirt, overall denim shorts, and neon pink sneakers that lit up every time her tiny foot touched the floor.

"Hey, pretty girl." Zuri slid in front of the child, cutting her off. "Where are you running to so fast?"

Kiley zig-zagged, trying to maneuver around Zuri, but she had met her match. Zuri scooped the toddler into her arms and tickled her tummy. Kiley giggled an infectious laugh that lightened the mood.

Reno and Skyler looked on with smiles plastered across their faces.

"Thank you so much," the woman panted, lowering a backpack, purse, and umbrella stroller to the floor.

"Is everything okay, Tia?" Reno asked, retrieving the items from the floor.

"Yes," she replied, sweeping box braids from her face. "I left the bus pass upstairs and was trying to go back to get it when Kiley took off."

"You have a future Olympian sprinter here," Zuri teased.

"I do." Tia grinned, tapping the tip of Kiley's nose, and the little girl squealed. "If you don't mind, can you watch her for a hot sec while I run upstairs?"

"No problem," Zuri said, carrying the toddler to the other end of the lobby where a colorful mural had been painted.

Soon as Zuri was out of earshot, Skyler asked, "What's this?" She waggled a finger back and forth from Zuri to Reno. "I see the difference in both of you."

"Skyler," he whispered, leaning over the front desk sighing, then glanced over in Zuri's direction, observing her interacting with the three-year-old.

"Before you say anything." Skyler tapped an ink pen against the marble desk, redirecting Reno's attention back to her. "I know Zuri isn't staying at the apartments, *and* she hasn't been there in days."

"It's complicated," Reno countered.

"That's what folks say when they know they've crossed the line or don't have an explanation for their actions," Skyler fired back, giving him a side-eye. "For real this time. Tell me the truth."

Reno rocked back on his heels, sliding a hand across the left side of his chest, where his heart thumped beneath. "I love her."

Skyler dropped the pen on the desk, completing a 360-degree turn in the office chair. Parting her lips, she asked, "How could you let this happen?"

"I didn't," he said, glancing over at Zuri for a second time, then back at Skyler. "It transpired on its own."

"Do you know how this is going to look to the other clients?"

"I know," Reno uttered, inhaling a deep breath and releasing it slowly from his mouth. "I tried to fight the feelings, but fate kept throwing us together. The circumstances aren't conventional, but I'm not sorry that it happened. I haven't felt anything like this— ever."

Skyler came around to the front of the desk. "You move quicker than the Bachelor. What's it been, three weeks?" she teased for a quick second.

Reno smirked at her attempt at making the moment light.

"But seriously, I've known you for a long time. I *knew* something was different, regardless of how much you protested. I'm happy for you—, the both of you, but please be careful," Skyler warned, embracing Reno and whispering in his ear. "Zuri's situation hasn't changed, and now, you'll have a target on your back as well."

"You don't have to worry about me. I can take care of myself," Reno replied, breaking the embrace, tilting his head as a smile lifted the corner of his lips. "Thanks for caring enough to look out for my best interest."

Skyler tucked a loose strand of hair behind her ear as she reclaimed the seat behind the front desk. "Always."

"By the way, Zuri wants to help at the shelter. Is there anything she can assist you with?"

Narrowing her eyes in Zuri's direction, Skyler commented, "She's a natural with Kiley. Maybe she can help in the evenings with the kids, giving the mothers a chance to unwind after they return from work or training."

"That sounds perfect," Reno replied, eyeing Zuri playing peek-a-boo with Kiley while Tia unfolded the stroller. Zuri placed Kiley in the seat and fastened her in, as her mom draped the purse and backpack straps over the handles. "Oh, yes. That's an excellent suggestion."

"Have a good day, Mr. DeLuca. Bye, Skyler," Tia said, pushing the stroller toward them, stopping at the front desk to sign herself and Kiley out for the day. Zuri stood close by. "Kiley, tell Ms. Zuri, thank you."

It was the protocol to sign yourself in and out. In the event of an emergency, Skyler would have an accurate count of who was in the building.

"Tank youuu," Kiley said with the brightest smile as she waved and swung her legs.

"You are welcome, cutie pie," Zuri replied, covering her eyes with the palm of her hands, then moving them away quickly and whispered, "Peek-a-boo."

Kiley giggled.

"Thanks again, Zuri, for your help," Tia said, checking her phone. "We have to go. The bus will be here in three minutes." She dashed toward the exit.

Reno skipped over and waited for Skyler to buzz the door. Once he heard the click indicating the door was unlocked, he pulled and held it open for them. "Be safe."

"I will."

"I'll see you this evening," Skyler shouted as Tia rushed from the building.

Tia barely cleared the exit when eight men bulldozed their way inside, almost knocking the door off its hinges, and grabbing Reno in the process.

"Get Zuri to the——"

Reno's speech was snuffed out by a gloved hand covering his mouth and nose. Immediately, he forced himself to remain calm, or else he'd pass out quickly from the lack of oxygen. A skill he'd learned from martial arts while at Macro. This is the second time in a manner of weeks that he had to fall back on his training.

He focused on Zuri, her eyes wide with terror as Skyler propelled her body in front of Zuri's as a human shield. Six men of African descent pinned Reno to the wall.

How did Reno miss this? He took in their style of dress. The men's attire was that of the hood's corner boys, low-slung jeans, white t-shirts, gawky chains, and baseball caps—— a stark contrast to the white and black classy garments that Reno had seen Godfrey and Djimon wear.

"Let him go," Zuri screamed, tears running down her face.

"This place has you confused," the familiar voice replied, removing a red cap that had been shielding the man's eyes from view. "You do not speak to me or any man in that tone."

"Djimon," Zuri whispered, inching forward, but Skyler swooped an arm around, keeping her in place.

"That is right," he scowled, removing his hand from Reno's airway as the others continued to restrain him. He approached Skyler and Zuri. "It is time for you to come home."

Reno gasped for air as he contemplated his next move.

"I do not have to do anything," Zuri spat.

"You will respect me."

A group of women entered the lobby from the residential staircase. "Oh my God," screamed a lady with short hair, pushing the other women back.

"Get over here," Djimon ordered, gesturing for his men to grab the women.

"Panic room. Now," Reno yelled, and one of the men punched him in the stomach.

The lady paused, seemingly confused about what to do.

"You heard him. Go," Skyler shrieked, backing away from the two men approaching her.

They gripped Skyler by both of her arms, but not before her fingernails raked one of them across the face, leaving red racetrack marks from his ear to his mouth.

"You bitch." He reared back to lay in a punch, but Zuri jumped forward and screamed, "I will go. Do not strike her. Please. I will come with you."

"Damn right you will," Djimon spat, grabbing Zuri by the arm with force, yanking her to his body, then licking the side of her face like a savage. "I have waited too many years to get a piece of this ass. Allah knows I paid a hefty penny for it."

Djimon gestured for his partner to lower his hand.

The man did as he was told, turning to walk away, then did an about-face and shoved Skyler so hard that she flipped over the desk.

"Skyler," Zuri and Reno called out in unison.

"That is cute," the muscular man said, snickering while applying more pressure to Reno's shoulder. The other men joined in with cruel laughter.

Zuri leaned toward the desk, and Djimon's clutch became even tighter. "I want to see if she is okay."

"Let's go," he growled, handling Zuri like a puppet. "He can look after her once we are gone," Djimon countered, glaring at Reno.

The look of fear in Zuri's eyes and the unknown state of Skyler's injuries were enough to send the already rumbling rage building within Reno, to the point of destruction. As much as it killed him to do nothing, he had to be strategic. He could easily overpower the five men holding him down, but the striking moment had to be just right for everyone's sake. Reno didn't know if they were armed.

No matter what, Reno wasn't going to allow Djimon to leave with Zuri.

"Skyler," Reno called out again. She still didn't respond. He was worried that she might have hit her head or broke her neck the way she fell over backward. "Skyler, please answer me if you can."

"Shut up," Djimon hollered, moving toward the exit.

"She may need medical attention. At least, check to make sure she's conscious," Reno pleaded, giving a slight head nod to Zuri, hoping she noticed the subtle hint.

"No," Djimon barked, stopping short of the door.

Zuri placed a hand on the one squeezing the life out of her arm, causing Djimon to flinch. "Can you do this for me, please?" she asked, batting her eyelashes. "I promise to leave with you, but I need to know that Skyler is not seriously hurt."

He hesitated for a moment.

"One of the men can hold me while you check," Zuri said, stroking his hand.

Reno smiled inwardly. Djimon was losing his resolve under Zuri's feminine aura. She laid it on him with just enough sweetness to be believable, but not too overt to cause suspicion.

"I will hold her," one of the men offered, leaving Reno's side.

"No one touches Zuri, but me," Djimon ordered, releasing his grasp and approaching the man.

Zuri darted around the desk, causing Djimon and the men closest to him to follow her. The intensity of the hold the remaining four men had on Reno lessened as they argued back and forth about what to do.

While they were distracted, Reno pressed his back firmly into the wall, using the men holding his shoulders as anchors, lifted his knees to his chest, and kangaroo kicked the two men in front of him. They flew across the room. Reflex caused the men on each side of him to release their hold.

Before they could react, Reno elbowed one man in the nose, causing an instant nosebleed. Then Reno jabbed the other man in the eyes. He stumbled backward, arms flailing trying to recover, but Reno finished him off with a round-house kick, knocking him to the floor.

"Get back," Skyler shouted, pointing that infamous Smith and Wesson at Djimon as he snatched Zuri to her feet. The men closest to her froze, and so did the others. At this point, Reno knew for certain that the men weren't armed.

Only the sound of heavy breathing floated in the air.

"You will not shoot as long as I have Zuri," Djimon countered, slowly moving toward the exit.

Skyler fired one round in the air, causing everyone but Reno to wince. Plaster fell from the ceiling like artificial snow. Then she put one in the kneecap of the man who had pushed her. He screamed and dropped to the floor.

Reno came over, removing the weapon from her hands while keeping the aim on Djimon. "You good?"

"Never better," Skyler replied, relinquishing control of the gun, but retrieving a bat from beneath the desk. "I've wanted to fire that gun for some time now, but I never had a good reason until," she smirked, glaring down at the man balled into a fetal position, holding what was left of his knee.

The door flew open. Reno pointed at the intruder who barreled in, Djimon spun around, still gripping Zuri's breast and body like a piece of property, and the men stood at attention.

"Get your hands off of my daughter," Godfrey ordered, snarling at Djimon, wearing a black suit and Kufi hat. "Once she is your wife, you may do as you wish, but now is *not* that time."

Djimon frowned, released Zuri, then glared at Reno, who gradually lowered the gun.

"And it never will be," Zuri added, running into Reno's waiting arms.

CHAPTER 27

"I am no longer pure," Zuri blurted out, resting her head against Reno's chest.

"What did you say?" Godfrey asked, moving in closer.

Reno lifted the gun, aiming the barrel at Godfrey's head.

"Put that thing down," he warned, waving him off, but Reno ignored the directive. "What do you mean *you are not pure?*" Godfrey barked, staring a hole through Zuri. "You foolish girl. Did you … give yourself to him?" he asked, gesturing at Reno.

Zuri's pulse raced, clutching fistfuls of the back of Reno's shirt to anchor herself. "Yes."

Godfrey's jaw tightened, and lips twitched. "Everyone out." His commanding tone reverberated throughout the lobby.

"I'm not going anywhere," Reno snapped, whipping Zuri behind him, then gripping the gun with both hands. "Skyler, take Zuri upstairs."

"Police. Don't move."

Ten uniformed officers rushed inside the shelter. They fanned out around the lobby.

"What is going on with this door?" Reno shouted, immediately, lifting his arms to the side, letting the gun flip downward, and swing on his index finger.

Zuri wrapped her arms around his midsection, afraid that the officers were with Godfrey and were there to deport her on his orders.

Skyler halted where she stood, and answered, "Humidity."

The men dressed as thugs held their hands in the air. Godfrey stood stoically near the front desk as if he belonged and was unfazed by it all.

Several officers rushed toward Reno. One relieved him of the gun, another guided Zuri away, while a third patted Reno down.

"What are you doing?" Detective Carter bellowed, darkening the entryway. "Release him and the young woman. He's the owner; one of the few people—— besides the women—— who belong here."

Zuri resumed her position next to Reno, taking in the disdained expression on her father's face.

Skyler inched forward, sliding a hand in Zuri's.

"Hello, Detective Carter," Reno said, placing an arm around Zuri's shoulder. "Your timing couldn't be more perfect."

"Mariano, tell me what happened here?" he asked, retrieving Reno's gun from the uniformed officer.

"I *demand* to speak with my daughter," Godfrey interrupted as if he were the one with a badge.

"You'll speak *if* and *when*, I allow you too," Detective Carter countered, moving with an aggressive stride toward Godfrey. "Or maybe I'll take you directly to lock-up. You and these men are trespassing. At least, they have enough sense to keep quiet."

Godfrey's dark brown eyes narrowed and face contorted as he pursed his lips. Zuri swallowed, taking in her father's challenging, but obedient stance. He wasn't accustomed to being on the receiving end of any directive. Godfrey was the one dishing out the orders and enforcing punishment when his instructions weren't followed to his liking.

Zuri whispered to Reno, "I will talk with him as long as you and your detective friend are close by."

"You don't have to do anything you're not comfortable with," he replied.

She glanced up at him. "I *need* to do this."

Reno kissed her forehead. "I'll be right over there," he said, pointing to the chair behind the front desk a few feet away.

Rubbing his arm, she replied, "Thank you."

Before stepping away, Reno asked the Detective, "Can you remove everyone, except Zuri's father?" He gestured in Godfrey's direction.

With a slight nod, he spoke in an authoritative tone, "You heard the man. Everybody out." He signaled for the officers to round-up the intruders.

"I'll be upstairs with the women," Skyler said to Reno.

Five of the men left the building without incident, but Djimon remained rooted where he stood.

"That means you, too," Detective Carter barked.

"She is my wife."

"No, I am not," Zuri shot back.

Detective Carter placed a hand on the handle of his service weapon. "Don't do anything stupid."

"Godfrey," Djimon called out, his wide eyes pleading.

"The only person you need to listen to is me," he said, stepping between Djimon and Godfrey. "You can leave voluntarily, or I can slap these cuffs on you and take you down to the station."

"Excuse me," Zuri said, standing amongst the three men. "He can stay."

The detective's focus pinned on her. "Are you sure?"

"Yes," she replied, glaring at Djimon. "He needs to hear what I have to say."

"Very well. I'll be right outside the door."

Detective Carter handed Reno his gun, then left the building.

Zuri gazed over at Reno, and a sense of calm gave her the courage to follow through with the conversation she needed to have with Godfrey. She maneuvered to the lounge chairs and claimed a seat. Godfrey and Djimon slowly followed.

"Baba. This will be the last time we speak in person," Zuri said, clearing her throat. "I want to free my mind of the things that have burdened me since I learned the truth."

Godfrey winced, then parked on the seat next to Zuri. Djimon stood behind him, looking more like Godfrey's security guard than a man who was trying to marry her.

"What are you speaking of?" he asked, placing a hand under his chin.

"Mama," Zuri said, fighting the overwhelming emotion that threatened to spill out of her quivering mouth and dampened eyes. "How could you take the life of a woman you vowed to love forever?"

"You know not of what you speak, Zuri," Godfrey responded; confusion crossed his face. "Suby died of natural causes."

"The kind that her body could no longer heal from after years of being abused by you," she fired back. "I know what it is like to be on the receiving end of your hand. I still have the scar as a reminder. I do not want to imagine the pain Mama endured."

"You cannot compare a spanking of a disobedient child to the inner-dealings of a husband and wife. You will not understand that until you are married, hence is why we," Godfrey said, gesturing toward Djimon. "Are here."

Gazing over at Reno, the man who showed Zuri what compassion and real love felt like, warmed her heart. He was the only man that had ever made her feel safe. Reno was everything Zuri didn't know she was missing, and he was now, everything she wanted. Deep in the soul of her heart, Zuri knew Reno was her forever love.

Then she glanced up at Djimon and shook her head. The fraction of a man that stood before her wasn't worthy of cleaning poop, let alone, her hand in marriage. Reno would have never handled Zuri the way Djimon had. Even when she cut him with the knife, he didn't lash out at her.

"What makes you think I would dedicate my life to Djimon?" Zuri asked Godfrey. "No man that thinks he can punch and grope me, is for me. He is not the marrying kind."

Zuri leaned forward in the seat. "I see what you did, Baba, trying to take the focus off of you. But I know you killed Mama for not making me come back home."

"Mama Winnie has filled your head with lies," Godfrey shouted, causing Reno to rise from his seat. "Suby was very much alive when I took her to Winnie."

Zuri raised her hand in Reno's direction to halt his movement.

"If you did not do anything wrong, it would not matter what Mama Winnie said or did not say," Zuri scooted to the edge of the seat. "Even when you are wrong, I have never known you to be a liar."

"Watch what you say, little girl," Godfrey howled, bounding to his feet, and pounded his chest. "I am your father."

Reno rounded the desk, and before Zuri could rise to a standing position, he was at her side within seconds. Djimon maneuvered around the chair and stood in front of Reno.

"None of it matters. I am not going back to Tanzania," Zuri said, glaring at Djimon. "I am not a virgin. My body is not pure. I have been with a man."

"You are only saying that to hurt me," Djimon commented, wearing an ugly scowl.

"I do not care about your feelings. I am only telling you the truth so you can move on to someone else who is *worthy* of your greatness and leave me alone."

Zuri hoped Reno didn't think the only reason she gave herself to him was to get away from Djimon and her father. She loved him.

Godfrey glared at Reno. "You have slept with the blue-eyed devil, and Allah will deal with your disobedience."

"My eyes are actually green," Reno sneered, taking Zuri's hand in his. "And I am nobody's devil."

Zuri stifled a laugh and found pleasure in Reno standing up to her father.

"I love your daughter. I know I'm not what you visualized for her, but I will treat Zuri a million times better than he ever could," Reno expressed, stepping forward, forcing Djimon to move aside. "You don't have to worry about her well-being. I am wealthy, so she will not want for anything. I'll love and respect Zuri and treat her like the queen she is, always."

Godfrey balled his hands by his side, nearly ready to implode.

"Baba, if you really love me, let me stay here. I am happy with Mariano. Please."

"You cannot replace me," Djimon chimed in, nudging Reno aside. "Zuri, you belong to me."

Reno lifted his index finger. "Let that be the last time you put your hands on me," he warned Djimon.

"Do you even *want* me now that I am not a virgin, or you just do not want another man to have me?" Zuri asked, glaring at Djimon. "You do not own me. I am not your slave or piece of property."

"I will restore whatever your family has paid for Zuri's hand in marriage, plus interest," Reno offered. "So, you can stop holding that over her head."

"I do not want your money," Djimon snarled.

"But you want a woman who clearly doesn't want you," Reno shot back. "That's control-freak behavior, and Zuri deserves better than that."

Godfrey silenced them all with the wave of the hand, then put his attention on Zuri. "You are not a citizen, so it is out of my hands. Besides, your student visa has expired."

"My immigration status is not your concern," Zuri countered.

Reno leaned over and whispered in Zuri's ear, "Shaz, is gathering information on what you need to receive a green card and become a permanent citizen. You're covered on all fronts."

Zuri's insides fluttered. Reno's thoughtfulness confirmed why Chicago was where she should be—— with him. "But if you must know, I applied for my work visa at the beginning of the final semester of school," she said, shooting a glance at her father.

"*Applied* for is not the same as *approved*," Godfrey shot back with a sinister glare. "You *are* getting on that plane."

"Why would I go back home with you?" Zuri asked Godfrey. "I would be shunned from the tribe. I would rather live here with Mariano, who loves me just the way I am, than set foot in Tanzania where I know I would be socially excluded because I am not what *tradition* says I should be."

Zuri didn't know why she was surprised that logic didn't mean anything to her father. How dare he continue to bully her? It's evident that Godfrey only cared about money and power.

"Let me reach out to President Magufuli's assistant and inform her that I am rejecting their generous job offer as an International Relations Diplomat between Tanzania and the United States because I am terrified of my father who killed my mother," Zuri said, leaning back in the chair, crossing one leg over the other. "Let's see if the government is still as eager to support you after learning your truth."

"You would not dare," Godfrey snapped, getting to his feet.

"I will if forced to." She stood, taking Godfrey head-on. "The way you are trying to *force* me to come back home and to marry *him,*" Zuri said, cutting her eyes at Djimon. "It does not feel good when someone is *forcing* you to do something against your will."

"This is ridiculous. I do not need an unchaste whore like you," Djimon barked, jumping in Zuri's face, aiming a finger at her forehead.

Godfrey gripped Djimon by the wrist, snatching him up as a farmer would a chicken by the neck. Reno jabbed him in the stomach, then in the jaw as he hunched over. Djimon groaned as Godfrey flung his hard body to the floor.

"Zuri." Godfrey cupped her face, and she flinched, then stepped backward. She shot a glimpse at Reno, who was standing over Djimon, rotating his wrist and stretching his fingers. "You will never have to deal with him again."

She searched Godfrey's eyes for a moment.

"Baba. What does that mean?" Zuri questioned, observing Djimon stagger to his feet. Reno escorted him to the exit and handed Djimon off to Detective Carter.

"Djimon has shown that he is not a good fit for you. Any man willing to disrespect you in front of me is not worthy of you. There is a way to do things," Godfrey explained, taking in a large gulp of air.

So, it is okay for him to abuse me in private, but not in public.

"Whatever you may think of me, Zuri. I do love you," Godfrey added.

In his twisted mind, she believed that to be true. Zuri reflected on Mama Winnie's explanation of why Godfrey was the way he was. He couldn't help most of his ways, being groomed since a young boy of certain traditions and rituals. One being that wives had to be subservient to their husbands. By that law, he had the right to punish Mama how he saw fit, but she would never forgive him for killing her.

But Zuri was no one's fool. She knew Godfrey's change of heart was more about him being exposed than his love for her.

"As long as you promise to keep silent about Suby, I will honor your decision to stay here in America."

Zuri smirked. "As if you had a choice."

Godfrey's face puffed, causing his eyes to flair. He was heated.

"Nothing better happen to Mama Winnie or any other women from the tribe," Zuri warned, placing hands on her hips. "If I hear otherwise, consider our deal void."

Godfrey stared at Zuri for several seconds. "You have the balls of a man. My colleagues have not spoken to me with such courage," he said with a slight upturn of his lips. "Maybe you are the future. I do not identify with the western world way of life, but you have embraced it." Godfrey paused, narrowing his gaze on Zuri. "Who am I kidding? You were born this way. No matter how hard I——." He sighed. "You are not molded for life back home."

Reno moved toward them. He wrapped an arm around Zuri's shoulder and asked, "Is everything okay?"

Godfrey shot a quick glance to Reno, then back to Zuri. "You have my word."

Zuri's insides were doing the happy dance. It was a shame that she had to stoop to his tactics, but she was thrilled, nonetheless.

Godfrey extended a hand to Reno. "Take care of my daughter. I know you are a warrior. I have witnessed first-hand your courage, enough to know that you are more than capable of protecting her."

Reno grabbed Godfrey's hand in a firm handshake. "You can count on that."

CHAPTER 28

Reno lifted Zuri in the air and spun her around.

"Did that just happen?" she asked, throwing her head back as Reno lowered her body just enough for their chests to meet before locking Zuri's lips in a passionate kiss.

"Yes, my love," he answered as their tongues danced. "You are mine. All mine. For as long as you want to be."

"That's forever," Zuri said, sliding down and burying her head in Reno's chest. "I never thought Baba would let me go—— self-preservation and greed will make you do all sorts of things."

"I'm happy about the outcome," Reno replied, stroking her hair. "It was quite different from the way they stormed in here."

Reno plucked a phone from his pocket and dialed Skyler's cell. "Hey. It's safe to come down."

"Okay, thanks," she replied before disconnecting the call.

He slid the phone in his back pocket and walked over to the door, turning the knob and checking the lock mechanism. Everything appeared to be in place.

"How are you feeling? Do you need to go to the hospital?" Reno asked as soon as Skyler's clicking heels announced her arrival.

"I'm fine," she replied, approaching him with a slight limp.

"Are you just saying that, or are you really okay?" he asked, shooting her a questioning glance. "Your body and facial expression say otherwise."

"My side hurts a little, but I'm good." Skyler rubbed her left hip and thigh. "Nothing a pain killer, and a heating pad can't fix."

"You've got forty-eight hours. If you don't feel any better, I'm taking you to the hospital myself."

"Roger that," she joked, giving him a mock salute.

Snickering at Skyler, Reno put his focus back on the door. "It's not catching."

"That's because you have to pull it closed until you hear the lock click," Skyler commented, pushing the door shut from the inside, then tugging on the handle, which had engaged. "It hasn't been automatically catching with the increased humidity the past week," she explained, opening the door, then letting it go, demonstrating the problem. "We've been pulling it closed behind us when we enter or leave, but those men didn't give Tia a chance."

"It wasn't her fault," Zuri chimed in; her soft voice was like a hummingbird's song, instantly bringing a smile to Reno's face.

"I know," he replied, gazing at Zuri for a moment. "Excuse me." He moved around the women and went to Skyler's desk, pressed the intercom button, then said, "Good morning. Can everyone please meet me in the lobby within the next five minutes. Thank you."

The disruption to the client's lives was not sitting well with Reno. He promised the women safety above all else, and the shelter had been anything but in the past several weeks.

Reno's phone rang as the women filtered into the lobby. He almost sent the call to voicemail, until his sister's picture popped up on the screen. Sofia didn't call him often, and when she did, it was never mid-morning because she had patients.

"Hey, Sofia. Is everything okay?" Reno asked, smiling and nodding at the women as they claimed seats.

"Yes. I wanted to tell you——"

"Can I call you later? This isn't a good time."

"Hold on, Mariano," Sofia shot back. "Frank Maddox just scheduled an appointment for his daughter."

"Wait a minute." Reno covered the phone, then leaned over to Skyler. "Can you get everyone situated. I have to take this."

"Sure thing," she replied.

"I'll be right back," he said, tapping Zuri's arm, then scurrying to his office.

"I'm assuming it's not the eleven-year-old, right?" Reno said, closing the door.

"No. This young lady goes by Irena Rodin, although I doubt that's a real name," Sofia added. "Her chart and ID says she's nineteen, but I have a feeling she's younger. She's Russian like his *other* daughter and speaks very little English. The last four times, I've seen her have been for urinary tract infections. I'm only breaking HIPAA because those are one of the symptoms in young girls who are being sexually abused."

"Why didn't you say anything about this before?"

"Because it's not conclusive. Many other factors could cause a UTI that have nothing to do with sexual abuse," Sofia explained. "God knows I had several as a teenager, and no one had ever touched me inappropriately."

"I didn't know that," Reno said, sinking into the office chair.

"Why would you?" she countered, sighing. "It's nothing that I would talk about with my little brother. Anyway, they are coming in tomorrow afternoon at three."

"Thanks for the heads up. I'm going to have to work fast."

"What does that mean?" Sofia asked; her voice hitched.

"I have a connect with a detective that I can trust," Reno said, whipping out his wallet and pulling Xavier Carter's business card out. "I'm enlisting his help with arresting Frank at the office and getting Irena away from him. Maybe she can tell us where he's holding the other girls hostage."

"When you asked for my help, I had no idea this is what you had in mind. I have other patients and staff here. I can't put their safety at risk."

"Sofia. Do you think I would do that?"

"Not intentionally, but things go wrong all the time," she retorted.

Reno marinated on her words for a second. Sofia was right. His life was proof of that, hence the fiasco that took place less than an hour ago.

"Some things you just can't predict, but I will do my best to assure everyone's safety."

"I'm holding you accountable," Sofia shot back.

"I know you will." He chuckled. "You always do.

Sofia couldn't help but laugh at that last remark. "Priyanka keeps nudging me to tell you hello."

"Tell my future sister-in-law; I said hey."

"From your mouth to the man above," Sofia said, her tone all of a sudden sounding sad. "What I wouldn't give to stop living in secrecy."

"Whenever you're ready, I'll be by your side."

"Mariano said hi," Sofia relayed to her girlfriend of three years, who was also her physician's assistant. "Papà makes life impossible."

"Who are you telling?" Reno shook his head. "Thank God for Mamma, who accepts us as we are. But I have to go, sis. Love you. I'll be in touch."

Reno ended the call, then made a beeline to the lobby. Immediately, he found Zuri sitting among the women, listening to Skyler speak. Reno stood next to Skyler and whispered, "Thank you. I'll take it from here."

"Ladies, thank you for your patience," Reno clasped his hands together. "I know we've had out of the ordinary activity around here the past few weeks, and I can promise you that it has come to an end. I want each of you," he said, scanning the crowd, giving every client direct eye contact. "To feel safe and protected."

"Mr. DeLuca, a lot has been going on, but I've never felt I was in harm's way," said a woman with Bantu-knots and a nosering.

"I'd have to agree with Nakida," another woman chimed in, resting hands in her lap. "You handled everything swiftly. We didn't have time to get caught up in whatever was going on."

"I disagree with that," said an older woman who had been at the shelter for almost a year due to arson in the senior building where she once lived. She was having problems with the Department of Aging finding her placement. "These old bones aren't made to be jumping up on a whim every time something goes wrong."

"My apologies, Ms. Violet," Reno walked over and knelt in front of the raven-haired woman. "I promise this will not happen again."

"You can't promise that," she warned, placing a hand on his shoulder. "You're not God. I know your intentions are good, Mr. DeLuca. Just do your best. That's all we ask."

"Yes, ma'am."

Reno rose to his feet. He was grateful that he hadn't lost the women's trust.

"Zuri, could you come to the front, please?"

He wasn't sure *how* he should introduce Zuri to the women. As his significant other? As a client? The only people he'd seen Zuri interact with were Olga, Tia, and Kiley. The other women didn't know her. Zuri rode in his car the day of the evacuation, she snuck back on an empty bus and stayed at the transitional apartments.

Zuri maneuvered through the women until she was at Reno's side. He smiled at her, then turned to Skyler, who stood in the background and waved her forward.

"This is Zuri Okusanya and ..." Reno paused, and Skyler took over.

"She will be helping at the shelter with the children in the late afternoon and early evenings. Zuri's been vetted and cleared, so get used to her friendly face. She's now part of the All-Star team."

Reno glanced at Skyler, and she winked at him. Again, she always knew what he needed.

"Hello, everyone." Zuri waved and smiled. "I look forward to getting to know all of you and your children."

The women gave Zuri a warm welcome, and from that moment, Reno knew she would be a good fit in personal life and business.

"Let's get this started, ladies." Skyler clasped her hands together in the same fashion as Reno had earlier. "If you need a statement for work or school, come see me at the front desk."

"Skyler, you rock," Reno said, patting his pants pockets for his phone and keys.

"Tell me something I don't know," she teased, moving behind the desk.

"I have to leave. Can Zuri be your copilot today?" Reno asked, observing Zuri engaged in conversation with the clients.

"Go handle your business," Skyler waved him off. "I got her."

CHAPTER 29

"Detective Carter, It's Mariano DeLuca," he said, sliding into the driver's seat of his Porsche.

"Hey, man, as much as I've seen you in the past several weeks, we should be on a first-name basis," he teased. "It's Xavier and that's from here on out."

"Gotcha."

"Did something else jump off after we left?" Xavier inquired in a concerned tone. "I'm not that far away. The squad can double back."

"Everything's good here, but I do need a huge favor. One that may change your career."

"Excuse me," he choked. "What kind of shit are you trying to drag me into, and please don't let it be something that has my wife coming for me?"

"I can't discuss it over the phone," Reno said, making a U-turn on Seventy-ninth Street, heading east to his condo on South Shore Drive. "This is FBI, CIA, classified confidential. I promise it'll be worth your time."

"I'm intrigued."

"Do you trust your partner?"

"Jason," he responded. "Yes. With my life."

"Great," Reno replied, making a left turn on Stony Island, inhaling the mixed aromas of cooked taco meat and greasy sliders and onions from the fast-food restaurants that sat on opposite corners of each other. "Bring him, too. I'll text you my address. Meet me there in an hour."

Reno ended the call, then dialed Kaleb, who answered on the second ring.

"Finally, he resurfaces," Kaleb teased, laughing hard into the receiver. "Every time I talk to you, I feel like I'm asking where've you been."

He'd have to update Kaleb on his relationship status another day.

"We got him," Reno boasted, zooming in and out of traffic like a professional race car driver.

"Who?"

"Frank Maddox."

"Hot damn," Kaleb shouted; enthusiasm dripped from his voice. "How?"

"Call the fellas, and y'all meet me at the condo in an hour."

"You're asking *me* to call everyone?" Kaleb said, sounding surprised. "This must be important."

* * *

Exactly, one hour later, Reno stared into the faces of his Macro brothers, Detectives Carter and Sharpe, all situated in spaces around his living room.

"Nice place," Jai said, touring the open floor plan. "I've never seen an apartment so roomy."

"Who needs the responsibility of a house when you have great living space and a view like this," Dwayne added, glancing out of the window at the glistening waters of Lake Michigan.

"Might have to borrow this sometime," Dro said, grinning.

"Though shalt not covet thy brother's condo," Reno said, pulling a barstool to the middle of the living room floor and taking a seat. "Hey, guys. Let's get started."

"The Bible said wife," Dro countered.

"That either." Reno chuckled, winking.

Everyone gathered around, giving Reno their undivided attention.

"Frank Maddox, The Castle Board Member and the leader of the Sovereign Kings." Reno paused, catching a shared, side-eyed glance between Detective Carter and Detective Sharpe at that last statement.

"He has been filtering drugs into the Chatham area, *and* is suspected of sex trafficking girls, has slipped up."

"How did you get this information?" Detective Carter asked, crossing his arms. His leather jacket stretched across his broad chest.

Kaleb scooted to the end of the couch, resting his elbows on his knees.

Reno would never disclose Kaleb's old affiliation with the Sovereign Kings or the fact that Daron illegally tapped Frank's phone with the detectives.

"Frank brings his *daughters*," Reno said, making air quotes. "To my sister's private practice. The young women are of Russian descent, passed off as eighteen, nineteen, and twenty-somethings. But my sister believes they are minors."

"Why would she suspect that?" Dro asked, shoving hands into his pockets.

"Because of the amount of control he has over the girls," Reno replied. "Frank never leaves them alone, even when having a vaginal exam, and he speaks for them. Granted, the girls speak little to no English, but what girl would have her father in the room while their private parts are being checked out?"

"That is over the top," Shaz shuddered, pursing his lips.

"He sounds like a person who's afraid of what the girls may say out of his presence," Grant said, raising a brow.

"Exactly," Reno agreed, lowering a foot to the floor. "Frank's bringing in a girl tomorrow for a three o'clock appointment. This would be a perfect opportunity to rescue the girl and arrest him."

"I see where you're going with this," Detective Sharpe chimed in. "But if we're going to do this right, we need to enlist the FBI's help. Their resources are limitless. Frank may already be on their radar."

"Normally, I would agree," Reno countered, getting to his feet. "But from what I understand, Frank has been doing this for years. He had to have the help of customs or some high-up government official or agency helping him get these girls into Wilmette."

"So, you think the FBI may be involved?" Daron asked, fiddling with a gadget in his hands.

"If not them, then who?" Reno shrugged. "I don't know who we can trust."

Reno zeroed in on Dro. "Where are we at with those Mexican connects I asked you about a few weeks ago?"

"On standby," Dro replied. "They're already here in Chicago, awaiting their assignment."

"Great." Reno pumped his fist. "I might give you my place for a few hours," he teased. "Restrictions apply."

"I know a few agents who could help," Detective Carter said, whipping out his phone. "These guys have assisted us in several undercover operations, and their intel had always been on point. We have two things to do in this case."

The room grew even more silent as everyone listened attentively.

"First, we need to make sure the girl is safe."

"Irena's her name," Reno added.

Detective Carter nodded. "We'll make sure Irena is safe, but from a distance. Maybe your sister can assist in that. She can let us know, or her nurse can let someone posing as a patient in the waiting area know her status," he said, looking at Reno. "Secondly, we need Frank to lead us back to the other girls. If we arrest him on sight, he may not reveal their location. We need his visit to run as smooth as usual, so he doesn't get spooked." Detective Carter sighed. "If that happens, he'll go so far underground that we'll never see him or the girls again."

"That's the last thing we want to happen," Detective Sharpe chimed in. "If Frank's running scared, the girls will be in more danger than ever. We'll be recovering bodies, instead of rescuing them."

"Understood." Reno frowned. "Now what?"

"Get in touch with your sister. See if there's a nurse or receptionist she trusts to relay information discreetly."

Priyanka.

Reno's body grew tense. He did not want to involve Sofia's girlfriend. The fewer people who knew about this situation, the better, but Reno also knew his sister. Besides family, Priyanka was the only person Sofia trusted.

"That shouldn't be a problem," Reno responded, walking behind the barstool and pressing his palms into the brown suede padding.

"Does Frank know you guys? Has he seen any of you before?"

"All of us, but especially me," Kaleb smirked, sharing a knowing glance with Reno.

The afternoon at Soul Nia Café was ever-present in Reno's mind. That was the first time Frank threatened him.

"What does that mean?" Vikkas inquired, eyeballing both of them.

"Nothing," they said at the same time.

"Well, none of you can be on the premises," Detective Carter countered, standing.

"Fellas, I'm going to need your eyes and ears open around The Castle and in the tunnels," Reno said, making eye contact with each of them. "Let me know if anything seems off tonight or tomorrow."

"I'll contact my FBI connects," Detective Carter added. "Send me the address to your sister's office. We're gonna have to bug the place."

"Sofia," Reno countered, moving toward Xavier, scrolling the contacts on his phone, then sharing the information. "Dr. Sofia DeLuca."

Detective Carter's phone chimed. "Got it. Thanks." He maneuvered through the men, walking to the door. Detective Sharpe followed. "Don't worry. We're going to catch this creep tomorrow."

"Hold on," Reno said, lifting his index finger. "That's her calling now."

The three of them returned back to the living room. Reno pulled the door up, leaving a small opening. "Hey, Sofia. We were just talking about you."

"Who's we?"

"Me and the detectives," Reno replied, taking in the defensive tone of her voice. "I gave them your phone number. They'll be in touch soon, and probably by the office to install some wiretaps."

"No one's bugging my office," Sofia shouted so loud through the receiver that Xavier and Detective Sharpe both turned their heads and arched their brows in Reno's direction.

"It's the only way to find out where——"

"Absolutely not," Sofia barked. "I have other patients before and after them. I won't invade their privacy like that. This is non-negotiable, Mariano."

Reno leaned against the wall, defeated. "I'm sorry. I didn't think about that." He lowered his eyes to the floor. "I'll find another way."

He disconnected the call, then paced the floor, mulling over a few scenarios. "Well, maybe my sister can simply text the outcome and possibly his next moves."

Dro held up a hand and said, "No can do." Then nodded to Daron who added, "Maddox has an interface blocking texts when his girls are anywhere outside of wherever he keeps them."

"So why is that an issue?" Reno asked.

"It ensures that they can't use anyone's phones to call or send for help," Daron explained. "And that means the nurses and the doctors can't use them either."

Dro continued with, "All this time, your sister has probably thought it was a temporary systems glitch."

Reno let out a long slow breath, and Daron gave his shoulder a reassuring pat.

"So, without that wire and getting that information while they're in your sister's office, we're dead," Xavier said, pacing the floor. "We might as well chuck the entire operation."

"Don't you all have any female undercovers? Ones who speak Russian who can tell us what's being said," Reno asked.

"Right now, all of them are on undercover assignments," Xavier said. "We can't just pull people off details like that. And you want someone we can trust and get them up to speed on short notice."

Reno swallowed hard. They would never have another opportunity like this. No way was he giving up, even if he had to stop Frank alone.

He stepped in Xavier's path, putting a cease to the pacing. "You'll have your wire, just not in the examination room."

Detective Sharpe hooked his thumbs through his belt. "Then where?"

"On a person in the waiting room," Reno answered. "I think I have someone who can get me to a woman who speaks Russian."

Xavier cocked his head, staring at Reno. "This better work."

"It has to," Reno said, breathing a sigh of relief.

"I hate to be the bearer of bad news but …" Shaz began and stood to face everyone. "But I don't think you all are taking in another part of the equation."

"What's that," Detective Sharpe inquired.

"You're out of your jurisdiction," he answered.

"So not only do you need the information, but whatever trail my sister can lay, it needs to be in a place where you'll are able to step in and take over," Reno replied.

Xavier rubbed a hand down his face, his frustration evident. "Do you think she will?"

"I'm not sure, but let's put everything in place and hope for the best," Reno said.

"This all hangs on a thread," Jai said. "But it's not like between all of us we can't make it work."

Once they were gone, Reno dialed the first several numbers of Olga's phone number, then paused, throwing his head back. He didn't want to involve her, but she was his best option to finding someone right away. Nodding as if giving himself the go-ahead, Reno finished punching in her number.

"Hello, Mr. DeLuca."

"Hi, Olga. I hope all is well," he said, leaning against the wall outside of his condo. "I have a huge favor to ask of you."

"Whatever you need."

Reentering the condo, Reno approached Daron, who was pouring himself a glass of Hennessey. "I need your Inspector Gadget skills tomorrow."

"How so?"

"I know what Detective Carter said, but I need you in the parking lot at Sofia's place of business. When Frank and Irena go inside, I want you to put a tracking device underneath his car."

"Consider it done."

CHAPTER 30

The following day, Reno picked up Olga and Yvengy, guilt filling his mind over the request he had made as he drove them back to his condo. He wanted everyone to be in a central location so they'd be prepared to make moves when the time came. He couldn't put her life at risk, but was well aware that the European community stayed connected. Olga knew someone who could help them with what he needed. Even though she was no longer associated with the life that she escaped from, Sarah was willing to assist them in ending the Frank Maddox nightmare once and for all.

Unfortunately, that person insisted on meeting him with Olga being present to put them at ease. That was making them a little pressed for time.

Reno smiled at Olga. "I want to thank you for helping out with this."

"I would do anything for you, Mr. DeLuca," she said, trying to keep the squirming toddler from moving about. "You have saved my life more than once." Olga stared at him eagerly. "But why this man?"

"He's a predator," he explained. "He's also the man responsible for the thugs hanging around your apartment." Reno glanced over at Olga, who was gripping the seatbelt so tight that her knuckles turned pink. "His name is Frank Maddox, and I've learned that he's a sex trafficker."

Olga's blue eyes grew several millimeters. "A special kind of scum," she scoffed in heavily accented English. "Men like him are the reason I will never go back to St. Petersburg. They make life hard for the everyday girl trying to survive. If you are poor and have no family support, they have you."

At seventeen, Olga had fallen into that trap. She answered a lipstick modeling ad that said no experience was needed. She went to an agency that looked the part. Olga had even been selected as one of the top ten models to go to the next level. Those auditions were held in Los Angeles. The agency paid for their flights, and when the girls met at the designated location to be taken to the airport, they were drugged and shipped in a freight car to New York.

"So, you did say that it was happening soon, yes?"

Reno nodded.

"Then why did you to meet with someone else," she asked. "Why not use me?"

"No," Reno said, pulling into the parking lot of his building. "I would *never* do that. The police are setting up a sting this afternoon at the doctor's office where Frank brings the girls for exams. We simply need Sarah to pose as a patient in the waiting room to wear a wire, so the physician's assistant who's working with us can relay information on the girl's condition, what Frank's wearing, and things that he said during the appointment that may help aid in his arrest, and so forth."

"No need for you to involve Sarah. I will help," Olga said, gazing into the backseat at her son sleeping in the infant carrier. "Yvengy is the only good thing that came from that horrid experience."

Reno's heart sank, absorbing the meaning of her words.

"You don't have to do this."

"No." Olga drew her focus from the baby to Reno. "I *want* to. If I can help one woman—— girl, not go through what I had to endure," she said, releasing the grip she had on the seatbelt. "I am more than willing to help. I wish someone were out there looking for me during the hardest two years of my life." She paused, shifting her eyes out of the window. "If it was not for a drunken, careless John leaving the door unlocked and a wallet with all of that money in it—— I would still be a sex slave. Maybe a dead one."

"I'm glad it didn't come to that," Reno said, turning the car off. "Know that I wouldn't put you in danger."

"I know," she countered.

Reno filtered every scenario of things that could go wrong, and couldn't see where it would where she was concerned. "Are you sure?"

"Yes. I will text Sarah and let her know she does not need to come."

Reno waited as she made contact, but also texted a photo to Olga's phone, then breathed a silent sigh of relief. Not having to wait for Sarah means they wouldn't cut it too close for time when setting things up.

When Olga was done, he angled his body toward her. "My sister, Sofia, has a private medical practice on the north side of town. Most of her patients are women," he explained. "I need you to wear a wire. The only thing you have to do is sit in the waiting room and observe your surroundings. The wire will tell us what we need to know."

"Sounds doable."

"Zuri's upstairs. I'll see if she'll keep the baby while we're gone." He smiled, stroking a finger down the chubby little guy's cheek. "Yvengy's familiar with her, so he should be comfortable in her care."

CHAPTER 31

Three hours later, Reno and Olga parked at an undisclosed location two miles away from Sofia's office. Detectives Carter and Sharpe were waiting for their arrival in a white surveillance van that had seen better days. Soon as they hopped out of Reno's car, they climbed into the cargo area.

"Detectives, this is Olga Smirnov," Reno introduced, trying to get comfortable on the tiny, padded seat cushion.

"Nice to meet you," Detective Sharpe said over his shoulder from behind the steering wheel. "But I thought there was someone else?"

"Olga's going to step in," Reno said.

"Thanks for helping us." Xavier reached past Olga and grabbed a small flat device that resembled a phone's sim card from the shelf. "Your contribution is of the utmost importance."

"I am happy to do it," she responded, scanning the different kinds of surveillance equipment. "I would be lying if I said I was not a little nervous."

"Don't be," Detective Sharpe said in a gentle tone. "We'll be listening the whole time, and if anything doesn't sound right, we'll be in there before you know it."

"Okay." A small smile crossed her face.

"An Indian woman in pink scrubs, named Priyanka, will come into the waiting area to call Dr. DeLuca's next patient, which will be *you*. This will happen while Frank is in the room with Irena, so you don't worry about your cover being blown," Detective Carter soothed, sliding the device in a small inconspicuous sleeve, then affixing it to the inside of Olga's shirt collar.

Reno watched Xavier's every move but became a little concerned, when Olga stiffened under his touch.

"Priyanka's been briefed on what we're specifically looking for. She will talk to you—to us through this little device," Detective Carter said, tapping the wire. "All you have to do is listen and make sure the wire isn't obscured by anything more than your hair."

"I can do that." Olga's trembling fingers tugged at the hem of her shirt. She glanced at Reno, and he gave her a reassuring nod.

"Let's go." Xavier tapped the back of the driver's seat, and Detective Sharpe pulled away from the curb.

"Did you study the photo of Frank that I sent to your phone?" Reno inquired.

"Yes," Olga placed a hand to her chest. "I wondered who that was, but now it makes sense."

They dropped Olga at the office an hour before the scheduled appointment just in case Frank and Irena arrived early.

Two and a half hours later, after bingeing on burgers, fries, and caffeinated drinks, and several texts from Daron to make sure he hadn't missed Frank and Irena, Reno scratched his head. "Frank's thirty minutes late. Do you think he's on to us?"

"No. These things happen," Xavier replied just as Detective Sharpe whipped his head to the left.

"There they are." He pointed to a man in dark denim jeans and a button-down shirt. The girl had on a flower print maxi dress with a lace shrug. Frank walked with his arm around Irena's waist in a way that appeared more forced than natural.

"He fits the description," Xavier whispered, taking photos with a high-end camera with a lens that extended several inches.

Detective Sharpe lifted a two-way radio from the dash and advised, "Frank and Irena are headed inside. Relax and act normal."

Reno was having second thoughts about pulling Olga into this. Concern must've been etched on his face because Xavier tapped his arm, and said, "She'll be fine. Don't worry." He handed Reno a pair of headphones.

People talking, phones ringing, and medical infomercials played in the background. The clarity was that of the wiretap that Daron had put on Frank's phone. Reno shuddered, shrugging that memory off to the far corners of his mind.

"What are you doing here?" Olga asked someone, alarming the detectives and Reno. What's the chance of her running into someone she knew at Sofia's medical practice?

"Where is Yvengy?"

"Zuri," Reno whispered, his heartbeat jumped into the back of his throat because Olga's question tipped him off.

"He is with Skyler," Zuri responded. "Isn't that your woman?" Xavier asked; his features scrunched in the middle of his face.

"Nothing is wrong. I could not let you do this alone," Zuri replied.

Xavier's eyes widened before his face darkened with anger. "She's going to blow our operation. Does Frank know what she looks like?"

"He's never seen her in person, but I'm not sure," Reno said, remembering the wiretap between Frank, Giacomo, and Godfrey. He didn't know if Godfrey had shared a picture of Zuri with them. That's a chance he wasn't willing to take.

"I'm going in," Reno said, hopping from his seat. He just missed hitting his head against the top of the van as Xavier yanked him down.

"You can't do that," Xavier warned, glaring at Reno. "Frank's already inside the building. You're gonna have to let this play out."

"He just walked in. He just walked in," Olga chanted, her voice quivering.

"Remain calm. Continue talking to your friend as if he isn't there," Detective Sharpe said through the two-way radio. "You'll be fine."

Reno drug his hands down his face. He couldn't believe Zuri had done this. She had given them a hard time about allowing her to help when they dropped off the baby. Reno gave her a hard "No."

"How's your woman under pressure?" Detective Sharpe asked over his shoulder.

Dropping his hands in his lap, Reno replied, "She'd make the hardest criminal crumble."

If Reno hadn't learned anything else about Zuri, he knew she was not to be messed with when her back was against the wall. Zuri had more strength than she gave herself credit for. Even knowing that, it still didn't keep him from worrying about her.

"Good," Xavier chimed in. "We may need her to keep Olga stable. Her voice sounds shaky."

"Ms. Rodin," a woman's voice called out.

The three men fell silent and listened intently at the new, feminine voice that transmitted through the radio.

"Right this way."

"That's Priyanka," Reno whispered as if the people in the van wouldn't already be aware.

"Good afternoon, Mr. Maddox," Priyanka said, sounding chirper like being at her job was the happiest place on earth.

For Priyanka, it may be. She was able to spend every day with the woman she loves without judgment. One day, Giacomo won't be so asinine, and all of his children could share the most important people in their lives with him, but Reno wouldn't hold his breath waiting for that day to come.

"Good day," Frank responded.

"Awesome job, Priyanka, confirming the suspect," Xavier commented. "She's a natural."

Their voices faded as the background noise of people talking, phones ringing, and infomercials came to the forefront.

"They're probably in the office now," Reno said, removing one speaker of the headphones from his ear. "Now what?"

"We wait," Xavier responded, leaning back into the seat, closing his eyes.

A text alert chimed from Daron. *All set. FYI: Kaleb, Shaz, Dro, and two sexy undercover cops dressed as working girls are here. Don't worry about us. I am the master of discretion.*

Reno chuckled. He had no doubt that Inspector Gadget knew how to be inconspicuous. He responded, *Thanks for the heads up. I'm about to lose my mind, Zuri's inside with Olga. Keep me posted.*

He closed the text message app, then called Zuri. The ringtone, My Love—— the one she has for him, echoed through the headphones.

"Not now, Reno," Zuri said into the phone.

Xavier and Detective Sharpe snickered, covering their mouths.

"You know this isn't cool, right?" he remarked, waving them off, then turning his body away from them. "I can't protect you when you disappear without me knowing."

"Mariano, I no longer need your protection, remember? I am free to move around how I please, and I wanted to help, so that is what I am doing."

Heat simmered under his cheeks. Reno loved her heart, but Zuri didn't understand the ramifications of her being there. Hell, he didn't want Olga there, either. If Frank knew who she was, their cover would be blown, and she'd be in danger.

"Ms. Smirnov."

Xavier snapped his fingers three times, getting Reno's attention.

Immediately, Reno ended the call and slid the other headphone speaker over his ear.

"Yes," Olga replied.

"Right this way."

Within seconds, the background changed from people talking to a shuffling echo in an empty space.

"Hi Olga, I'm Priyanka, Dr. DeLuca's assistant," she said, then Reno heard what he believed to be the sound of a door closing.

"Nice to meet you," Olga responded.

"Listen up. I don't have much time," Priyanka said. "I'm supposed to be calling in Irena's prescription for Frank to pick up at the MedRx on North Avenue and Wells for a specific dosage, that's only available at that store."

"That's my wife's location," Xavier whispered, covering the transmitter.

"I've already spoken to Patricia Carter. She's the head pharmacist."

Reno's head swiveled in Xavier's direction. "Do you need to call her?"

Xavier held up a hand to halt the conversation.

"Dr. DeLuca just came up with an idea that she thinks might help you all out. She's giving Irena a placebo injection of antibiotics, then she'll tell Frank that he needs to pick up the remainder by seven tonight because the pharmacist has to specially compound the medication for the strain of infection. If Irena is, indeed, a sex slave, Frank will make sure she has what she needs to keep her out there, turning his profit," Priyanka explained, sighing. "That should give y'all plenty of time to get over there and do whatever it is you need to do. The pharmacy closes at seven-thirty."

"What do you want me to do now?" Olga asked.

"Go back into the waiting room." Priyanka replied, "I have to get back in there. I've already been gone too long. Be safe."

CHAPTER 32

"We're going to have to regroup and come up with another plan," Xavier said with a shake of his head. "I'm not comfortable having this take place at my wife's job."

"Oh, but it's perfectly fine when everyone else is at risk," Reno snapped back causing Xavier to bristle. "My woman's ass and my client's ass was on the line and you didn't have any problem putting them all in the mix." Reno grabbed Xavier's arm, commanding his attention. "I'm going to need you to give more than lip service. We did our part. Now, do yours."

Detective Sharpe let out a low whistle and Xavier gave him the evil eye.

"Frank's on his way. Let's catch this bastard," Reno said to Xavier, reading a text message from Daron as they cleared MedRx of civilians, and replaced the shoppers with plain-clothes cops.

"Wait a minute," Detective Sharpe said, eyes narrowing as both he and Xavier gaped at Reno. "How would you know that?"

"I had Daron place a tracker on his car at Sofia's office," Reno admitted with a sheepish grin. "Frank dropped Irena off at a house in Skokie two hours ago, and now he's on the move."

"We know," Xavier shot back. "We also know about the two undercover female cops from Mexico that are breaching the property in

Skokie, along with the FBI, soon as Frank hits US-41 South."

"That gives us exactly thirty-six minutes before he arrives," Detective Sharpe commented, adding his two cents.

Reno's mouth fell open.

"You're not the only one who knows how to manipulate a situation," Xavier taunted. "We wouldn't be top-notch detectives if we didn't."

"Noted."

"I'm aware you don't know who you can and can't trust, but remember," Xavier said, angling a finger at Reno. "You called me."

Xavier was right. He'd already proven that he was trustworthy. If Reno could depend on him to protect his woman, then everything else was a given. He took in a large breath, thankful that Zuri didn't put up a fight when he insisted she and Olga make tracks back to the shelter. Reno couldn't afford for anything to go south. He'd lose it if anything happened to those women. Frank had to go down, but not at the expense of people he cared about.

"No more secrets," Reno agreed, giving the detectives each a fist bump.

"Now, let's get this asshole," Xavier growled.

* * *

Reno watched from behind the pharmacy counter, between the prescription bays as Frank approached the register at ten minutes to seven, with a serious chip on his shoulder. Reno's focus veered to the left at Xavier sitting in the waiting area, wearing a fedora, silk shorts, knee-length dress socks, and a pair of steppers.

Xavier really does know how to play his part.

"How may I help you?" Patricia asked, moving to the out window.

"I'm picking up for Irena Rodin," Frank replied, glancing over his shoulder.

"Ah, yes," Patricia said, smiling. "I just finished it. Let me grab it from the refrigerator."

Xavier's beautiful wife walked pass Reno, wiping the plastered smile from her face. She retrieved a white paper bag from the fridge and handed it to him. Then, Patricia opened the emergency exit door and slipped into the stockroom where she had been instructed to wait.

Reno emerged from the back and stood in front of Frank. "Are you waiting for this?" he asked, holding up Irena's prescription.

Frank's expression morphed from surprise to anger, to fear. He turned to run, bumping into Xavier, Detective Sharpe, and a slew of other undercover cops closing in on him.

"You have nothing on me," Frank uttered as Xavier yanked his arms behind his back, slapping handcuffs on his wrist.

"We'll see about that," Xavier replied, speaking over Frank's shoulder. "But a lot can happen in forty-eight hours."

"You'll never find them," he whispered.

The arrogance on Frank stank worse than cow manure.

"We already have," Xavier said, shoving him toward the FBI agents. "He's all yours."

* * *

Reno drove straight to the shelter.

"Don't be mad at me," Skyler pleaded as Reno entered the building and approached her desk. "Zuri wasn't at fault. I tried to talk her out of it, but she would've just found another way."

He glanced down at her. "I know." He chuckled, crossing his arms as she breathed a visible sigh of relief. "But I'm still baffled. How did she know my location?"

Skyler tapped the inside of her wrist. "Your tracking tattoo."

"Say no more." He shook his head. "The only time I remember this thing is there is when it's itching."

Reno forgot he'd given Skyler and Zuri the code to the King tracking tattoo Daron had branded on his inner wrist, along with the rest of the Kings. They could access his movement from any smartphone or computer through the special app that Daron and Dro perfected.

"Where are they now?" he asked, scanning the area.

"Upstairs with the rest of the women," Skyler said, coming from behind the desk. "Olga really likes it here. She told me she'd rather be here among the residents, than by herself at the apartment."

"I'm sure Yvengy's soaking up the social interaction with the other babies."

"He is," Skyler said, grinning like she'd won an all-inclusive trip to Fiji. "Olga said this is the most she's seen him smile."

Reno pulled out his phone. "Let me check with Shaz and see if he can let me know the status of Olga's paperwork. Maybe it can be expedited. In the meantime, she can stay."

"I don't understand why it's taking so long," Skyler countered, reclaiming the seat behind the front desk, then sliding her fingers across the keyboard and narrowing her eyes at the screen. "Her online status says that she is a citizen."

"You know the way the current Presidential Administration is set up," Reno remarked, smirking. "Let's not talk about that before I become angry," he said, dialing Shaz's number. "I'll be in my office."

"Hey, Shaz."

"Wow, man," he said in an undecipherable tone. "Today was nothing like I've ever experienced." He paused and the rustle of papers sounded in the background. "And I've seen a lot."

Shaz accompanied Kaleb, Daron, and Dro to the home in Skokie. He was enlisted just in case there was a problem with Homeland Security. Anything was possible with the FEDS being involved.

"I'm still here at the hospital. Thirteen girls were rescued. They were drugged, pale, and much skinnier than the average Russian woman," Shaz said, recounting the events of the sting. "Most of them are underage and afraid to speak with law enforcement, except for one girl. She said some of the Johns were cops and judges, which explains why the girls were hesitant to trust us," Shaz explained. "God bless you, Reno— these girls may have never been found without your help."

The victory was bittersweet. A sick feeling coursed throughout Reno's body. There wasn't a punishment harsh enough for Frank Maddox, and death would be too easy. He wanted him to suffer as much or more than he had made these girls suffer.

"I'm having a hard time assuring the girls that I am here to help, and not deport them," Shaz said, sounding defeated. "I'm struggling to get their family information. They don't trust anyone—— and I can't blame them."

"What if the girls were brought to the shelter?" Reno suggested. "Skyler, Zuri, and Olga could help them adjust. Speaking with other women, especially ones who've had similar experiences, might encourage them to open up and it wouldn't be so intimidating."

"I like that idea," Shaz replied. "I'll run it past the crisis counselor."

"Speaking of not trusting folks, that brings me to the reason I called," Reno said, turning on his computer and checking emails. "My client, Olga Smirnov, the one that helped us today, her immigration paperwork is in the wind. If you look up her status, she has been deemed an official US citizen. Can you find out what's holding up her documentation?"

"Sure," Shaz replied, then his voice dropped to a whisper. "I also have that information on Zuri."

Reno's fingers stopped moving across the keyboard, and he sat straight up in anticipation of the news. "Hello," Reno said, but received no response from Shaz. He was greeted with a shuffling sound as if the phone had been covered or put into a pocket.

"Sorry about that. I had to move to someplace private," Shaz explained. "I see the application for Zuri's work visa hasn't been approved yet, but she's still covered under the F1 student visa for up to sixty days after graduation."

"That's good," Reno whispered, leaning back in the chair.

"If you guys get married," Shaz said slowly. "Zuri's F1 visa is eligible for transitioning to a green card directly because *you're* a US citizen. There aren't any limits or waiting periods for spousal green cards."

Reno rocked in the chair a moment, mentally flipping through the best scenario to make that happen. "So, marrying the love of my life will solve her citizenship problem. That's what you're telling me?"

"It will solve the immediate problem, yes. The green card can then lead to citizenship, but there are other stipulations."

"Like what?" Reno inquired just as Zuri knocked on the office door, then came in, and settled onto his lap.

He held a finger to his lips. Zuri propped an elbow on Reno's shoulder and twirled her fingers in his hair.

"Nothing that should be major," Shaz replied. "First and foremost, make sure Zuri hasn't done anything that would make her inadmissible—like committing a crime or have any communicable diseases."

Reno's mental rolodex flipped to the image of Zuri slashing him with the knife, and the one she put to Djimon's neck, and the golden gun that she'd pulled on her father. Then he brushed those memories aside, glanced up at his lady and smiled. "No, none of that. What else?"

"There are several forms the both of you will need to fill out, medical exams, fees, and individual interviews to make sure the marriage is legit and not a sham."

"I love this woman," Reno confessed, resting his head on her breast. "None of that should be a problem."

"Good," Shaz commented. "Let me get back. I'll keep you posted."

Reno placed his phone face down on the desk, then wrapped his arms around Zuri's waist. "I love you."

She smiled. "I love you, too."

"Why don't we make this arrangement permanent?"

Zuri's eyes sparkled as she traced Reno's jawline with the back of her hand. "Are you asking me to marry you?"

"I want to," he said, taking her hand and bringing it to his lips. "Being your husband would give me tremendous joy. And what if I told you that your visa could be transitioned to a green card without any delay?"

"I would say sign me up," Zuri responded, searching his eyes.

"Marrying me would also make everything I just mentioned *possible*, but I don't want you to feel like that's the only reason I want to."

"Mariano, I would do it in a heartbeat." Zuri spoke the words so softly that he thought he'd melt from underneath her. "The moment I decided to be with you was the moment I *knew* you were my forever love. Regardless of how our marriage comes to pass, I desire it just the same. I want to be Mrs. Mariano DeLuca."

EPILOGUE

Reno and Zuri tied the knot at the place they vowed to live, The Castle. Though Khalil was in a wheelchair, he insisted on officiating the ceremony. Reno opted to seal the most important day of his new life at the bridge over the lake. That's a place where Khalil spoke to him about being a man and protecting the people he love, especially his woman. Reno was happy Khalil was there. He was in desperate need of that extra father figure.

He wasn't sure if Giacomo would show after the ambush that had taken place at the family home, at least, that's what he called it. Emma prepared a feast for Reno, his siblings, and their significant others. Automatically, Giacomo was on the defensive, refusing to eat with people who weren't *his kind*. The siblings tried to reason with their father, but he wouldn't listen.

Reno couldn't fathom getting married without speaking with his family first, including his racist father.

Zuri insisted that Reno try to get through to him.

* * *

"I can take whatever Giacomo dishes out," Zuri insisted. "I love Emma, Sofia, and Vicente. Maybe one day, I will love your father too, if he gives us a chance. But we will never know if you do not talk to him."

"I'll need reinforcements," Reno replied, conferencing a call with his brother and sister, telling them his plans.

"It's past time," Vicente agreed. "I'll bring Shanise home to meet everyone officially. "She has told me more than once that she's tired of being a well-kept secret. No matter how many times I've explained that wasn't the case."

"Papà is a special breed," Reno chimed in. "I know you were trying to protect her from his evilness, but unless they've experienced his judgmental ways, then they'll never understand."

"I know first-hand," Sofia added. "In high school, my friend came over to study. Mama had made us lunch. We were sitting at the kitchen table when Papà came home from work. He said she looked like a dyke and needed to leave his house. From that moment on, I knew I could never come out of the closet or tell him who I was dating. Well, Mama always knew."

"She always does," Vicente said, and they all erupted in laughter.

Once the shared moment subsided, Reno said, "Tomorrow, with our significant others." He glanced at Zuri, and she gave him an approving smile.

"Dinner's at six, Mariano," Sofia reminded him. "I'll give Mama a heads-up."

"I know what time to be there," Reno chided. "Just because I don't live there, doesn't mean I don't know what time dinner has been served every day, since before I was born," he teased.

"Mama has coveted our secrets since forever," Vincente added. "So, no throwing Mama under the bus."

"Well, that won't happen because I drive a Bentley," Sofia shot back.

"And I roll in Porsche." Reno grinned at Zuri. "No bus drivers here. And talk to your girlfriends and make sure they're not holding any bus passes. Let Mama be the one to acknowledge what she knew and when she knew it."

* * *

Reno stood in front of a white gazebo, adorned with sheer drapes, and pink and purple flowers. The calm waters of the lake hummed in the background as the ducks and swans floated on the gentle ripples. He watched in awe, as The Kings and their beautiful women, marched down the center aisle, and took their places on each side.

Time hadn't diminished Reno's relationship with his brothers. In fact, it was much stronger. After everything he'd been through, the Kings were right by his side. These extraordinary men had his back, which is why he couldn't pick just one of them to be his best man. They all were.

The picturesque view of their loved ones sitting in white chairs with matching floral décor on the end seats, all awaited the bride to make her grand entrance.

Reno shot a glance to the left side of the aisle, locking eyes with his mother and then the woman sitting next to her. He smiled and winked, and he swore they could feel the happiness in his heart by the returned smiles. The empty seat where his dad should've been tugged at his soul, but he wouldn't allow nothing and no one, to ruin this day.

Men and women alike gasped at Skyler's daughters, Tru and Sahara, when they appeared at the beginning of the aisle in white tulle flower girl dresses, with pink petals encased in the hem. They plucked matching rose petals from white satin baskets, dropping them along the runner as they moved forward.

"Could everyone please rise to receive the bride?" Khalil asked, raising his arms toward the audience.

Reno and Zuri were from different religious backgrounds, so they decided to have a nondenominational ceremony.

Zuri stood gracefully, like the goddess she was, with her arm interlocked in Vicente's. Reno inhaled so loudly that his mother turned around and asked, "Are you alright?"

All he could do was nod because Zuri's beauty had snatched his breath and was holding it hostage.

She was so beautiful in a luxurious, gold lace beaded, African mermaid wedding dress with a sheer neck and long sleeves.

Vintage. Sexy. Elegant.

Dro nodded at Reno, then stepped out of the groomsmen line, and sat at the grand piano. His fingers graced the keys, playing the chords to the classic song, You and I, by Stevie Wonder.

Watching Zuri float down the aisle on his brother's arm seemed surreal. Smiling, Reno's eyes held her gaze until the Khalil spoke, breaking the trance.

"Who gives this woman to this man to be his lawfully forever mate?"

"I do."

Zuri's head whipped to the direction of the familiar voice.

A woman in a red tribal print ruffle trim African dress, with a red satin headwrap, stood in the front row.

Zuri's hands trembled, dropping the bouquet. Skyler caught it before it hit the ground.

"Hey, it's a little early for that," Kaleb teased and Skyler gave him a major side eye.

"Mama Winnie," she said as tears trickled down her face.

"Oh chile," Mama Winnie said, taking the handkerchief clutched in her hand, and dabbed Zuri's cheek. "You did not think I would miss your wedding day?" She smiled. "Now stop that crying before you ruin your makeup."

"Yes, ma'am."

Mama Winnie took Zuri's hand, guided her back to the place by Reno's side, then put it in his hand. "He who finds a wife finds a good thing and obtains favor from the Lord. Love and respect each other always," she advised before returning to her seat.

Zuri mouthed, "Thank you."

Reno's heart swam with love. There wasn't anything he wouldn't do for her.

Khalil gave his opening remarks and addressed the couple. Reno and Zuri exchanged vows and rings. Then the Khalil said, "Will all of you witnessing these promises do everything in your power to uphold these two persons in their marriage? Will you bring out the best in them, share their happiest moments, and offer comfort and support during hardships? If so, answer, We will."

The resounding response, "We will," radiated like an alto choir singing praise.

"I now pronounce, Mariano and Zuri, husband and wife," Khalil said with such joy. "You may kiss your bride."

Reno gazed into those russet eyes that he could never tire of, pulling Zuri into a kiss that would make somebody's grandmother grab the church fan or clutch the proverbial pearls. He dipped Zuri back like a professional dancer. He couldn't get enough of her. Finally, coming up for air, Khalil introduced Mr. and Mrs. Mariano DeLuca.

After the ceremony, the bridal party gathered for pictures.

Reno was speaking to Kaleb and Skyler with his arm draped across Zuri's shoulder, when a familiar voice said, "Welcome to the family."

Reno's pulse raced. Zuri pinched his backside, which made Reno shift his focus on her. They shared a silent conversation that spoke volumes. The anxiety that had started to build decreased enough to the point that Reno didn't feel like he would cause a scene.

"Thank you," she replied, wearing a smile.

"What are you doing here?" Reno whispered through gritted teeth. "This is not the place or the time for foolishness, Papà. You told me you couldn't accept Zuri, so that means you disapprove of me, as well."

"Son, I know what I said, and——I'm sorry," Giacomo expressed, moving in closer. "Give me a chance to make it right."

"The only way you can do that is to change your ways," Sofia said, maneuvering past the ushers, scattered guests, and around the chairs while holding Priyanka's hand. "You may not like our life choices, but they are ours."

Giacomo stood silent.

"This beautiful woman, who I plan to marry one day, thought I was ashamed of her because I never brought her home to meet my parents," Vicente said with Shanise by his side. "Papà, I love you but——"

"I'm sorry," Giacomo said for the second time and his expression became remorseful. "Nothing is worth losing my children. I cannot promise that those changes will happen overnight but I can work on being a better man and father to the three of you," he said, looking at each of them. "I can't imagine my life without any of you in it."

The siblings looked from one to the other.

"Zuri, you are a beautiful bride, and Reno is lucky to have you," Giacomo added, then turned and walked away.

Reno didn't know if Giacomo's change of heart was from acceptance or fear of his children disowning him, but either way, he'd take it. He loved his Papà, and if Giacomo was able to humble himself, owning his part *and* still show up at his wedding, Reno could meet him the other half of the way.

"Papà," Reno called out, halting Giacomo where he stood. Reno went to him and wrapped his arms around his father. They stood that way for several moments and Reno opened his eyes and saw his mother smiling and dabbing tears from her eyes.

"We'll find our way back," Giacomo whispered, clasping Reno's shoulder.

"Instead of trying to capture what once was," Reno countered, gripping Giacomo's shoulder. "Let's start fresh. Right here. Right now."

"Ehhh, look at my men," Emma beamed, holding praying hands to her chest.

"Sorry to interrupt," Skyler said, standing off to the side. "The photographer's ready to take the family photo."

"Thanks, dear," Emma replied, maneuvering between Giacomo and Reno, sliding her arms under both of theirs as they moved toward Zuri. The photographer was smoothing the train on her dress in a specific pattern.

"I'm proud of both of you," she said and then leveled a steely gaze. "Maybe the threat of having to do his own cooking from now on worked its magic."

Giacomo swore in his native language, then leaned in to kiss his wife as he said, "Yes, and that wasn't your only threat."

"Something tells me we're about to hit the TMI Zone," Reno teased and his siblings chuckled as Giacomo's face bloomed with reddish color.

They all lined up in front of the gazebo. Reno and Zuri were centered with his parents and siblings on the sides.

"One sec." Reno stepped out of place. "This isn't the whole family."

Reno hopped in a golf cart that was used to transport the elders to the grand ballroom on the other side of the estate. The guests gathered there, awaiting the reception. It was like walking into a royal palace. Everything was made of gold, the plush red carpet felt like heaven beneath his feet, and human angels were suspended in the air, playing harps.

Scanning the large crowd, Reno found the person he was searching for by the fountain.

"Mamma Winnie, please come with me," Reno said, extending his hand for her to take hold. "We're taking the family portrait. It isn't complete without you."

* * *

The Kings, their women, and the bride and groom gathered at the entrance of the grand ballroom, awaiting the wedding coordinator to introduce the bridal party.

After the final couple had been called to the floor, the room grew silent.

"Everyone on your feet. Grab your flutes and raise them high in the air," Giacomo shouted with cheer.

Reno and Zuri gazed into each other's eyes; both were pooled with tears, daring to overflow.

"Thanks for pushing me to talk to my father," Reno said, resting his forehead against Zuri's. "I believe the happiness I hear in his voice is genuine."

"And thanks for saving my life, loving me through it all, and bringing Mama Winnie to me."

The disco beat to Kool & The Gang's song, Celebration, pulsated through the speakers. Zuri snapped her fingers and whipped her hips side to side.

Reno smiled at his wife, then peered through the door. "Why are The Kings standing in the middle of the dance floor?"

"What are they up to?" Zuri grinned, shimmying her shoulders.

The music lowered a little.

"Not quite Cali," Vikkas teased.

"And not quite Vegas," Shaz added.

"It's Mr. and Mrs. Reno DeLuca, all the way, baby, from now and forever, loving each other for the rest of their lives," all of The Kings chanted, parting the dance floor, making an aisle, and holding their champagne flutes in the air.

London St. Charles

National Bestselling Author, London St. Charles, has published three works of fiction in multiple genres. She has contributed to two anthologies, *Sugar* and *Just One Kiss* with *New York Times* and *USA TODAY* Bestselling authors. Her debut novel, *The Husband We Share*, hit the AALBC Bestsellers List within six months of release and was followed by her recent literary offerings: *Sugarcoated Deception* and *Betrayal of Trust*. She is a Licensed Daycare Provider and operates a Transportation Service on the South Side of Chicago. In addition to being an author, she is a beta reader and a proud member of several writer's groups.

She loves to engage with readers. Visit London on the following:

Website: www.londonstcharles.com
Facebook: Author London St. Charles
Instagram: london_writes
Twitter: @LSCharles2017

The Husband We Share

Xavier Carter is a Chicago detective who is leading the ultimate double life. He is married to not one, but two beautiful, intelligent, professional women. Over the years, he has taken extreme measures to keep both homes happy--and separate.

Patricia, the first Mrs. Carter, believes that Xavier has left his playboy ways in the past. She had been warned to stay away from the "Campus Casanova," but didn't listen. Now she's finding that something's not quite right in their world. Unfortunately, Patricia can't focus on him, when she has a secret of her own that has shadowed her since age sixteen. Fate has been unkind in the fact that her "secret" is actually watching her every move, waiting for the chance to destroy Patricia and her family.

Lauren, the second Mrs. Carter, is an independent, down to earth, home girl from New York with enough passion and sassiness to keep her husband intrigued, and the presence of mind not be taken for a ride. She gave Xavier an ultimatum and Mr. Carter managed to put a ring on it, even though, unknown to her, he'd already made a lifetime commitment to his college sweetheart.

Shawn Johnston has a unique and intricate connection to both "wives" and the husband, which only stirs an already complicated pot. She survived, by coming out on the opposite end of a turbulent past within the foster care system. Her quest for the one thing she has craved more than anything, may cause everyone's world to collapse and send someone to an early grave.

All in all, when the skeletons come creaking out of the closet, two of the women will wonder if the man they share is worth dying for.

bit.ly/thehusbandweshare

Sugarcoated Deception

Walking a tightrope of a career, a husband, and fulfilling a life-long dream is never easy. Balancing a lie, a child out of wedlock, and public scandal is almost unforgivable.

Cadence Goldsmith, a young, successful automotive engineer for a European car manufacturer, learns in the middle of an awards ceremony that her husband fathered a child with a woman he claims to have stopped seeing long before he married Cadence.

Weighing her options, she's paralyzed by the tug of war between present life and future possibilities. She must either have blind faith in her husband and trust him when he swears he hasn't touched the other woman in seven years or cut her loses. Not willing to simply walk away, she works to uncover the sinister plans of a woman who is out to destroy them. Cadence is now racing the clock to save her marriage ... and herself.

Purchase your copy today.
bit.ly/sugarcoateddeception

Betrayal of Trust

What do you do when you've committed a heinous crime? You run and never look back.

At least, that's what Uwezo Omari and his mother planned when they fled their hometown of Reno, Nevada and planted roots in the Midwest, far away from their tumultuous past. Or so they thought.

Fifteen years later, Uwezo, now known as Chef Cedrick Dalton, is a loving husband, father, and successful businessman. Still haunted by the sins from his childhood, he treads carefully by keeping a low profile. Unfortunately, having a booming restaurant in an affluent neighborhood, the anonymity that he once coveted is now a thing of the past.

With the anniversary of the worst day of his life nearing, Cedrick's feelings of guilt and paranoia are triggered and kick into high gear. The mysterious phone calls and anonymous notes stating that someone is looking for him doesn't help. The belief that his mind is playing tricks on him vanishes when he runs into Victoria, his childhood friend who knows his secret. Turmoil is brewing because Cedrick's wife, Sierra, is unaware of his past and Victoria now threatens his freedom and puts the people he loves in danger.

Cedrick is left with life-altering decisions: tell Sierra and jeopardize her safety, or risk losing her because of this betrayal of trust? Or does he take his secret to the grave?

All options have dire consequences.

Purchase your copy today: bit.ly/betrayaloftrust

ABOUT THE KINGS OF THE CASTLE SERIES

Books 2-9 are standalones, no cliffhangers, and can be read in any order.

Book 1 – Kings of the Castle, the introduction to the series and story of King of Wilmette (Vikkas Germaine)

USA TODAY, *New York Times*, and National Bestselling Authors work together to provide you with a world you'll never want to leave. The Castle. Powerful men unexpectedly brought together by their pasts and current circumstances will become a force to be reckoned with. Their combined efforts to find the people responsible for the attempt on their mentor's life, is the beginning of dangerous challenges that will alter the path of their lives forever. Not to mention, they will also draw the ire and deadly intent of current Castle members who wield major influence across the globe.

Fate made them brothers, but protecting the Castle and the women they love, will make them Kings.

www.thekingsofthecastle.com

King of Chatham - Book 2

While Mariano "Reno" DeLuca uses his skills and resources to create safe havens for battered women, a surge in criminal activity within the Chatham area threatens the women's anonymity and security. When Zuri, an exotic Tanzanian Princess, arrives seeking refuge from an arranged marriage and its deadly consequences, Reno is now forced to relocate the women in the shelter, fend off unforeseen enemies of The Castle, and endeavor not to lose his heart to the mysterious woman.

King of Evanston - Book 3

Raised as an immigrant, he knows the heartache of family separation firsthand. His personal goals and business ethics collide when a vulnerable woman stands to lose her baby in an underhanded and profitable scheme crafted by powerful, ruthless businessmen and politicians who have nefarious ties to The Castle. Shaz and the Kings of the Castle collaborate to uproot the dark forces intent on changing the balance of power within The Castle and destroying their mentor. National Bestselling Author, J.L. Campbell presents book 3 in the Kings of the Castle Series, featuring Shaz Bostwick.

King of Devon - Book 4

When a coma patient becomes pregnant, Jaidev Maharaj's medical facility comes under a government microscope and media scrutiny. In the midst of the investigation, he receives a mysterious call from someone in his past that demands that more of him than he's ever been willing to give and is made aware of a dark family secret that will destroy the people he loves most.

King of Morgan Park - Book 5

Two things threaten to destroy several areas of Daron Kincaid's life—the tracking device he developed to locate victims of sex trafficking and an inherited membership in a mysterious outfit called The Castle. The new developments set the stage to dismantle the relationship with a woman who's been trained to make men weak or put them on the other side of the grave. The secrets Daron keeps from Cameron and his inner circle only complicates an already tumultuous situation caused by an FBI sting that brought down his former enemies. Can Daron take on his enemies, manage his secrets and loyalty to the Castle without permanently losing the woman he loves?

King of South Shore - Book 6

Award-winning real estate developer, Kaleb Valentine, is known for turning failing communities into thriving havens in the Metro Detroit area. His plans to rebuild his hometown neighborhood are dereailed with one phone call that puts Kaleb deep in the middle of an intense criminal investigation led by a detective who has a personal vendetta. Now he will have to deal with the ghosts of his past before they kill him.

King of Lincoln Park - Book 7

Grant Khambrel is a sexy, successful architect with big plans to expand his Texas Company. Unfortunately, a dark secret from his past could destroy it all unless he's willing to betray the man responsible for that success, and the woman who becomes the key to his salvation.

King of Hyde Park - Book 8

Alejandro "Dro" Reyes has been a "fixer" for as long as he could remember, which makes owning a crisis management company focused on repairing professional reputations the perfect fit. The same could be said of Lola Samuels, who is only vaguely aware of his "true" talents and seems to be oblivious to the growing attraction between them. His company, Vantage Point, is in high demand and business in the Windy City is booming. Until a mysterious call following an attempt on his mentor's life forces him to drop everything and accept a fated position with The Castle. But there's a hidden agenda and unexpected enemy that Alejandro doesn't see coming who threatens his life, his woman, and his throne.

King of Lawndale - Book 9

Dwayne Harper's passion is giving disadvantaged boys the tools to transform themselves into successful men. Unfortunately, the minute he steps up to take his place among the men he considers brothers, two things stand in his way: a political office that does not want the competition Dwayne's new education system will bring, and a well-connected former member of The Castle who will use everything in his power—even those who Dwayne mentors—to shut him down.

AUTHOR BIOS

Naleighna Kai is the *USA TODAY* Bestselling Author of Every Woman Needs a Wife, Open Door Marriage, Loving Me for Me, Slaves of Heaven and several other controversial novels. She is founder of NK Tribe Called Success, The Cavalcade of Authors, and is a publishing and marketing consultant. www.naleighnakai.com

S. L. Jennings is a military wife, mom of three, coffee addict, Willy Wonka enthusiast, and real-life unicorn. She's also the New York Times and USA Today Bestselling author of Taint, Fear of Falling and the Se7en Sinners Series, along with a few other titles that she's too lazy to type. She's been with her high school sweetheart for almost twenty years, and he still can't get her Subway sandwich order right. But he's cute and brings her vodka, so she keeps him around. They currently reside in Spokane, WA with their three stinky boys and their equally stinky cat. www.sljenningsauthor.com

Martha Kennerson is the bestselling and award-winning author who's love of reading and writing is a significant part of who she is. She uses both to create the kinds of stories that touch the heart. Martha lives with her family in League City, Texas. She believes her current blessings are only matched by the struggle it took to achieve such happiness. To find out more about Martha and her journey, visit her website at www. marthakennerson.com and you can follow her on Facebook and Twitter.

J. L. Campbell is an award-winning Jamaican author who has written over thirty books in several romance subgenres. Campbell, who features Jamaican culture in her stories, is a certified editor, and also writes non-fiction. Visit her on the web at www.joylcampbell.com.

National bestselling author, **Lisa Watson**, is a native of Washington D.C., and writes in the Multicultural & Interracial, Contemporary, Romantic Suspense, and Sweet Romance genres. Her memorable novels for the Harlequin's Kimani line, The Match Broker series was listed as one of 2014's Top 25 Books of the Summer, and Top 50 Best Reads. Lisa lives in Raleigh, North Carolina with her husband of twenty-two years and two teenagers, and is avidly working on book one, Alexa King: The Guardian, in her second new Romantic Suspense series, The Lady Doyen and Book 2 in the Love and Danger Series. www.lisawatson.com

Karen D. Bradley is a national bestselling author and screenplay writer. English and Grammar were never her strongest subjects, but as life would have it, her weakest link would become her saving grace. Writing fiction became one of her favorite forms of therapy. She has penned several contemporary fiction, suspense, and romantic suspense novels. Visit Karen on the web at www.karendbradley.com

Janice M. Allen is a National Bestselling Author who has always been an avid reader of fiction. She even edited the work of other authors for several years. But she gets an incomparable thrill from creating stories that entertain readers and cause them to reflect on real life issues. No Right Way To Do A Wrong Thing is her first novel, followed by her short story Cayenne. www.janicemallen.com

London St. Charles has always had a passion for the pen, paper, and books. She is a Chicago native who uses the Windy City as a backdrop to the romance, suspense, and contemporary fiction stories she writes. London published her debut novel, The Husband We Share in 2017 and is one of nine authors in the anthology, Sugar. She also composes an online newsletter, London Writes, that keeps readers abreast of what's going on in her world. www.londonstcharles.com

MarZe Scott is a lifelong resident of Ypsilanti, Michigan and Graduate of University of Michigan. A lover of all things creative, MarZé enjoys reading, free-hand illustrating, jewelry making and makeup artistry.

Known for her vivid and captivating storytelling, MarZé has been writing short stories and poems since elementary school and developed a taste in high school for writing about provocative topics like the consequences of casual sex. You can find Gemini Rising, MarZé's debut novel, and short story Next Lifetime wherever books are sold. www.marzescott.com

SERIES MENTORS:

LaVerne Thompson is a *USA Today* Bestselling, award winning, multi-published author, an avid reader and a writer of contemporary, fantasy, and sci/fi sensual romances. She loves creating worlds within and without our world. She also writes romantic suspense and new adult romance under the pen name Ursula Sinclair also a USA Today Bestselling Author. www.lavernethompson.com

Kassanna is a strong believer in love at first sight and happily ever afters. Writing has always been her passion but fate sometimes has other roads that must first be taken .Navigating the road less traveled was not only unexpected but in the end extremely rewarding. Her books are mainly contemporary romance but she has delved into the paranormal, fantasy, and plans on expanding into other areas as the ideas come to her. Right now she is enjoying life and seeing her works come into fruition make it that much more pleasurable especially when her books make others smile. Kassanna wouldn't have it any other way. www.flavorfullove.com